Warriors of the Tempest

ORCS
FIRST BLOOD

Book 3

Warriors of the Tempest

STAN NICHOLLS

VICTOR GOLLANCZ
LONDON

The right of Stan Nicholls to be identified as the author
of this work has been asserted by him
in accordance with the Copyright, Designs and Patents Act 1988.

First published in Great Britain in 1999 by
Victor Gollancz
An imprint of Orion Books Ltd
Orion House, 5 Upper St Martin's Lane,
London WC2H 9EA

To receive information on the Millennium list, e-mail us at:
smy@orionbooks.co.uk

A CIP catalogue record for this book
is available from the British Library

ISBN 0 575 07069 2

Typeset by SetSystems Ltd, Saffron Walden, Essex
Printed in Great Britain by Clays Ltd, St Ives plc

The Blooding of the Orcs

The social structure of Maras-Dantia, cradle of the elder races, was near collapse. Its fragile balance had been disrupted by the inflow of a rapacious species called humans. They laid waste to natural resources, despoiled cultures and fomented conflict. Many gravitated to opposing religious groups, the Manis and the Unis, that waged bloody civil war.

And they ate the land's magic.

Human pillaging upset the flow of earth energies which fed the magical powers most of the other races enjoyed. Now the spring of enchantment was dying. In turn the climate soured, throwing the seasons into confusion. The prospect of endless winter hung over Maras-Dantia, and beyond that the threat of an ice age, heralded by glaciers creeping southward.

Orcs had no magic abilities to lose. What they did have were unparalleled martial skills and bloodlust.

Captain Stryke led the Wolverines, a warband of thirty orcs serving sorceress queen Jennesta, a tyrannical sadist and Mani supporter. Stryke's fellow officers were sergeants Haskeer and Jup, the latter the band's only dwarf member, and corporals Alfray and Coilla, the group's sole female. The balance of the command, at the outset, numbered twenty-five common grunts. On Jennesta's orders, the Wolverines seized a mysterious object contained in a message cylinder they were commanded not to open. They also came into a quantity of pellucid, or crystal lightning, a powerful hallucinogenic.

I

When the cylinder was stolen by kobold bandits, Stryke's decision to track them down and recover the prize was the first step to the Wolverines going renegade. Aided by a gremlin scholar called Mobbs, the band opened the cylinder and found it held an instrumentality, an artifact said to embody great magical properties. To the orcs this strange object looked like a simple representation of a star, and they dubbed it such. Discovering it was one of five which, when gathered together, might free the elder races in some unexplained way, the band cast off their fealty to Jennesta. Against a background of Maras-Dantia's descent into anarchy, they set out to search for the remaining pieces of the puzzle.

Their mission was fraught with peril. They were dogged by a party of warriors Jennesta had sent to kill or capture them. Armies of Unis and Manis, aided by fellow orcs and opportunistic dwarves, sought their heads. Human diseases, against which the elder races had little defence, endangered their survival. And impatient with the failures of her own minions, Jennesta employed a trio of merciless human bounty hunters who specialised in tracking rogue orcs.

All the while, Stryke was plagued by inexplicable dreams that showed an idyllic orc homeland, untainted by humans or a worsening climate. These visions were so lucid he questioned his sanity.

The band snatched a second star from Uni extremist Kimball Hobrow, causing him and his followers to pursue them relentlessly. A third instrumentality was located in Scratch, the troll race's underground kingdom. The Wolverines only escaped by taking troll monarch Tannar hostage.

Haskeer, crazed after recovering from a fever, seized the two original stars and made off with them. Coilla rode after him and was captured by the bounty hunters. She bluffed them into believing that the band had gone to the freeport of Hecklowe. Having betrayed Jennesta and struck out to exploit the situation themselves, the bounty hunters needed Coilla to identify her comrades. They set off for Hecklowe with her as their prisoner.

Stryke led the remainder of the band in search of Haskeer and Coilla. King Tannar, trying to bargain for his freedom, told them that a centaur called Keppatawn possessed a star, and that it was guarded by his clan in Drogan Forest. Stryke refused to release Tannar, who attempted to escape and died in the process, adding tyrannicide to the Wolverines' infractions.

In a deranged state, Haskeer became convinced that the stars were communicating with him in some way, and that he should take them to Jennesta, though this would mean certain death. Before he could carry out the plan, Huskeer was taken by Hobrow's zealous followers, the custodians, and the stars fell into Hobrow's hands.

The Wolverines had bloody encounters with Hobrow's men too, and discovered that Jennesta had officially declared them outlaws, with prices on their heads. Stryke decided to temporarily split the band, something he had previously set his face against. He took half the troop and continued looking for their companions; Alfray was sent to check on the possibility of a star at Drogan.

Jennesta stepped up the hunt for the Wolverines, including more dragon patrols under the direction of her mistress of dragons, Glozellan. She also maintained telepathic contact with her brood sisters, Adpar and Sanara, queens of their own domains in different parts of Maras-Dantia. Adpar, ruler of the nyadd realm, was making war against a neighbouring race, the merz. Jennesta offered her an alliance to help find the stars, promising to share their power. Not trusting her sister, Adpar refused. Enraged, Jennesta used sorcery to cast a harmful glamour on her sibling.

Coilla and the bounty hunters came across an enigmatic human named Serapheim, who claimed to be an itinerant storyteller. But the encounter ended before they could learn more about him, and the party pushed on to Hecklowe. The freeport, a neutral meeting place for all races, was policed by an assembly of Watchers, magically created homunculi who enforced order with lethal force. In one of the town's seedier quarters, the bounty hunters negotiated to sell Coilla to goblin slaver Razatt-Kheage.

Stryke's group located Haskeer and saved him from lynching by Hobrow's custodians. They also recovered the stars. Haskeer couldn't give a coherent explanation of his actions. Stryke put his behaviour down to the fever and allowed him to rejoin the band, though under observation. Later, during an unseasonable snowstorm, the mysterious

Serapheim appeared. He told Stryke that Coilla had been captured by the bounty hunters, whose existence was previously unknown to the band, and that they had taken her to Hecklowe. Then he disappeared, impossibly. Stryke sent a message to Alfray's group postponing their rendezvous at Drogan, and with an even more depleted company headed for Hecklowe. They saw Serapheim there. Following him at a distance, he led them to the slaver's lair where Coilla was being held. After a bloody battle they rescued her, but Razatt-Kheage and the bounty hunters escaped. Serapheim too had disappeared. Fighting their way clear of the Watchers, the Wolverines fled Hecklowe.

Stryke and Alfray's groups reunited at Calyparr Inlet, near Drogan Forest. Shortly after, while hunting, Stryke was ambushed by a vengeful Razatt-Kheage and his goblin henchlins. But Stryke overcame his captors, and killed the slave trader. Entering Drogan Forest, the band made contact with Keppatawn's centaur clan. Keppatawn, a renowned armourer hampered by lameness, did prove to have a star. He stole it from Adpar when he was a youth, barely escaping with his life. But a spell cast by her left him crippled, and only the application of one of her tears would right him. Keppatawn declared that if the Wolverines could bring him this bizarre trophy he would trade the star for it. Stryke agreed.

The band made their way to the nyadd's domain, where Scarrock Marsh met the Mallowtor Islands. Chaos reigned there. Nyadds and neighbouring merz fought each other, and Adpar had slipped into a life-threatening coma as a result of Jennesta's magical attack. As she had eliminated all rivals, her death promised to throw her realm into turmoil, with opposing factions vying for power. Fighting their way to her private chambers, the Wolverines found the queen on her deathbed, abandoned by her courtiers. When the cause looked lost, she shed a single tear of self-pity, which Coilla caught in a phial.

Adpar's death sent a telepathic burst to Jennesta and Sanara. It revealed to Jennesta that Stryke and the band were in the nyadd's realm. She set out for Scarrock at the head of a Mani army ten thousand strong, determined to annihilate the Wolverines once and for all. Dragon Dam Glozellan and a squadron of dragons were sent on ahead. Kimball Hobrow discovered that the band had been in the area of Drogan. He led his own army of Uni followers there.

4

The band fought their way out of the nyadd realm, only making it because merz warriors intervened to help them. But Wolverine grunt Kestix was killed in the process. The band rode for Drogan Forest with the tear and stars. En route they were attacked by a group of Hobrow's custodians. Vastly outnumbered, the orcs made a run for it, but Stryke's horse tumbled and threw him. As the custodians bore down, a dragon descended and Glozellan rescued Stryke. She flew him to a remote mountaintop and deposited him there, leaving without explanation. Despite the peak being impossible to scale, the mysterious Serapheim appeared and urged the orc not to give up hope. Then he vanished. Stryke almost didn't notice the human's inexplicable exit.

Because the stars he had were singing to him.

1

They rode like harpies fresh out of hell.

Jup turned in his saddle and looked back at their pursuers. He reckoned there were maybe a hundred of them, outnumbering the Wolverines four or five to one. They wore black and were heavily armed, and the length of the chase had done nothing to cool their fire.

Now the leading humans were near enough to spit at.

He glanced at Coilla, riding abreast of him at the band's rear. She leaned forward, head low, teeth resolutely clenched, bunched hair flowing like rippled bay smoke. The angular, tattooed corporal's stripes patterning her cheeks stressed her stern features.

Ahead of Coilla, sergeants Haskeer and Alfray galloped headlong, their foaming mounts' hooves pounding the frigid turf, kicking up clods of mud. The rest of the orcs were spread out on either side, grim-faced, bent into the lashing wind.

All eyes were on the distant shelter of Drogan Forest.

'*They're gaining!*' Jup bellowed.

If any but Coilla heard, they didn't show it. '*Then don't waste breath!*' she yelled, glaring at the dwarf. '*Keep moving!*'

Her mind was still on the spectacle they had witnessed earlier, of Stryke unhorsed, then carried off by a war dragon. They had to assume it was one of Jennesta's, and that he was lost.

Jup shouted again, puncturing her brief reverie. He had an arm thrust out, pointing toward her neglected left side. She swung her head. A custodian had drawn parallel with her. His sword was raised and his horse was about to barrel into hers.

'*Shit!*' Coilla snapped. She pulled hard on the reins, turning herself aside. It got her clear and bought enough time to unsheathe her own blade.

The human pressed in. He was waving the weapon and roaring, his words obliterated by the thunder of the chase. His first swing was wide, the blade tip hewing air just short of her calf. A rapid second stroke came closer and higher, and would have cleaved her waist if she hadn't tilted from him.

That made Coilla mad.

She whipped round and sent out a stroke of her own. The man ducked and it cut a whistling arc inches above his head. He returned a thrust meant for her chest, but Coilla blocked it, knocking aside his sword. He made another pass, and another. She deflected both, their blades connecting with a jarring, steely clatter.

Hunters and hunted sped on, pell-mell. They entered a small ravine perhaps a dozen horses wide. The terrain flashed by, a blur of green and brown. On the edge of her vision Coilla was aware of more humans crowding the band.

She stretched out and swiped at her antagonist again. The stroke missed, and overreaching she almost toppled. He countered. Their weapons clashed, edge to edge, metal ringing. Neither found an opening.

There was a fleeting respite as they realigned themselves and Coilla checked the way ahead. It was as well she did. The forward riders were splitting to either side of a dead tree square in their path, flowing around it like fast-running water against a huge ship's prow. She tugged the reins to the right, throwing her centre of balance in the same direction. The horse swerved and skimmed past the trunk. For an instant she had sight of the bark's scabrous grain. A skeletal branch raked her shoulder. Then she was clear.

Where Coilla passed to the tree's right, the human took a route to the left. But it was an obstacle for the rest of his kind. Their greater numbers clogged at the bottleneck, and for a moment he was alone. Set on being rid of him, Coilla steered his way. They recommenced their duel as the gully gave way to open plains.

Trading blows, she was aware of the decamping Wolverines, with Jup staring at her over his shoulder. At the same time the main body of custodians, coming up behind, was renewing speed. Coilla settled on a bold move. She let go of her reins, giving the horse its head, and clasped her sword two-handed. Inviting a fall was a risky ploy, but she took the gamble.

It paid off.

This time, putting all her strength and reach into the swing, the blade bit flesh. It made contact at the elbow joint of the custodian's sword arm, hacking deep. Blood jetted. Crying out, he dropped his weapon and clamped the wound. Coilla's follow-up struck his chest, shattering bone, freeing a copious ruby gush. He swayed, head rolling. She made to strike again.

There was no need. The bridle slipped from the wounded human's fist. For a second he bumped along insensibly, a mere passenger, carried like a rag doll by his racing horse. Then he fell. A confusion of askew limbs and tangled clothing, he hit the ground tumbling.

Before he came to rest, the custodian vanguard rode over him. Some went down in the collision and were trampled in their turn. A chaotic scrum of screaming men and horses formed.

Coilla snatched her flailing reins and spurred onward, several riderless mounts in her wake.

She reached the tail end of the fleeing band to find Jup hanging back for her. As they rode on together the enemy regrouped behind them.

'They're not gonna quit,' Jup decided.

'Do they ever?' She surveyed the land ahead. It was turning boggy. 'And this isn't running country,' she added.

'We're not thinking.'

'Eh?'

'We can't lead 'em to Drogan.'

Coilla frowned. 'No,' she agreed, her gaze flicking to the tree line. 'Bad way of repaying Keppatawn.'

'Right.'

'What, then?'

'Come *on*, Coilla.'

'*Shit.*'

'Got another plan?'

She eyed the mob of humans. They were closing. 'No,' she sighed. 'Let's do it.'

Urging her horse, she put on a burst. Jup followed. They weaved through the ranks of grunts to the band's head, where Alfray and Haskeer were leading the charge. The marshy footing was checking progress, yet still the pace smarted Coilla's eyes.

'Not the forest!' she called across. '*Not to the forest!*'

Alfray understood. 'A stand?' he shouted back, hefting the band's streaming war banner.

It was Jup who answered. 'What else?' he bawled.

'Stand, yes!' Haskeer chimed in. 'Orcs don't run! We *fight!*'

That was enough for Coilla. She curbed her mount. The others took her cue and reined-in. At their hind the custodians were coming up rapidly.

Wheeling about, she boomed, '*Stand fast! We're meeting 'em!*'

It wasn't her place to command. As the highest-ranking officers, Jup or Haskeer should have given the order. But nobody was thinking of formalities.

'*Spread out!*' Jup barked. '*Make a line!*'

With the enemy almost on them, the troop swiftly obeyed. They produced slingshots, throwing knives, short spears and bows, though in spears and bows they were miserably equipped, having no more than four of each among them. Snub blades and shot were more plentiful.

The custodians were baying as they swept in. Individual faces could be made out, twisted with bloodlust. Their horses' steaming breath was visible. The earth rumbled.

'*Steady!*' Alfray cautioned.

Then they were a rock's lob from the orc line.

'*Now!*' Jup yelled.

The band loosed its meagre armoury. Arrows were fired, spears soared, clusters of stones flew.

There was a moment of chaos as the humans braked. Several were tossed from their horses by the sudden halt. Others were felled by arrows and stinging shot. Here and there, shields went up.

Retaliation was swift, if ragged. A few arrows winged back, several spears sailed over; but from their sparseness it seemed the custodians were as badly supplied as the Wolverines. Where they had them, orcs raised their own shields. Projectiles rattled off them.

Soon the stockpiles were exhausted, and the sides fell to swapping jeers and taunts. Hands were filled with close combat weapons.

'I give it another two minutes,' Coilla predicted.

She was wrong. The stand-off was broken in half that time.

Emboldened by their greater numbers, the humans suddenly rushed forward, a black tide thick with steel.

'This is it,' Jup muttered darkly, hiking a butterfly axe from its saddle scabbard.

Haskeer drew a broadsword. Scooping back a sleeve, Coilla plucked a throwing knife from her arm sheath.

Alfray levelled the spiked banner spar. '*Hold fast! And watch those flanks!*'

Any other advice was drowned by the onslaught.

The custodians' larger numbers and lesser discipline had them grouping together as they came in to confront the lesser force, hampering themselves. It didn't change the fact that each Wolverine faced towering odds, but it did buy a few seconds grace.

Coilla used it to try picking off some of the enemy before

they reached her. She flung her knife at the nearest human. It smacked home in his windpipe and he plunged from his mount. Quickly snatching another blade, she pitched it underarm at the next foe, spiking his eye. Her third throw was wide of its mark, and proved the last. Now they were too close for anything but hand-to-hand. Shrieking a battle cry, she brought her sword into play.

The first warrior to reach Jup paid for it dearly. A blow from the dwarf's weighty axe split his skull showering blood and bone shards on all in range. Two more custodians waded in. Dodging their blades, Jup sent out a wide horizontal swing that severed the hand of one and stove in the other's chest. There was no pause. More opponents replaced the fallen. His weathered, bearded face straining with effort, Jup laid into them.

Haskeer's savage rain of blows downed both his initial attackers. But the second took the blade with him as he fell, leaving Haskeer to face his next assailant bare-handed. The man had a pike. They wrestled for it, knuckles white, the barbed spear jerking back and forth. Plumbing all his strength, Haskeer drove the butt into the man's stomach, breaking his grip. With a dextrous flip, the weapon was delivered to its owner's innards. Prised free, it served again on another custodian. But this victim's writhing snapped it, leaving Haskeer with a useless length of shank.

Then two things happened at once. Another human moved in on him with flashing sword. And a lone arrow zipped from the scrum to pierce Haskeer's forearm.

Howling more with fury than pain, he wrenched out the gory shaft. Brandishing the arrow he lurched forward and employed it like a dagger, stabbing at the custodian's face. The distraction let Haskeer snatch away the wailing man's blade and gut him. His place was instantly taken. Haskeer fought on.

Favouring a hatchet over the spar for close combat, Alfray wielded it with deadly precision. But in truth it was all he could do to hold back the storm. Though he had an orc's lust for bloodletting, his years were beginning to tell. Yet despite his waning stamina he matched any in butchery. For now.

He scanned the mêlée and saw that he wasn't the only one overextended. The whole band was on the point of being overwhelmed, with fighting especially brutal at the wings, where the enemy was trying to outflank them. The Wolverines may have had little option other than a stand, but it was proving too bold a move. They were taking wounds, though so far none of them had gone down. That wouldn't last.

Though only a corporal, Alfray was on the point of ignoring protocol and shouting the order himself. Jup beat him to it, yelling words that stuck in an orc's throat.

'*Fall back! Fall back!*'

The instruction spread along the besieged line. Grunts hastily disentangled themselves and withdrew. The face-off became a rearguard action. But the custodians, suspicious of a feint, were wary of going after their quarry with any zeal. The band knew their reluctance was temporary.

Arms aching from the exertion of slaughter, Coilla retreated with the rest, reopening the gap between the lines. The Wolverines moved closer together.

She came to Jup. 'What now? Run again?'

'No chance,' the dwarf panted.

Coilla ran a palm over her cheek, wiping blood. 'Thought so.'

Their opponents were working themselves up for the final assault.

At Coilla's shoulder, Alfray said, 'We got a good few.'

'Not enough,' Haskeer responded gruffly.

In undertones, some of the grunts were calling on orc deities to guide their blades. Or to make their deaths suitably heroic and swift. Coilla suspected the humans were appealing to their own god in similar vein.

The custodians began advancing.

There was a keening sound in the air. A fast moving shadow

passed over the Wolverines. They looked up and saw something like a swarm of elongated insects sweeping across the sky. The dark cloud had already reached its apex and was curving down towards the enemy.

It fell upon them wrathfully. The forefront of the custodian line was riddled with lethal bolts. They bored into upturned faces and chests, arms and thighs. Their velocity took them through the paltry defences of helmets and visors. Shields could have been made of paper for all the good they did. Peppered with numerous shafts, men and horses succumbed wholesale in a struggling, bloodied mass.

A large force was riding, hell-bent, from the direction of the forest, and even as the band spied them they unleashed another deadly cloud. The arrows' great arching path was well above the Wolverines, yet still they instinctively ducked. Once more death rained mercilessly on the heads of the humans, bringing further mayhem and chaos.

As their allies approached, the band began to make them out.

Squinting at the reinforcements, eyes shaded with a hand, Alfray exclaimed, 'Keppatawn's clan!'

Jup nodded. 'And well timed.'

The small army of centaurs at least equalled the humans in strength of numbers. And they would reach the fray in minutes.

'Who's at their head?' Alfray wondered.

Knowing him to be lame, the band didn't expect Keppatawn himself to be leading the offensive.

'Looks like Gelorak,' Jup reported.

The young centaur's muscular physique and distinctive flowing chestnut mane were now plain to see.

Haskeer finished wrapping a piece of dirty cloth around his wound. 'Why talk when there's killing undone?' he grumbled.

'Too right,' Coilla agreed, breaking ranks. '*At the bastards!*'

They weren't slow in following her lead.

The custodians were in bedlam from the arrow blizzard, their dead and maimed littering the plain. Loose horses and walking wounded added to the anarchy, and those custodians still mounted milled in a directionless daze. They were easy pickings for a vengeful warband.

No sooner had the orcs waded in and commenced their slaughter than they were joined by the troop of centaurs. With clubs, spears, short bows and crooked blades they assured the rout. The rump of the custodian force soon turned and fled, chased off by a knot of fleet-footed centaurs.

Exhausted, battle-grimed, Coilla surveyed the aftermath. The auxiliary chief of the Drogan clan trotted to her side and sheathed his sword. He pawed the ground a couple of times.

'Thanks, Gelorak,' she said.

'Our pleasure. We have no need of such unwanted guests.' He gave a flick of his plaited tail. 'Who were they?'

'Just a bunch of humans serving their god of love.'

He smiled wryly, then asked, 'How went your journey to Scarrock?'

'Well and . . . not so well.'

Gelorak cast his eye over the warband. 'I do not see Stryke.'

'No,' Coilla replied softly. 'No, you don't.'

She stared at the darkening sky and tried to hold back her despair.

2

He was in a narrow tunnel that stretched endlessly before and behind him.

His head almost touched the ceiling, and when he extended his arms he could lay his hands on either wall, which felt cold and slightly clammy. Ceiling, walls and floor were made of stone but the tunnel seemed to have been bored rather than constructed because there were no joints or sign of blocks having been fitted together. There was no illumination of any kind either, yet he could see quite clearly. The only sound was his own laboured breathing.

He didn't know where he was or how he came to be here.

For a while he stood quite still, trying to make sense of his surroundings and uncertain of what to do. Then a white light appeared far ahead. No such light showed in the other direction, so he assumed he was facing the tunnel's exit. He began walking towards it. Unlike the slippery smoothness of the walls and ceiling, the floor was rough in texture, giving him purchase.

It was hard to keep track of time but after about ten minutes, as best he could reckon, the light didn't look any nearer. The features of the tunnel remained absolutely uniform, and the silence was unbroken save for his footfalls. He pressed on, moving as fast as he could in the confined space.

His lack of a sense of time became timelessness. All notion of the passing of minutes and hours deserted him. There was only an endless now, *and a universe consisting solely of his pursuit of a light he could never reach. His body became a trudging automaton.*

At some indefinable point in his monotonous journey he was roused by a fancy that the light had grown brighter, though not necessarily larger. Soon he found it hard to look directly at it for more than a few seconds.

With each step he took, the pure white light grew stronger and stronger, until walls, floor, ceiling, everything was obliterated. He closed his eyes and still saw it. Keeping on, he clamped his hands to his face to shut it out, but that made no difference.

Now it pulsated, throbbing to a beat he could feel pounding at his chest, tearing at the very core of his being.

The light was pain.

He wanted to turn and run away. He couldn't. He was no longer walking but being sucked into its blinding, agonising, searingly cold heart.

He cried out.

The light died.

Slowly, he lowered his hands and opened his eyes.

Before him stretched a vast barren plain. There were no trees, no blades of greenery, nothing he could equate with any landscape he had ever seen before. It resembled a desert, though the sand was pewter-coloured and very fine, like volcanic ash. All that broke the desolate scene were numerous jagged, ebony-hued rocks, large and small, strewn across and partly buried by the sediment.

The atmosphere was tropical. Tendrils of yellowish-green mist crept sluggishly at ankle level, and there was an unpleasant odour in the air that reminded him of sulphur and rotting fish. Way off in the distance towered black mountains of impossible height.

But what shocked him most was the sky.

It was blood red and cloudless. There were no stars. But close to the horizon hung a moon, and it was vast. He could see every pockmarked, scarred detail of its glowing, tawny surface. So large and near was it that he half believed he could pierce the great globe with an arrow. He wondered why it didn't fall and crush this forsaken land.

Tearing his eyes away, he turned and looked behind him. The view was exactly the same. Silver-grey sand, craggy rocks, distant mountains, crimson sky. There was nothing that could have been a tunnel mouth.

Despite the moist warmth, an ominous thought chilled his spine. Could he have died and gone to Xentagia, the orcs' hell? This certainly looked like a place of eternal purgatory. Would Aik, Zeenoth, Neaphetar and Wystendel, his race's holy Tetrad, descend on fiery war chariots and condemn his spirit to everlasting punishment?

Then it occurred to him that if this was Xentagia it appeared sparsely populated indeed. Was he the only orc in history to deserve being consigned here? Had he alone committed some crime against the gods, of which he was unaware, that warranted damnation? And where were the tormenting demons, the Sluagh, that some said inhabited the infernal regions and whose single pleasure was making misery for errant souls?

Something caught his eye. Across the blasted expanse there was movement. He strained to make it out. At first he couldn't. Then he realised he was watching a cloud of the yellow-green, all-pervasive smog. Only this was thicker and travelling with purpose. His way.

Had he been right? Was he about to be judged? Denounced by the gods? Horribly tortured?

His instinct was to put up a fight. On second thoughts how futile a plan that would be if he really was going to be confronted by the gods. The idea of running seemed just as stupid. He determined to face whatever it was. Whether deity or demon he wasn't about to betray his creed with an act of cowardice.

He squared his shoulders and readied himself as best he could.

There wasn't long to wait. The cloud, which billowed but somehow remained compact, rolled directly to him. There was no question of it being blown by the wind. It moved too precisely for that, and there was no wind anyway.

The cloud settled in front of him, perhaps a spear's measure short. It continued to spin, and he would have expected to feel the misplaced air, but didn't. This close he could see there were uncountable numbers of golden pinpoints woven into the swirling smoke. He was less sure of what the cloud contained. But there was a shape of some kind.

Almost immediately the sphere's rotation slowed. The dense mist began stripping off, layer by layer, and melted into the air. The darker form it surrounded gradually started to reveal itself. It became obvious that it was a figure.

He tensed.

The last wisps dissolved and a creature stood before him.

He had imagined many things, but not this.

The being was short and stocky. It had green-tinged, wrinkly skin and a large round head with spiky, projecting ears. Its attenuated, slightly protruding eyes had inky orbs with yellow-veined white surrounds and pulpy lids. No hair covered the pate or face, but there were bushy, reddish-brown sideburns, turning ashen. The nose was small and pinched, the mouth had the quality of hardened tree sap serrated with a file. Its clothing consisted of a modest robe of neutral colour, held with a cord.

The creature was very old.

'Mobbs?' Stryke whispered.

'Greetings, Captain of the orcs,' the gremlin replied. He spoke softly, and a faint smile lightened his face.

Myriad questions filled Stryke's mind. He settled on, 'What are you doing here?'

'I have no choice.'

'And I do? Where am I, Mobbs? Is this some kind of hell?'

The gremlin shook his head. 'No. At least not in the sense you mean.'

'Where, then?'

'This is a . . . between land, neither of your world nor mine.'

'What are you talking about? Aren't we both Maras-Dantians?'

'Such questions are less important than what I have to tell you.' Mobbs indicated their surroundings with an absent sweep of his hand. 'Accept this. See it as a forum that enables us to meet.'

'More riddles than answers. You're ever the scholar, Mobbs.'

'I thought I was. Since being here I've realised I knew nothing.'

'But where—'

'Time is short.' With hardly a pause he added, 'Do you remember our first meeting?'

'Of course I do. It changed everything.'

'Helped a change already underway, more like. An act of midwifery perhaps. Though neither of us knew the magnitude of what was to come once you chose your new path.'

'I don't know about magnitude.' Stryke pronounced it with the faltering respect due a word he'd never used before. 'All it's brought me and my band is trouble.'

'It will bring you more, and worse, before you triumph.' The gremlin corrected himself: 'If you triumph.'

'We're holding together with spit and gumption, running around looking for pieces of a puzzle we don't understand. Why do we want more trouble when we don't even know what we're doing?'

'But you know why you're doing it. Freedom, truth, the unveiling of mystery. Big prizes, Stryke. And they have a price. In the end you may or may not think that price worth paying.'

'I don't know that it's worth it now, Mobbs. I've lost comrades, watched order crumble, seen our lives torn apart . . .'

'You think it wasn't coming to that anyway? The whole of Maras-Dantia is on a downward track, the incomers have ensured that. You have a chance to make a difference, at least for some. If you stop now, you guarantee defeat. Carry on and you have a slim chance of victory. I won't pretend it's more than that.'

'Then tell me what to do.'

'You want to know where to find the last instrumentality and what to do with them all once you have?'

Stryke nodded.

'I can't tell you. I have no more knowledge than you in that respect. But have you considered the possibility that the objects of your search want to be found?'

'That's crazy. They're just . . . things.'

'Perhaps.'

'So you've nothing to offer me but warnings?'

'And encouragement. You're so close. You will be given the chance of completing your task, I don't doubt that. Though there will be more blood, more death, more heartache. Despite this you must keep on.'

'You speak with such certainty. How do you know these things?'

'My present . . . state brings me a small insight into events yet to be. Not particulars, but a glimpse of the larger currents shaping future times.' His face darkened. 'And a fire is coming.'

Stryke's backbone prickled again as realisation dawned. 'You said you had no choice in being here,' he mouthed, half aloud.

Mobbs didn't reply.

Stryke repeated his earlier question, this time with some force. 'Where are we, Mobbs?'

The aged scholar sighed. 'You might call it a repository. A realm of shades.'

'How long have you been here?'

'Since just after we parted. Courtesy of another orc, a Captain Delorran.'

The gremlin pulled aside the edges of his robe and revealed his chest. He bore a wound, dry of blood now, so deep and pernicious it could have had only one effect.

Confirmation of his suspicion had the colour draining from Stryke's face. 'You're . . .'

'Dead. Undead. Between two worlds. And not likely to rest until things are resolved in yours.'

'Mobbs, I . . . I'm sorry.' It seemed such a weak thing to say.

'Don't be,' the gremlin replied gently, closing his robe.

'Delorran was chasing me. If I hadn't involved you—'

'Forget that. I have no ill will for you, and Delorran himself has paid. But can't you see? Free yourself and you free me.'

'But—'

'Whether you like it or not, Stryke, the game is afoot and you're a player.' Mobbs stretched an arm to point over the orc's shoulder. 'Heed!'

Mystifed, Stryke spun around. And gaped at insanity.

The gigantic moon, just beginning to set behind the mountain range, had transformed into a face. It had the features of a female, and one he knew too well. Her hair was black, her eyes were unfathomable. She had skin that glinted with a faint emerald and silver lustre, as though flesh had commingled with fish scales.

Jennesta, hybrid queen, opened her overly broad, canine-toothed mouth and roared with silent laughter.

A hand rose from behind the range. It was of the same incredible scale as the face. Its unnaturally slender fingers, tipped with nails half as long again, clutched some vast object. With an almost casual flip, the hand pitched its load toward the plain.

Stryke stared, dumbfounded, as the thing tumbled end over end and hit the ground at an angle. A massive plume of dust went up. The earth shuddered. Then the object bounced, spun in the air, came down and bounced again.

When it had done that half a dozen times two things dawned on Stryke.

First, he recognised the object. It was what Mobbs called an instrumentality and the Wolverines had dubbed a star. It was the first one the band found, at Homefield, a Uni settlement. But whereas Stryke knew it as something he could easily fit into his palm, now it was of titanic proportions. Its sandy-coloured central sphere would have taken a team of horses to move. The seven projecting spikes were as big as mature oaks.

Second, he realised it was coming straight at him.

He turned to where Mobbs was standing. The gremlin had vanished.

Tumbling, rocking the ground like a small earthquake every time it touched down, the star bounded closer. It didn't seem to lose momentum.

Stryke started to run.

He pelted across the bizarre wasteland, zigzagging boulders, arms pumping. The star gained on him, beating the ash with bone-jarring blows, crushing rocks, throwing up clouds of dust, spiralling through the air with awesome splendour.

Stryke could hear it, feel it, at his back. Straining to outpace it, he sneaked a look over his shoulder. He saw two of the mighty spikes smashing down like the legs of a giant, fall forward, rip out of the ash and fly off again. A wave of dust blinded him for a second, then another crash tossed the ground and the star was close enough to touch.

He threw himself aside using every ounce of muscle power the sprint had left him. As he rolled in the clinging ash his fear was that the star would turn and continue the chase. He came to rest and scrambled to his feet, ready to bolt.

The star kept to its path, flattening every obstacle, drumming a thunderous rhythm as it careered away. He watched as it sprang across the plain. When it was a distant speck he let out the breath he'd been holding.

His eyes were drawn back to what he hoped would be a restored moon. That hope was dashed. Jennesta's enormous form remained, floating in an ocean of blood, glaring down at him.

Once more, she raised her hand. It held more than before. She cast again, and this time a trio of stars cascaded, striking the ground in a ragged line. Triple puffs of ash erupted. The stars bounced and headed for Stryke.

He recognised these, too. The first was green with five spikes, the second dark blue with four spikes, the last grey with two spikes. They were the other stars the band had collected.

As they ranged in on him it seemed there was an intelligence at work, guiding them more cunningly than the first star. One came in an unerringly straight line. The ones on either side of it travelled in a more meandering fashion, bouncing far out and then back close. It was a classic pincer formation. And Stryke was sure they were moving at much greater speed than the initial star.

Again he ran. He took an erratic, unpredictable route to make it harder for them. But every time he looked back they were still on his trail, and they remained in the same relationship to each other, like a trawl net ready to scoop him. He put on all the speed he could muster. His limbs throbbed with pain. When he gulped for breath it felt like inhaling fire.

Then one of the tremendous stars bounced down on his right-hand side, erupting ash. He veered to the left. Another landed, blocking his way. The third was spinning above him. Stumbling, he fell awkwardly. He rolled onto his back. A shadow covered him. Helplessly he saw the airborne star plunge towards him, knowing that in an instant he'd be pulverised.

He was trapped like an insect, watching as a great boot descended to grind him to pulp.

And he thought he could hear a strange, lilting, faraway song.

He was yelling.

It took him a moment to realise he was awake. And alive. A few seconds more passed before he was sure of where he was. Sitting up, he used his sleeve to wipe at the sweat that covered his face despite the cold. He was panting, his breath clouding in the thin, chill air.

The dream wasn't like the others, but it was just as vivid, every bit as real. He tried to make sense of it, running through it in his mind. Then he thought of Mobbs.

More blood on his hands.

Stryke checked himself. It was stupid to feel guilty because of a dream. For all he knew, Mobbs was alive and well. But somehow he couldn't quite bring himself to believe that.

He was still muddled and had to get a grip. Climbing to his feet, he walked to the edge of his prison.

The mountaintop plateau he'd been deposited on by Glozellan, Jennesta's Dragon Dam, was quite small, perhaps a hundred paces long by sixty wide, with only a couple of rock outcrops to give some protection from the wind. He didn't know why Glozellan had brought him here. The probability was that he had been snatched at the behest of her mistress, and it was just a matter of time before he faced her wrath.

He surveyed the view, not really sure where he was, beyond it being some way north of Drogan. Maybe one of the peaks in Bandar Gizatt or Goff. The fact that he had a glimpse of ocean to the west, and could clearly see the looming ice field further north, seemed to confirm this. Not that it mattered.

The temperature was low and the keen wind stung. Stryke was glad of his fur jerkin, and pulled it tighter about himself as he pondered the last few hours' events. Glozellan had left without explanation. Shortly after, the mysterious human who called himself Serapheim had been here, though how he came and went from such an inaccessible place was beyond Stryke's understanding. Then there were the instrumentalities, the stars.

The stars.

He remembered them singing. Just before he slept they were making some kind of sound. But it wasn't out loud, it was in his head. It wasn't singing either, but that was the nearest he could come to describing it. Just like Haskeer.

That gave him pause.

Stryke slipped a freezing hand into his belt pouch and brought out the stars. He examined them. The one they got at Homefield, sandy-coloured with seven spikes of varying lengths; the Trinity star, green with five spikes; the dark blue one with four spikes, from Scratch. They weren't 'singing' now.

He frowned. Nothing to do with these things made any sense.

Then he saw something approaching, several miles distant. A great black shape with lazily flapping saw-toothed wings. There was no mistaking it.

He stood ready, hand on sword.

3

The band was escorted into Drogan Forest.

Guards had been doubled in case the humans returned, and the centaurs were on a war footing.

Alfray took Haskeer away to dress his wound properly, and to tend to the injured grunts. The other Wolverines scattered through the settlement, looking for food and drink. Accompanied by Gelorak, Coilla and Jup made their way to the clan chief.

Keppatawn was found at the entrance to his weapons forge, barking orders and despatching messengers. Once fit and muscular, age had greyed his beard and lined his face. He was lame, his withered right foreleg dragging uselessly.

After greeting Gelorak, he turned to the pair of Wolverines. 'Sergeant. Corporal. Welcome back.'

Jup nodded.

'Sorry to bring you trouble, Keppatawn,' Coilla told him.

'Don't be. A good fight now and again sharpens our mettle.' The centaur grinned roguishly. 'So, how went your mission?'

'We got what you wanted.'

'You *did*?' Keppatawn beamed. 'Wonderful news! Everything they say about you orcs—' He saw their faces. 'What's wrong?'

Neither answered.

Keppatawn looked about the clearing. 'Where's Stryke?'

'We don't know,' Jup admitted glumly.

'Meaning?'

'His horse fell when we were trying to outrun the humans,' Coilla explained. 'Then a war dragon came out of nowhere and took him.'

'You're saying he was captured?'

'We didn't see him being forced, if that's what you mean. Too busy running for that. But Jennesta's one of the few with command of dragons these days.'

'I got a look at the handler,' Jup said. 'I'm pretty sure it was Glozellan.'

Coilla sighed. 'Jennesta's Dragon Dam. That settles it.'

'Maybe not,' the dwarf offered. 'Can you imagine a *brownie* making Stryke do something he didn't want?'

'I . . . I just don't know, Jup. All I know is Stryke's gone, and the stars and the tear have gone with him.' To Keppatawn she added, 'Sorry. Should have said.'

The chieftain betrayed no obvious disappointment, but they all noticed his hand absently rub against the thigh of his ravaged leg. 'I can't miss what I've never had,' he replied stoically. 'As to your Captain, we'll scour the area.'

'The band should be doing that,' Jup said. 'He's one of our own.'

'You need rest, and we know the terrain.' He addressed his second-in-command. 'Muster search parties, Gelorak, and post lookouts on higher ground.' The young centaur nodded and galloped off. Keppatawn returned his attention to Jup and Coilla. 'There's nothing more we can do at the moment. Come.'

He lead them to an oak trestle-table. They slid wearily onto its bench seat. A centaur was passing, towing a small two-wheeled cart loaded with rations. Keppatawn reached out and yanked a narrow-necked stone jug from the creaking load.

'I think you could use ale,' he ventured. Sinking his teeth into the jug's cork stopper he drew it out and spat it away, then slammed the jug on the table.

'What the hell,' Jup responded. He raised the jug two-handed and drank. It was offered to Coilla. She shook her head.

Easily hoisting the jug with one hand, Keppatawn gulped a long draft. He wiped the back of his arm across his mouth. 'Now tell me what happened.'

Coilla took the lead. 'Stryke wasn't the only band member we lost. On the way back one of our grunts, Kestix, was killed by nyadd warriors in Scarrock Marsh.' She felt a stab of anguish. Kestix had died saving her.

'I'm truly sorry,' Keppatawn said. 'The more so as you undertook the task for me.'

'We did it as much for ourselves. You're not to blame.'

'Frankly, I'm surprised our casualties weren't heavier,' Jup put in, 'given the chaos down there.'

'How so?' Keppatawn asked.

'Adpar's dead.'

'*What?* Are you sure?'

'We were there when she died,' Coilla told him. 'And no, it wasn't us.'

'You had an eventful journey indeed. How did she die?'

'It was Jennesta's doing.'

'*She* was there?'

'Well . . . no.'

'Then how do you know it was her?'

It was a good question. Coilla hadn't really had time to think it through. Now she realised there was a mystery. 'Stryke said so,' she replied distantly. 'He seemed certain of it.'

Apparently Jup hadn't given it much thought either. 'Yes, but how?'

'Must have known something we didn't,' Coilla decided, though she couldn't imagine how.

'Anyway, there was anarchy in the nyadd realm,' she summed up tersely. 'We only got out because the merz helped us.'

Keppatawn looked reflective. He stroked his full-bearded chin with thumb and forefinger. 'We'll have to be even more alert after this. Adpar's death changes the whole power structure in this region. And not necessarily for the better.'

'But she was a tyrant.'

'Yes. But at least we knew where we were with her. Now others will move to fill the void she leaves, and they're an unknown quantity. It can only bring more instability, and Maras-Dantia already has plenty of that.'

They were interrupted by the arrival of a swaggering Haskeer. He had his arm in a sling and was wolfing a hunk of roast meat. His lips and cheeks shone with grease.

'Where's Alfray?' Coilla said.

'Bimbing whoons,' Haskeer replied with a full mouth.

She nodded at his arm. 'How's yours?'

He swallowed, tossed away the stripped bone and loudly belched. 'All right.' Without asking he snatched the jug and guzzled heartily, head back, ale dribbling down his face. He belched again.

'As ever, your courtly manners put us all to shame,' Jup commented.

Haskeer looked dimly baffled. 'You what?'

'Forget it.'

There was a time when the dwarf's gibe would have had the two sergeants at each other's throats. Perhaps Haskeer was mellowing, or simply didn't understand he was the butt of sarcasm, but in the event he just shrugged and asked, 'What do we do now?'

'Try to find Stryke. Apart from that, we don't know,' Jup confessed.

Haskeer wiped his oily fingers on his fur jerkin. 'Suppose we can't find him?'

'Don't even *think* that,' Coilla rumbled ominously.

The truth was that she could think of nothing else herself.

Stryke watched as the behemoth sank through the air and touched down on the mountain plateau.

The dragon's sinewy wings crackled as they folded in on themselves. Its great head slowly turned to regard him, slitty yellow eyes unblinking, milky smoke curling from cavernous nostrils. The creature was panting, dog fashion, a glistening tongue the size of a horse blanket lolling from its massive jaws. It brought with it a smell of raw fish, halitosis and broken wind.

Stryke retreated a few steps.

The beast's handler disengaged herself and slid from its scaly back.

Almost everything she wore comprised shades of brown, from jerkin and trews to high boots and thin brimmed hat. The hat's white and grey decorative feather, and simple gold strands at her wrists and neck, were the only departure.

It was an enigma that brownies, a hybrid race born of elves and goblins, neither of which excelled in height, should be so lanky. She was even taller than the norm, and her height was more striking because she held herself totally erect. Her frame looked deceptively delicate and she was overly thin. As with all brownies her proud expression could be mistaken for conceit.

'*Glozellan!* What the *hell's* going on?' Stryke demanded.

She seemed unfazed. 'I'm sorry to have left you so long. I couldn't avoid it.'

'Am I a prisoner here?' He still clutched his sword.

She arched her almost non-existent brown eyebrows. Otherwise she stayed glacial. 'No, you're not a prisoner; *I'm* hardly capable of holding you captive. And there are no dragon squadrons on their way, loaded with Jennesta's troops, if that's what you think.' Her voice took on an even more caustic edge. 'It looks like you've not fully understood that I was trying to help you. Perhaps I didn't make that clear.'

'You didn't make *anything* clear.'

'I thought rescuing you from those humans was clear enough.'

'Yes . . . Yes, it should have been. Thank you for that.'

She gave an almost imperceptible nod of acknowledgement,

then said, 'Now put that sword away.' He lingered and she added in a mocking tone, 'You're quite safe.'

Contritely he sheathed his blade. 'But you can't blame me, you being the Queen's Dragon Mistress and—'

'No longer.' Her face was unreadable.

'Explain yourself.'

'Too many slights, too many blows. I've had enough, Stryke. I've left her. As a member of a race that prides itself on its loyalty, it wasn't an easy decision. But Jennesta's cruelty and misrule have overridden that. So, I'm a deserter. Like you.'

'These really are strange days.'

'Two other dragon handlers and their beasts deserted with me. I left you here to go and aid them.'

'That'll be a blow to Jennesta.'

'Others are deserting too, Stryke. Not in hordes, but there's a steady bleed.' She paused. 'Many would rally to you.'

'They don't *know* me, I'm no saviour. I didn't even *mean* to desert.'

'But you're a leader. You've proved that commanding the Wolverines.'

'Heading a warband isn't the same as running an army or a realm. Most who do are false, wicked. Jennesta, Adpar, Kimball Hobrow . . . I don't want to be like them.'

'You wouldn't. You'd be helping to remove their kind.'

'The elder races shouldn't be fighting amongst themselves. It's the humans we have to stand against. Or at least the Unis.'

'Exactly. And to do that the races have to be united.'

'Well let somebody else do the uniting. I'm just a simple soldier.' He looked to the advancing ice sheet and the unnatural glow suffusing the gloomy sky above it. As though on cue, a few flakes of snow began falling. The dragon gave a rumbling snort.

'Humans are mad, irrational, needlessly destructive. They eat the magic. But they aren't alone in destroying Maras-Dantia. Other races—'

'*I know.* You're not going to change me on this, Glozellan, so don't try.'

'As you wish. Though it could be that you'll have no choice in the matter.'

He let that go and changed the subject. 'Talking of humans, do you know the name Serapheim?'

There was no hint of recognition. 'I've known few humans, and certainly none called that.'

'You didn't bring anybody else here last night, before or after me?'

'No. Why should I? You mean a human?'

Half suspecting the story-weaver's appearance had been some kind of delusion, he backed off. 'I expect I . . . A dream. Forget it.'

She stared at him curiously. The snow swirled thicker. After a moment she said, 'The rumours are that you have something Jennesta wants.'

He weighed his response before deciding she could be trusted. After all, she'd likely saved his life. 'It's more than one thing,' he said, digging into his belt satchel.

The three stars filled his cupped palm. Glozellan gazed at the strange objects.

'I don't really know what they are or what they're for,' he confessed, 'except they're called instrumentalities. My band calls them stars.'

'These are instrumentalities. *Really?*'

He nodded. It was the first time he'd seen her express anything approaching awe. No mean achievement with a brownie.

'You've heard of them?' he asked.

She gathered herself. 'The legend of the instrumentalities is known to my folk.'

'What can you tell me about them?'

'In truth, not much. I know there are supposed to be five, and that they're very old. There is one story connecting them with my race. We have a famous ancestor, Prillenda, though little is known about him either. He was . . . well, a kind of philosopher seer, and it's said he was inspired to make prophecies by one of these things.'

'Prophecies? About what?'

'If they were predictions, they were lost long ago. But they were supposed to have something to do with the End Days, the time when the gods roll up this world and play another game.'

'We orcs have a similar myth.'

'Anyway, how the instrumentality came to him or where it went isn't recorded. Some say it led to his death in some way. I always thought the whole thing was a tale told by pollen-crazed fairies, to be honest.' She stared at the stars. 'But now you have three of the things. Are you sure they're genuine?'

'I'm sure.' He put them away.

'I have no better idea of what they're capable of doing than you, Stryke, but whoever possesses them commands power. The stories always made that plain if nothing else.'

After his latest dream, if it was a dream, he reckoned that power was greater than either of them could guess. But he didn't mention that to her. Nor did he say anything about the stars 'singing' to him.

'I can see why Jennesta thinks them such a prize,' Glozellan said. 'Even if they have no magic they have power as totems. They could restore her crumbling authority. If *you* were to use them to muster opposition—'

'Enough.' His tone invited no further comment. 'What are you going to do now?'

'I'm not sure. I'd like to return to my kith for a spell of contemplation. But we brownies are southerners, and as you know there are more humans in the south than anywhere else. My folk have scattered long since. So perhaps I'll go to a dragon fastness, stick to high-up places.' She turned and gave her charge an affectionate pat. With drooping eyes the slumbering dragon accepted it passively. 'Brownies and dragons have always had a kind of understanding. They're the only other race we really trust, and they seem to feel the same way about us. Perhaps we see each other as allies in adversity.'

Stryke realised she was as much an outcast as the orcs had become, and felt a pang of sympathy for her.

'Will you keep on opposing the Queen?' Glozellan said.

'When I have to, and I'll fight humans and any other race that gets in my path. But I'm not going out of my way to do it. All I'm really trying to do is keep my band alive.'

'The gods might have other ideas.'

He laughed. It was a little sour. 'Whatever. But first things first. I have to get back to the Wolverines.'

'Then we should leave before the weather gets too bad. Come, I'll take you.'

4

Now she rode a black chariot embellished with arcane symbols in silver and gold. It was pulled by a pair of sable horses, leather face masks smothered with pyramid barbs, iron studs peppering their leggings. Burnished scythes jutted from the chariot's wheels.

At Jennesta's back marched an army above ten thousand strong, comprising orcs, dwarves and a goodly smattering of humans dedicated to the Mani cause. The horde bristled with standards and spears. White canvassed ox-drawn wagons swayed in the flow. Regiments of cavalry shepherded the flanks.

They had skirted Taklakameer, the vast inland sea, and crossed most of the upper Great Plains, keeping Drogan well to their south and Bevis to the north. Soon she would lead them to the shores of Norantellia and the Scarrock peninsula. In that marshy realm of the nyadds, so recently governed by Adpar, the sister she killed with sorcery, Jennesta would hunt the Wolverines and her prize.

She knew they were there, or at least had been. Adpar's dying psychic burst revealed it.

Jennesta's Dragon Dam, Glozellan, had been sent on ahead with three of her beasts to spy out the land. Reinforcements had been summoned and would swell Jennesta's army. Elite warbands were on their way from Cairnbarrow, her seat of power. All was in hand. Contingencies had been planned for. She was as near as she had ever been to revenge and advancement. The army she headed was testament to her authority.

Yet she was not content.

The butt of her displeasure rode alongside the chariot. General Mersadion, horde Commander, was in his prime but serving a mistress so demanding had made him careworn. More than the usual number of lines creased his forehead and he was hollow-eyed. If male orcs had hair, his would be greying.

Jennesta harassed him.

'Whenever it shows itself, crush it. Disloyalty's a canker that quickly festers if it isn't cut out.'

'With respect, ma'am, I think you overestimate the problem,' he dared to suggest, quickly appending, 'The *majority* are loyal.'

'So you keep saying. Yet still we have sedition and deserters. Make every hint of disobedience, every whisper of rebellion a capital offence. With no exceptions, whatever the rank.'

'We're doing that, Majesty.' He might have added that she well knew it, had he felt suicidal.

'Then you can't be applying the principle rigidly enough.' Withering was too poor a word to describe the look she gave him. 'A fish rots from the head, General.'

She meant him, of course, but Mersadion saw the unintended irony. He kept his reply to a prudent, 'Ma'am.'

'Those who serve me well are rewarded. Bad servants pay the price.'

It was news to him that there were rewards. He'd had none apart from an unasked for promotion to an impossible job.

'Do I need remind you of your predecessor, Kysthan, and his protégé Captain Delorran?' she went on, and not for the first time.

'No, Majesty, you don't.'

'Then ponder their fate.'

He did. Often. It was part of living on the edge of a volcano. He was starting to think the deserters could hardly be blamed, and that her increasing harshness was worsening the situation.

Swiftly he checked that line of thought. He knew it was irrational, but he had an abiding fear that she might be able to read his mind.

She spoke then, and he almost started. But it was more to herself than him. 'When I get what I want, none of you will have a choice in the matter of loyalty or anything else,' she muttered. In a clearer tone she ordered, 'Get them moving! I want no more delay.'

Her whip cracked on the back of the horses and the chariot surged ahead. Mersadion had to move smartly to avoid the scythes. As he spurred to catch up, he glanced at the display she'd arranged.

A line of fourteen 'dissidents', all dead now, hanging in cages suspended by gibbets over large open fires.

The subdued army was being made to pass by them to appreciate their mistress's justice. Some looked away. Many held cloths to their noses and mouths against the fearful odour.

Ash fluttered in the wind. Clouds of orange sparks twisted skyward.

Orcs were meant for the ground.

Stryke had that confirmed for the second time as Glozellan took him to Drogan. The wind was brutal, and the beating of the dragon's wings added an updraft that made him wonder if he could hang on. His rear was numb from the beast's knobbly back, swirling snow made his eyes water and it was so cold he lost feeling in his hands. When he tried to talk to the Dragon Dam he couldn't make himself heard over the buffeting.

He concentrated on the view. The glacier in the north looked like a milk spill inching across the landscape, and he was startled by how great an area it covered. Then the dragon wheeled about and he was looking down at lesser mountain ranges with white-tipped peaks. They gave way to sheer cliffs falling to rugged ground dotted with scrub.

Lines of hills passed beneath, and valleys resembling long, ribbed leaves. Mirror-surfaced lakes swathed in cottony mist.

Waving woods. At length they came to the rolling Great Plains. Later he spotted the silver thread of the Calyparr Inlet, the green cluster of Drogan Forest.

The dragon roared. It blasted his ears and shook his bones. Glozellan shouted something he couldn't make out.

They fell, it seemed to him, then dived, the rush of air stopping his breath. He felt the dragon realigning itself, levelling, and the dive became a glide. The ground sucked them closer, the tops of trees grew from raindrops to barrel lids. Screeching flocks of birds scattered.

Then the land was parallel, moving underneath faster than a charge. They were flying away from the forest, but in a banking arc that would eventually encircle it. He understood Glozellan was scouting for lingering custodians or other hostile forces, and lent his eyes to the cause.

Their girdling of Drogan took them briefly over a lip of ocean. He glimpsed waves hammering craggy rocks; pebbly beaches; an expanse of land; grass; trees. The slash of the inlet appeared, straight at this point, a god's burnished blade. Then the plains again, and the closing of their circle.

There was an exodus from the forest even before they touched down. Centaurs, and orcs on horseback and foot, raced to meet them.

The dragon landed with a gentle bump. Stiff-limbed, Stryke clambered down from behind Glozellan. She stayed perched on the rumbling giant.

He looked up at her. 'Thank you, Glozellan. Whatever you do, good luck with it.'

'And you, Captain. But I've something else to say that you must heed. Jennesta is heading for Scarrock, and she's leading an army. She's only a couple of days behind us, and could easily pick up your trail. You aren't safe here.'

Before he could reply she whispered something in the dragon's capacious ear and urged it away. It lifted, sturdy wings working their rhythm, fleshy legs gathering in. The backwash had Stryke retreating a few paces and shading his eyes with a hand.

He watched the leviathan impossibly rise, and saw its bulk convert to grace. It climbed, swung, described a courtly circuit overhead. Glozellan's arm went up and out. He returned the farewell. Then she took an eastward bearing and soared away.

Stryke was still staring when the others arrived.

Alfray, Haskeer, Jup and several grunts had ridden. Coilla had too, on Gelorak's back. There were scores of other centaurs with them, and the first of the running orcs approached at speed. They gathered around him, everyone's relief palpable. A clamour went up.

He waved them quiet. 'I'm fine! It's all right, I'm fine.'

Coilla slid from the centaur's back. 'What's been happening, Stryke? Where have you been?'

'Learning that an enemy turned out to be a friend.'

'What—'

'I'll explain. But over food and drink.'

He was given a horse and they headed for the forest.

The short journey allowed him a little time to think about Glozellan's news, and the fact that there seemed no rest.

Not far from the forest stood a crooked line of low hills topped with copses. On one, hidden in the trees, three figures stretched out, watching events below. They had their horses hobbled in the thicket behind, and were vigilant for patrols.

The watchers were human.

'Those *bastards*,' one of them rumbled vehemently.

He had a look of depravity that matched his companions', but he was shorter and scrawnier, and had a wiry, nervous energy they lacked. His sickly yellow hair was as thin as his near-transparent goatee, and his teeth were ruins. What nature and self-neglect hadn't given him was provided by enemies; a black leather patch covered his right eye, most of his left ear had been torn off, the little finger of his right hand was grubbily bandaged.

'Makes me want to puke looking at the things,' he went on, staring at the retreating centaurs, and especially at the orcs. 'Damned filthy, lousy—'

'Will you shut the *fuck* up, Greever?' hissed the man lying next to him. 'I can't think for your never-ending whine.'

The first human wouldn't normally take that kind of talk, but the group's self-appointed leader wasn't somebody to gainsay. He was beefy, if starting to run to seed through dissipation. A scar branded his pockmarked face, travelling from the centre of his cheek to the corner of his mouth. He had greasy black hair and an unkempt moustache. His eyes were dark and harsh.

'*You* ain't lost what *I* have, Micah,' the other returned in a grating whisper. He indicated his eye, ear and finger. 'All because of that orc *bitch.*'

'Not your eye though, Greever,' the third human reminded him.

'What?'

'Not your eye. She didn't do that.'

'No, Jabeez, she didn't.' The reply was delivered as though to a wilful and brainless child. 'It . . . was . . . another . . . orc. *Same difference!*'

Forehead crimped, the third man took a few seconds to absorb that, then said, 'Oh, yeah.'

In appearance he was the most conspicuous of the trio. Had the other two been combined into one being he would still easily outweigh them. But his huge bulk was due to muscle, not fat. His head and face were completely hairless. His nose had been broken at least once and set badly. He had a banal mouth, like a knife slash in dough, and the eyes of a newborn hog.

'Mind you,' he added, 'as for the *new* wound—'

Big and dim as he was, the first human's expression stopped him.

Greever Aulay and Micah Lekmann returned their attention to the forest scene. The last of the orcs and centaurs were entering the forest. Jabeez Blaan fidgeted, impersonating a flesh molehill trying to flatten itself.

'So what do we do, Micah?' Aulay wanted to know. 'Attack?'

'Attack? You got a death wish? Course we don't attack!'

'They're only fucking *orcs*!'

'*Only* orcs? You mean only the best fighters in Centrasia, after our kind? Only the ones that done for your good looks?' He sniggered unpleasantly. 'Them the orcs you mean?'

Aulay took that but looked murderous. 'We've killed enough of 'em in our time.'

'Yeah, but not by going square against a band that size, and never in anything like a fair fight. You know that.'

'So what do we do, Micah?' Blaan asked.

'Use our heads.' He regarded the questioner. 'Or some of them, anyway. Which is what Greever here ain't doing. He's all fired up, and that clouds his sense.' Lekmann nodded at the forest. 'What we gotta do with this bunch is the tried and tested. Bide our time, take 'em down singly or in small groups. Play our cards smart, we could still turn a coin or two on this.'

'This ain't about coin no more,' Aulay growled. 'It's about getting even.'

'You bet. And I want those freaks as much as you do. But maybe we can pick up some bounties too. And that relic thing they stole, that's gotta have value. Revenge tastes sweet and all that, but so does food, drink, the finer things We need wherewithal.'

'Who's going to give us bounty or buy that relic except Jennesta? And I reckon we ain't her favourites since we double-dealed her.'

'I prefer "left her service",' Lekmann corrected.

'Whatever you call it, I don't think it was too wise a move.'

'Careful, Greever, you're straying into thinking and that's my territory. I can handle Jennesta.'

His companions looked doubtful. Aulay replied, 'Maybe you

can, maybe you can't. I'm beyond that now. I just want that orc bitch, that Coilla.'

'But if there's spoils too you'll take 'em, right?' His voice hardened. 'Don't go fucking this. We work together or we're lost.'

'Don't fret about me, Micah.' He brought up his left hand. Or rather what had been. Now a cylindrical metal plug extended from his wrist. Attached to its end was a sharpened curve of steel, part billhook, part blade. Its polished surface caught and amplified the dismal light. 'Just get us near enough to those freaks and I'll earn my keep.'

5

As Stryke dug in his belt pouch he was afraid the phial might have broken. But the miniature ceramic bottle was intact and its tiny stopper was still in place.

He laid it in Keppatawn's outstretched palm. The centaur stared at it for a moment and seemed uncharacteristically lost for words. Then in an undertone he managed, 'Thank you.'

'We try to keep our word,' Stryke told him.

'I never doubted that. But I regret you losing one of your band doing it.'

'Kestix knew the score. All orcs do. And the mission suited our aim as much as yours.'

Coilla nodded at the phial and asked, 'What do you do with it?'

'Good question,' Keppatawn replied. 'I'll have to consult our shaman about that. In any event we need him to complete our bargain. Gelorak, fetch Hedgestus.'

His second-in-command moved across the encampment toward the seer's coop.

Stryke was relieved that attention had shifted from him to some extent. He had been fed, watered and generally fussed over. Then, with a sizeable audience looking on, he explained what had happened. But he didn't say anything about Sera-pheim appearing on the mountaintop, or his strange dream.

Nor did he mention the stars 'singing', although the memory of it had him eyeing Haskeer with something like sympathy.

Most of the others had melted away to their chores, leaving just the Wolverine officers, Keppatawn and Gelorak. Stryke preferred a small group. He didn't know how the centaurs would take the news about Jennesta.

Gelorak re-emerged from the shelter with the ancient seer in tow. Hedgestus moved slowly and falteringly on uncertain legs. A small ornamented chest was tucked under one of Gelorak's arms; he used the other to steady his ward.

Hedgestus greeted the orcs as Keppatawn took the box. He opened it and showed them the star. It was as they remembered; a grey sphere with two spikes of irregular lengths, made from unidentifiable matter.

'We keep our word too,' Keppatawn said, holding the box out to Stryke.

'We never doubted it,' Stryke told him dryly.

'Before you take this,' the centaur added, 'are you sure you want to?'

'*What?*' Jup exclaimed. 'Course we do! Why do you think we went through all that mud and shit?'

'Stryke knows what I mean.'

'Do I?'

Keppatawn nodded. 'I think so. This could be a poisoned chalice. More harm than good may come from it. That's the reputation of these things, and our experience.'

'We already figured that out,' Coilla said, hinting mild sarcasm.

'We've chosen our path,' Alfray put in, 'we can't stop now.'

Unusually for him, Haskeer voiced no opinion. Stryke thought he knew why.

He reached out and took the star. 'As my officers say, we didn't come this far to give up. Besides, we've no option, no other plan.'

But then Haskeer offered, 'We do. We could toss those things away. Ride out of trouble.'

'Where would we ride to that isn't trouble for us?' Coilla asked. 'Outside a dream, that is.'

Stryke stiffened, then decided she meant nothing by it. 'Coilla's right,' he told Haskeer. 'There's nowhere for us to go, not the way Maras-Dantia is now. And we'd never get Jennesta and the rest off our backs. The stars give us an edge.'

'We hope,' Jup murmured.

'The band agreed,' Stryke continued pointedly, '*all* of us. We said we'd go after the stars.'

'Never liked the idea,' Haskeer grumbled.

'You've had plenty of chances to get out.'

'It's not the band. It's those fucking things. There's something wrong about 'em.'

'Something wrong about *you*,' Jup mumbled.

Haskeer caught it. 'What'd you say?'

'All you've ever done is whinge,' Jup said.

'Not true,' Haskeer fumed.

'Oh, come on! And then there was all that cracked stuff about the stars singing at you—'

'Who you calling cracked?'

Haskeer was showing a flash of his old volatile self. Stryke wasn't displeased with that, but could see the name-calling about to escalate. It was a complication he didn't need. 'That's enough!' he snapped 'We're visitors here.'

He turned his attention to Keppatawn, Gelorak and Hedgestus, who looked slightly perplexed. 'We're all a bit tense,' he explained.

'I understand,' Keppatawn assured him.

Freeing the cover on his belt pouch, Stryke put the star with its fellows. He was aware of the others watching him do it, and especially of Haskeer, who wore an expression resembling distaste.

As the pouch was secured, Keppatawn sighed, 'Good riddance.'

That had Jup raising an eyebrow and the orcs exchanging looks, but none commented.

'Here,' the centaur chieftain said, handing the phial to Hedgestus, 'a tear shed by Adpar.'

The old seer accepted it gingerly. 'I confess I thought it impossible. That she was capable of something as humane as crying, I mean.'

'Self-pity,' Coilla informed him crisply.

'Ah.'

'But what am I supposed to *do* with it?' Keppatawn asked.

'There are precedents in lore to guide us. As with the blood of a warlock or the ground bones of a sorceress, we must assume this essence to be very powerful. It should be employed as a dilution, combined with ten thousand parts of purified water.'

'Which I drink?'

'Not if you value your life.'

'Or your bladder,' Jup let slip.

Stryke fixed him with a stern gaze but Keppatawn took it in good humour and smiled.

Hedgestus cleared his throat. 'The potion is to be applied to the afflicted limb,' he went on. 'Not all at once but over three days, and for the best effect during the hours of darkness.'

'That's it?' Keppatawn said.

'Naturally there are also certain rituals to observe and incantations to be chanted which—'

'Which serve to do nought but fill the forest with caterwauling.'

'They have an important function,' Hedgestus objected indignantly, 'and they—'

Grinning, Keppatawn waved him down. 'Easy, easy. You know how I enjoy pulling your tail, old charger. If there's a chance of your concoction working you can wail for a month for all I care.'

'Thank you,' the seer responded doubtfully.

'So when do we start?'

'Preparing the solution should be a matter of . . . oh, four or five hours. You can have the first application tonight.'

'Good!' Keppatawn gave the seer's shoulder a genial if

weighty slap. Hedgestus tottered slightly and Gelorak lent his arm again. 'Now we celebrate! Feast, drink, swap lies!' He scanned their faces and paused. 'You seem less than keen, Stryke, from your look. I know you lost a trooper, but this isn't disrespect. It's just our way.'

'No, it's not that.'

'What's up, Stryke?' Coilla said.

'The tear isn't all we brought.'

Haskeer gawped at him. 'You what?'

Keppatawn was puzzled. 'Really?'

'I should have told you earlier,' Stryke admitted. 'Jennesta's on her way to these parts, with an army.'

'Shit,' Jup whispered.

'How do you know this?' Alfray asked.

'Glozellan told me. She'd no reason to lie.'

'How long before she arrives?' Keppatawn wanted to know.

'Two, three days. I'm sorry, Keppatawn. She's after us—' he patted his belt bag '—and these.'

'She has no fight with us, nor we with her.'

'That wouldn't stop her.'

'We're used to defending ourselves, should it come to that. But if it's you she's after, why squander her followers' lives? Why divert herself?'

'In search of us. I reckon she's somehow found out we were in Scarrock. When she sees we're not there, she could end up at your door.'

'Then we'll make it clear you aren't here either. And if Jennesta wants to argue the point she'll find it costly.'

'We'll stand with you,' Haskeer promised.

'Yes,' Stryke agreed, 'we should stay and fight. There are Hobrow's custodians too. They could return.'

Keppatawn considered that for a moment. 'It's good of you to offer, but . . . no. The stars are important, I see that. We can fight our own battles. You have to get away from here.'

There was a brief silence, then Jup said, 'Where to?'

Stryke sighed. 'That's our next problem.'

'But not one you need worry about now,' Keppatawn told him. 'Join us in food and ale, shrug off your cares for a few hours. Call it celebration or wake, it's your choice.'

'With the enemy bearing down?'

'Is whether we feast or not going to stop Jennesta's coming? I don't think so. No more than supping on gruel would.'

'It's a good way of looking at it, Stryke,' Alfray opined. 'And the band could do with unwinding.'

Stryke addressed Keppatawn. 'Celebrating a warrior's life or a victory isn't unknown to us orcs. Though it's possible to celebrate too well.' He was thinking of Homefield and how that particular occasion had lead to all their later troubles. Before the centaur chief could question his remark, Stryke added, 'We'd be honoured to join you.'

The passing hours brought mellower moods.

Fowl, game and fish bones littered the banqueting boards, along with nut husks, discarded fruit and scraps of bread. Honeyed ale had been downed and spilt in quantity.

Now servers moved among the tables with tankards of mulled wine, and fires were banked against the creeping cold. At Alfray's suggestion Stryke had some of the band's cache of pellucid broken out. Smouldering cobs were handed round.

Off to one side a troupe of centaurs made low music with pipes and hand-harp. Others used muffled beaters to pound drums fashioned from hollowed tree trunks.

As repleteness, liquor and crystal subdued the revelry, Keppatawn hammered his table with a flagon. The babble and music died.

'Long-winded speeches don't suit us,' he boomed. 'So let's just toast our allies, the Wolverines.' Tankards were raised, ragged cheers went up. He directed his gaze at Stryke. 'And a salute to your fallen.'

Stryke got unsteadily to his feet. 'To lost comrades. Slettal, Wrelbyd, Meklun, Darig and Kestix.'

'May they feast in the halls of the gods,' Alfray responded.

A more sombre toast was drunk.

Another tankard was placed in front of Stryke. The server dropped in spice, then plunged a red-hot iron brand into the wine to mull it, releasing its aromatic tang in a little cloud of steam.

Stryke held up the brew. 'To you, Keppatawn, and your clan. And to the memory of your revered father . . .'

'Mylcaster,' Keppatawn whispered.

' . . . Mylcaster.'

The name was echoed reverently by a number of the centaurs before they drank.

'To our enemies!' Keppatawn declared, drawing perplexed glances from the orcs. 'May the gods confound their senses, dull their blades and bung up their arseholes!' That brought ribald laughter, particularly from the grunts. 'Now take your ease, and let tomorrow look after itself.'

The music struck up again. Chatter resumed.

But a cloud darkened Keppatawn's face as he turned to Stryke. 'My father,' he sighed. 'The gods alone know what he would have made of the changes we've seen. *His* father would barely recognise the land. The seasons ailing, war and strife, the dying of the magic—'

'The coming of the humans.'

'Aye, all our ills stem from that infernal race.'

'But you don't seem to be doing too badly here in the forest,' Alfray observed.

'Better than many. The weald nourishes us, protects us; it's our cradle and our grave. But we don't live in isolation. We still have to deal with the outside world, and it's going to hell. The chaos can't be held at bay forever.'

'None of us will be free of it until the humans are driven out,' Alfray replied.

'And perhaps not even then, my friend. Things may have gone down too far.'

'We meant it when we offered to stay and fight,' Stryke reminded him. 'Just say the word.'

'No. You have to move on and finish what you've started.'

Stryke didn't tell him he had no idea how to do that. 'Then at least let us help you beef up your fortifications,' he suggested, 'in case Jennesta does attack. We've a few days in hand.'

'That I will agree to. Your special skills would be welcome. But I don't want you lingering too long for our sakes.'

'All right.'

'And while that's going on we'll forge new weapons for you.' Pointedly, but with good humour, he added, 'Seeing as you've been so careless with the last batch we made you.'

'We get through a lot of weapons,' Jup informed him. 'It's an overhead of our trade.'

'Thanks, Keppatawn,' Stryke said. 'It's good for us to kick in something. We seem to have taken much from you and given so little in return.'

The centaur waved that aside. 'Weapons are nothing, we'll be making plenty in any case. As to giving, if you bring about the healing of this wretched limb—' he laid a hand on his blighted thigh '—you will have given more than I could ever hope for.'

There was a stir at one of the paddocks. A small group of chanting centaurs appeared. Hedgestus was at its head, supported by Gelorak, with four or five acolytes bringing up the rear. They began making their way across the clearing at a stately pace.

'Ah, the moment of truth,' Keppatawn said, signalling the music to stop.

With everyone looking on, the procession arrived at his table, their chanting lowered to a murmur. Two of the aides were carrying between them a stout wooden tub with curved iron handles. The table was cleared and the tub carefully set down. It was two-thirds full of what appeared to be unremarkable plain water.

'Don't look like much, does it?' Haskeer remarked.

Stryke placed a finger to his lips and glared at him.

'Come on,' Keppatawn urged the shaman, 'let's get on with it.'

A stool was brought and the chieftain lifted his leg onto it. Hedgestus held out his hand. One of the acolytes passed him a yellow sea sponge. He immersed it in the liquid, squeezed out the excess and with an effort bent to apply it. As he gently dabbed, the chanting swelled again.

If the onlookers expected an instant result they were disappointed.

After two or three swabbings Hedgestus noticed Keppatawn's quizzical expression. 'We must be patient,' he advised. 'The enchantment will need a little time to effect itself.'

Keppatawn tried to look stoical. The shaman continued with his ministration. Chanting droned on.

Eventually many of the bystanders started to melt away. Alfray sidled off with a clutch of grunts. Yawning cavernously, Haskeer went in search of more drink. Jup slouched, chin in hands, looking vacant.

Coilla, eyes as limpid as opals despite the alcohol and crystal, caught Stryke's attention. They quietly withdrew.

'I was getting worried about you,' she confessed, 'disappearing like that.'

'To be honest, so was I.' It was the first time he'd spoken to any of the band with nobody else around. He was glad to drop his defences a bit.

'I thought we'd really lost it this time,' she said. 'Not knowing if you'd gone willingly, and having the stars with you.'

'Now we've got four.' He fingered his belt pouch. 'I never thought we'd get this far.'

She smiled and indicated the others. 'Don't tell them that.'

His mood stayed doleful. 'But we're no nearer knowing what they do.'

'Or where we go next.'

He nodded. After a moment he continued, 'Something

strange happened on that mountaintop. That human, Sera-pheim, was there.'

'Glozellan took *him* there too?'

'That's the thing. She didn't. He just . . . appeared, somehow. Went the same way. And there was no getting off that peak without a dragon, believe me.'

'You spoke to him?'

'Yes. But what he said wasn't plain. I sort of understood what he was getting at, but I . . .' He trailed off, lost for words. 'He said I should carry on searching for the stars.'

'Why would he do that? Who *is* he?'

Stryke shrugged.

Coilla studied his face. 'You don't look too good,' she decided. 'What's wrong? Apart from all the shit we're going through, that is.'

'I'm all right. Except . . .' He wanted to tell her about the dreams and how he feared for his sanity.

'Yes?' she coaxed.

'It's just that I'm—'

A grunt jogged up to them. 'Sir! Corporal Alfray wants a rota for the work parties tomorrow.'

'Very good, Orbon. Tell him I'll be right there.'

'Chief.' The trooper went off again.

'What were you going to say, Stryke?' Coilla asked.

The moment had passed. 'Nothing.' She was about to speak again. He stopped her. 'It'll keep. Meantime, there's work to be done. Then we've got to get out of here. Jennesta's coming.'

6

Kimball Hobrow looked on as the stragglers drifted into the bivouac.

He knew what had happened. Forward riders from his custodian regiment, bloodied and dispirited, had reported on the debacle at Drogan. The indignity of being bested by sub-humans cut deep with him and his rage had been towering. Then he fell to brooding on revenge and planning his next move.

At length he turned from the scene and trudged to the tent that served as temporary field command.

Weighed down by the mission he had taken upon himself and the sour taste of a defeat, his back was a little less straight and his eyes lacked a mite of their usual steel. For all that, he couldn't help but be a striking figure. He was arrestingly tall and almost preternaturally thin. Black garb and a stovepipe hat added to his imposing appearance. His face was weathered and leathery, like a farmer's, though recent exertions had made it sallow. He had a slash of a mouth and a tapering chin adorned with silvering whiskers. It was a mien unwarmed by laughter or any of the gentler emotions.

But looks and dress were superficial in his case. Hobrow was the kind of man who, had he gone naked and wreathed in smiles, would still be marked out by the cold fervour in his heart.

'Father! *Father!*'

Sight of his daughter, standing at the tent's entrance, softened him to a small degree. He strode over and laid a hand on her shoulder.

'What's happening, Father?' she said. 'Are the savages coming?'

'No,' he assured her, 'the heathens aren't coming. You have nothing to be afraid of, Mercy. I'm here.' He steered her back into the tent and sat her down.

Mercy Hobrow resembled more the mother they didn't talk about than him. There was nothing of the cadaverous about her. She had yet to fully cross the divide between childhood and adolescence, or shed her puppy fat. With honey blonde hair, a porcelain complexion and unclouded blue eyes, she appeared vaguely doll-like but that was offset by a certain malevolence in her face, and a mean mouth.

Compared with everyone else her father surrounded himself with, her clothing seemed almost flamboyant. Eschewing black, she wore restrained patterned fabrics, and even a hint of plain jewellery. It spoke of his indulgence towards her, in contrast to the way he dealt with the rest of the world.

'Did they beat us, Father?' she asked, wide-eyed. 'Did the monsters beat us?'

'No, darling, they didn't. The Lord has punished us, not the sub-humans. He used them to send us a warning.'

'Why is God warning us? Have we been bad?'

'Not bad, no. But not good enough. He has found us lacking in undertaking His work, I see that now. We must do more.'

'How, Daddy?'

'He would have us grind the orcs and their like into the dust forever, along with the degenerate humans allied with them. I've sent for reinforcements from Trinity, and messengers have gone out to Hexton, Endurance, Ripple, Clipstone, Smoke-house and all the other decent, God-fearing settlements in Centrasia. When they heed the Lord's appeal we'll be more than an army, we'll be a crusade.'

Mercy's face had clouded at the mention of orcs. 'I *hate* them Wolverines,' she hissed.

'You are right to, child. Those beasts have particularly incurred God's anger. They ruined my scheme to cleanse this land in the Lord's name, and they stole the relic.'

'And that freak, that dwarf, he held a knife to my throat.'

'I know.' He gave her shoulder a squeeze. It was an action at once affectionate and distanced. 'They have much to answer for.'

'Make them die, Daddy.' There was a pitiless edge to her voice.

'Their souls will burn,' he promised.

'But we don't know where they are.'

'We know where they were last; somewhere around Drogan, with that other band of ungodly brutes, those half horse, half men abominations. We'll look for their trail there.'

'If God detests the inferior races so much, why did He create them?'

'As a test for us, maybe. Or it could be they aren't the Lord's work at all. Could be they're kith of the Horned One.' He dropped to a whisper. 'Satan's issue, sent to plague the pure.'

Mercy shuddered. 'Lord preserve us,' she breathed.

'That He will, and have us flourish too, providing we spread His Word. With blade and spear if need be. That's His command.' Hobrow's eyes took on a different light. He fixed them on a point above. 'Hear me, Lord? With Your guidance we'll bear the glorious burden of racial purity You have laid upon us. Arm me with Your sword of vengeance and Your shield of righteousness, and I will bring down the fire of Your wrath upon the savages!'

His daughter stared up at him with something like awe. 'Amen,' she whispered.

'Scurvy fat arse!'

'Shit breeches!'

Fists balled, Jup and Haskeer advanced on each other, eager to turn insults into action.

'*As you were!*' Stryke barked.

Glowering, the pair of sergeants lingered on the edge of mutiny. Stryke elbowed between them, palmed their chests and shoved them apart. 'Are you *officers* in this band or what? Eh? You want to stay sergeants, act like it!'

They backed off, scowling.

'No way am I taking brawling from you two,' Stryke told them. 'If you've got a beef, save it for the opposition. And if you've got energy to spare, you can work it off. You're on fatigues.' He flashed them a look that stifled their groans. 'Haskeer, muck the horses.' Jup smirked. Stryke turned to him. 'See that tree, Sergeant?' He pointed at one of the tallest in sight. 'Climb it. You're on lookout. Now *move!*'

They loped off, stony-faced.

'Their truce didn't last too long,' Alfray said.

Coilla nodded. 'Just like old times.'

'I think they like being at odds,' Stryke reckoned. 'Gives 'em something to kick out at. And there's not a lot else going on right now.'

'There's been a bit of unrest among the grunts too,' Alfray reported. 'Nothing serious. Squabbles, bitching, minor stuff.'

'We've only been here thirty-six hours, for the gods' sake!' Stryke complained.

'It was a good thing we had work to do on the defences. They would have boiled over earlier without the vent. But now that's done—'

'I won't have indiscipline just because they have to cool their heels for a while.'

'They're not *bored*, Stryke,' Coilla corrected, 'they're frustrated. About what we do next. Aren't you?'

He sighed. 'Yes,' he admitted. 'I haven't a clue what we're going to do or how we go about finding the last star.'

'Well, we can't stay here much longer while we figure it out.

We've got to head somewhere. Unless you want to hang around for a parley with Jennesta.'

'We're moving out today. Even if we have to toss a coin for where.'

'And end up doing what?' Alfray wondered. 'Pointless wandering? Spending the rest of our lives running from her and everybody else who wants what we've got?'

'You got a better idea, let's hear it,' Stryke flared.

'Heads up,' Coilla interrupted.

They looked the way she indicated. Keppatawn was approaching. Already his withered leg had improved noticeably. New, healthy skin was forming, and he walked with less of a limp. His whole demeanour seemed more robust.

When he reached them, Stryke commented on this.

'My affliction improves by the hour,' the centaur replied, 'though it's not entirely healed yet. Hedgestus tells me tonight's final application will complete the process.'

'That's good.'

'It's thanks to you.' He included Alfray and Coilla in his smiling approval. 'All of you. I'm in your debt for this miracle.'

'You owe us nothing.'

'How go your preparations?' Keppatawn enquired. 'Have you decided on your next move?' He added hastily, 'Don't think we're being inhospitable.'

'We don't. And in truth, no, we haven't settled on a destination. But we'll be going today, in any event. We know having us here would only make our enemies your enemies.'

'I'm glad you understand. The weapons we're forging for you are ready, and—'

A shout stopped him. Jup ran to them, arms pumping.

Stryke glared at him. 'I thought I told you—'

'Look what's coming,' the dwarf panted.

Centaurs were escorting a group into the clearing. Four or five of the newcomers had the unmistakable physique and gait of pixies. They led strings of mules and horses, laden with saddlebags, bolts of cloth, sacks and chests.

Grunts abandoned their chores and came to watch, followed by Haskeer. Stryke didn't reprimand them.

'See?' Jup nodded at a knot of figures, a dozen strong, marching at the caravan's rear.

They were orcs.

Alarm spread through the band. Weapons were drawn.

'Betrayal!' Haskeer growled.

Keppatawn reached out and grasped Stryke's sword hand. 'No, my friend. You aren't in danger. These traders are regular visitors.'

'And them?' He indicated the orcs.

'Not all of your kind are in hordes, you know that. Some manage an independent existence. These are freelance body-guards. What better protection could the merchants buy? Trust me.'

Stryke slowly resheathed his blade, then ordered the rest of the band to do they same. With some reluctance, particularly from Haskeer, they did as they were told.

The bodyguards were looking on, their bearing tense.

'It's a comedown for orcs,' Alfray remarked, 'reduced to hiring themselves out as chaperones for peddlers.'

Pixies and centaurs began unpacking the wares. Silks and rugs were shaken out, boxes levered open, sacks upended. An orc moved away from the crowd and headed for the band.

'Please remember that they are guests too,' Keppatawn said.

'Of course,' Stryke replied. 'We don't pick fights with our own kind.'

'Unless they pick one with us,' Coilla appended.

Keppatawn seemed a little pained at that, but held his tongue.

The orc arrived. He kept his hands well away from his weapons and looked as diffident as his nature allowed.

'Well met,' he offered.

Stryke returned the greeting. The rest of the Wolverines contented themselves with wary nods.

'I'm Melox,' the orc went on, 'leader of our group. I was surprised to see you here.'

'The feeling's mutual. I'm Stryke.'

'Thought so. Wolverines, eh?'

'What of it?'

'We're out of Jennesta's horde too. Not in a band. Footsoldiers.'

'How did you come to this?' Alfray wanted to know, a hint of disdain in his voice.

'Desert a horde and what's an orc to do? Still got to eat. Anyway, I could say the same about you. No disrespect.'

'None taken,' Stryke decided. 'Nobody's judging you. These are hard times.'

'Why did you leave Jennesta?' Coilla asked.

'Same reason you did, I reckon. Couldn't take no more.'

'Wasn't quite like that with us. But it came out the same.'

'Well, we think what you're doing's right. Should have happened long ago.' He nodded the caravan's way. 'This job, we'd drop it in a minute, all of us, if you'd take us on, Captain.'

'We're not recruiting,' Stryke told him. His tone was dismissive.

'But that's why you went AWOL, ain't it? To go against Jennesta? To get things back the way they were for us?'

'No.'

'It's what everybody thinks.'

'They think wrong.'

A strained silence descended. Jup broke it. 'You're being called.'

The bodyguard's comrades were waving him back.

'Maybe we can talk later,' Melox said.

'We're moving out today,' Stryke replied.

'Oh. Right. Well, if you change your mind about letting us join . . .' He turned and walked away.

Coilla directed, 'Good luck!' at his back. Then, 'You were a bit hard on him, Stryke.'

'I'm not leading a crusade, I've told you that.'

'Looks like not everybody agrees.'

'Another visitor,' Haskeer rumbled.

One of the merchants was coming their way.

Keppatawn smiled. 'This is somebody you should meet.'

The individual who joined them was short and fairly robust, yet somehow gave an impression of fragility. His features inclined to the feminine, with lush lips, slightly tapering, dreamy eyes and smooth pale skin. His nose was pert and just a tad upturned. His ears were small and swept back to a point. A green felt cap didn't entirely confine his mop of black hair. His tunic and leggings were green too, but the effect was offset by a wide brown leather belt with a gleaming buckle, and by a black cape, lined in green. The ankle-length soft hide shoes he wore, whose necks curled outward petal fashion, were known universally as 'pixie boots'.

It was impossible to tell his age because all his race had faces like infants. The voice was no clue either. It could have been a child's, albeit a rather knowing one.

'Keppatawn!' the pixie gushed. '*Wonderful* to see you again, you old *knave* you!' His pitch rose to a near shriek. 'And your *leg*! *Such* an improvement! How *delightful*!' He winked theatrically. 'Suits you.'

Laughing, Keppatawn accepted the pixie's delicate, outstretched hands in greeting. They were tiny compared to his. 'Welcome back. It's good to see you.' He wheeled his guest around. 'Meet some friends, the Wolverines.'

'I've *heard* of you,' the pixie exclaimed. 'Aren't you *outlaws*?'

'This is Stryke, band captain,' Keppatawn explained. 'Stryke, this is Katz, master merchant.'

'Honoured, Captain.' Katz thrust out a limp hand.

Bemused, Stryke took it, but didn't shake too vigorously for fear of fracture. 'Er, me too.'

The other officers were each introduced, and the grunts *en masse*. Katz simply nodded this time and didn't try offering his hand to any of them. Which in Haskeer's case was probably wise. He looked as though he might have bitten it off.

'You know, for a race with such a fearsome reputation, you orcs aren't at all bad,' Katz prattled. 'I've found that with my own retinue. Splendid fellows, every one of them. Always happy to oblige, nothing's too much trouble, and the best protection coin can buy, naturally. We pixies aren't warlike by nature, as I'm sure you know, and we—'

'Don't you ever shut up?' Haskeer grumbled.

'Of *course*, how thoughtless of me. Here I am engaging you in idle chit-chat when all you want is sight of my goods.'

'Wha—?'

'I know what you're thinking. You're asking yourself how you can afford the amazing commodities I'm about to lay before you. Don't worry about it. My prices are so reasonable you'll think I'm robbing myself, which in truth I am, and if even the paltry cost is too much I'm open to trade.'

'But I don't—'

'What's your need?' Katz ploughed on. 'Cooking pots? New boots? A saddle? The finest handwoven horse blankets?' He prodded Haskeer's chest with a tiny finger. 'How about a length of high quality cotton fabric with attractive flower patterns?'

'What would I want with *that*?'

'Hmmm, well, it might improve that dowdy uniform for a start.'

A series of expressions crossed Haskeer's face as he tried to decide whether he'd been insulted. Shoulders heaving, Jup clamped a hand to his mouth. Coilla found her feet of great interest.

'How . . . how's business?' Alfray quickly put in.

Katz shrugged philosophically. 'If you were selling hats they'd be born without heads.'

'Sure as the sun rises,' Keppatawn said, 'merchants complain about trade.'

'These are tough times,' Katz protested. 'The gods should give us honest tradesbeings a break.' He sighed. 'But it's preordained, I suppose.'

Glad to shift the conversation away from Haskeer, who'd settled on fuming, Coilla took the bait. 'You don't believe in free will?'

'Some. But I think most of what we do is set by the gods and the stars.'

'Sol signs?' Haskeer sneered. 'That's all . . . *pixieshit.*'

Katz ignored the slur. 'Ah, there speaks a true Seagoat.'

'Wrong,' Haskeer grunted.

'A Viper then.'

'Nope.'

'Er, an Archer?'

'No.'

'Balladier, Grapnel, Scarab?'

'No, no and no.'

Katz massaged his temple. 'Don't tell me . . . uhm . . . Bear?'

'Wrong again.'

'Eagle? Charioteer?'

Haskeer folded his arms and rocked on his heels.

'Basilisk? Longhorn? *Ah!* Yes! I see I hit the target there! Longhorn. Of course. I can always tell. It's a gift.'

Haskeer mumbled something low and threatening.

'Anyway,' Katz continued, 'as a discerning Longhorn I know you'll appreciate the benefits of the exquisite fabrics I can offer you for only—'

Haskeer snapped. With a roar he lurched forward and seized Katz by his throat, hoisting him clear of the ground.

'*Sergeant, please!*' Keppatawn shouted. 'Don't forget that pixies—'

There was a loud sound like ripping cloth and a spume of yellow flame shot from the merchant's hindquarters. Grunts standing three yards back scattered, then danced on the ignited grass.

'—have fire-starting abilities.'

Haskeer dropped the pixie and swiftly retreated.

Katz grinned sheepishly. 'Oops. Sorry. Nervous bowel condition.'

Keppatawn stepped in. 'I think it might be best if we got on with our business,' he stated diplomatically, ushering Katz away.

The band and Haskeer, open-mouthed, watched as the pixie moved off with smouldering breeches and a slight hobble.

'They must have behinds like quartz,' Jup remarked admiringly.

Gelorak placed a finger to his lips and quietly *shushed* her.

At first Coilla couldn't make anything out as she squinted through the tangled undergrowth. Then there was movement and she saw their quarry.

There were two of them. They stood as tall as centaurs and looked muscular, particularly in the arms and legs, the latter completely covered in dark shaggy fur and ending in cloven feet. Their chests were bare and ordinarily hairy, again like a centaur, or an hirsute human. Both angular faces had pointed beards and upswept, bushy eyebrows. Their jet black, curly hair finished above their foreheads in widow's peaks. They had eyes that were penetrating, with a somewhat cunning attitude to them. One of the creatures clutched a set of wooden musical pipes.

'I've never seen one before,' Coilla whispered.

'Satyrs are an extremely retiring race,' Gelorak replied. 'Even we rarely encounter them though we often hear their piping.'

'Is there ever conflict between you?'

'No. They are forest dwellers too, and have as much right to be here as us. We leave each other alone.'

She leaned forward for a better look and trod on a fallen branch. It gave a dry crack. The satyrs froze. Two pairs of yellow-green eyes, almost feline, briefly flashed in their direction. Then the creatures vanished with startling speed and remarkably little noise.

'*Damn.* Sorry.'

'Don't worry, Coilla. We were fortunate to find them at all. You can count yourself as privileged.' He looked up through the leafy canopy to patches of sky. 'It's been over an hour. Your band will be readying to leave. Shall we go back?'

She nodded, smiling. 'Thank you, Gelorak.' Her mind was on whether Stryke had worked out where they were heading.

They battled their way through the scrub and came eventually to the clearing.

The Wolverines were packing up their gear. Most of the grunts clustered around the horses. Stryke, Alfray and Jup were talking with Katz. Haskeer stood off to one side, eyeing the pixie with suspicion.

Gelorak went off on a chore. Coilla joined the band.

Stryke was stuffing gear into his saddlebags.

'Decided where we're going yet?' she asked.

'I thought maybe north.'

'Why?'

'Why not?'

'Fair enough.' She wandered to Alfray and Jup.

Stryke crouched and emptied his belt pouch, placing the stars on the grass in front of him. Katz came over and watched, vocally restrained for once. After a moment he remarked casually, 'I've seen one of those before. Couple of months ago.'

Nobody really took that in, least of all Stryke, absorbed by sorting. 'Hmmm?'

'One of these things. Here.' He pointed with his toe. 'Or similar anyway. In the hands of humans.'

Stryke looked up. 'What?'

'It was different to these. But near enough.'

'These? The stars?'

'That what you call them? Yes, one of these.' He saw Stryke's face, then straightened and looked at the others. 'What's wrong?'

A small window opened on bedlam.

7

The band crowded round him, firing questions. Numbed by the onslaught, Katz gaped, wordless.

Haskeer pushed through and grabbed him by the scruff of the neck. '*Where? Who?*' he demanded, shaking the terrified pixie.

'Careful!' Alfray shouted.

'Don't point his arse at me!' Jup yelled.

'*Steady, all of you!*' Stryke ordered.

Haskeer checked himself and gingerly put the merchant down. The hubbub calmed.

'I'm sorry, Katz,' Stryke said. He forced the others back, giving him air.

The pixie swallowed and took a breath. He rubbed his neck.

His bodyguards were running towards the band. Stryke held up his hands placatingly and called, '*It's all right! No problem!* Katz?'

'Yes.' the pixie croaked, waving the bodyguards away. 'Yes, I'm fine.'

They stopped, and after a moment's hesitation reluctantly dispersed.

Stryke laid a hand on Katz's shoulder. He winced slightly. 'We shouldn't have acted that way, but what you just said is very important to us. Can we go through it?'

Katz nodded.

'You say you've seen one of these before.' He indicated the stars at his feet.

'Yes. Well, like them. Different colour and different number of bits sticking out. But the same sort of thing.'

'You're sure?'

'It was a couple of months ago, but yes.'

'Where?'

'Ruffets View. Know it?'

'Mani township, down south.'

'At the tip of the inlet, yes. There's a lot of building going on there, thought it might be a good place for trade.'

'What kind of building?'

'You haven't heard?'

'Heard what?'

'They've got a breach. Earth energy escape. Big one. They were going to try capping it, store the magic somehow.'

'Did they?'

'I don't know. When I left they weren't ready. They won't manage it, if you ask me. Nobody else has. Anyway, they were putting up some kind of holy place there, a temple, and that's where I saw the star. The Manis didn't like me seeing it, mind you. They had me out of there pretty quick.' He stared at the stars. 'So what are these things?'

'Some call them instrumentalities.'

'Instru— *The* instrumentalities?'

'You've heard of them?'

'Who hasn't? But I thought they were a myth. They can't be genuine.'

'We think they are.'

'I've seen lots of so-called authentic relics all over Maras-Dantia. Not many of them turn out to be real.'

'These are different.'

A covetous light kindled in the pixie's eyes. 'If these really are the genuine items they'd be worth a fortune to the right buyer. Now if you let me act as your agent—'

'No way,' Stryke replied firmly. 'They're not for sale.'

Katz obviously found that a hard concept to come to terms with. 'Why seek them if you don't want to realise their value?'

'There's different kinds of value,' Coilla told him. 'Theirs isn't reckoned in coin.'

'But I've told you where there might be another one. Isn't that worth something?'

'Yeah,' Haskeer drawled. 'You get to live.'

Keppatawn arrived, curtailing any unpleasantness. 'What's happening?' he said.

'Looks like Katz here might have put us onto another star,' Stryke explained.

'What? Where?'

'Ruffetts View.'

'Have you heard about a magic escape there, Keppatawn?' Alfray wanted to know.

'Yes. It's been going on for some time.'

'Why didn't you tell us about it?'

'Why should I? I had no reason to think it would interest you. Such fissures aren't as rare as they used to be, sadly, with humans interfering with the energy.' He turned his attention to Katz. 'You're certain about your information?'

'I saw something that looked like them.' He pointed at the stars. 'That's all I know.'

'Why should he be any more right about this than the sol signs?' Haskeer complained.

'Maybe he isn't,' Stryke replied. 'But it's the only lead we've got. We either roam without point or head for Ruffetts View. My money's on Ruffetts.'

There was a murmur of agreement from the band. Stryke had nothing else to say.

'There's a purpose here,' Keppatawn declared. 'The instrumentalities emerging from obscurity. It's no coincidence.'

'That's hard to believe,' Alfray countered.

'You orcs have many admirable qualities. But if I may say so, you take too practical a view of life. We centaurs are down to earth too, but even we acknowledge that there is an unseen side to things. The hands of the gods may not be visible, yet they are behind much of our affairs.'

'Can we stop flapping our jaws and decide?' Jup pleaded.

Stryke began scooping the stars back into his pouch. 'We're going to Ruffetts View,' he said.

A couple of hours later Drogan Forest was behind them.

The band had newly-forged weapons, fresh horses and replenished rations. They also had a rekindled sense of purpose.

The route they followed was south-west, straight down the peninsula, with the Calyparr Inlet on their left. To their right, modest cliffs marked the shingled coast of the darkly lapping Norantellia Ocean. If they kept to a fair pace, Ruffetts View was about two days' ride.

Stryke continued pondering whether to tell the others about his dreams, and he hadn't mentioned to anybody that the stars had sung to him. He had talked to Haskeer again about *his* experience, although the Sergeant was no nearer making sense of it and proved unusually tight-lipped. It seemed he wanted to bury the incident. But Stryke drew some comfort from the fact that it was unlikely both he and Haskeer should go insane in exactly the same way. With that in mind, and somewhere to go, he felt he had more of a grip. But not entirely. There were still his dreams.

All of it lay heavily on him as they rode, and he was distracted enough not to hear himself spoken to.

'Stryke? *Stryke!*'

'Huh?' He turned and saw Coilla staring at him. Riding on her other side, Jup, Alfray and Haskeer looked on too.

'You were half the land away,' she gently chided. 'What's on your mind?'

'Nothing.'

He obviously wasn't inviting discussion on the subject. She changed tack. 'We were saying it was tough on Melox and the others, having to take on that kind of work.'

'You mean I should have let them join us.'

'Well . . .'

'We're not a refuge for waifs and strays.'

'They're hardly that, Stryke. You could at least have thought about it.'

'No, Coilla.'

'I mean, what's going to become of them?'

'You could ask the same about us. Anyway, I'm not their mother.'

'They're our own kind.'

'I know. But where would it end?'

'With you leading a serious revolt, maybe. Against Jennesta, and the humans, and anybody else holding us down.'

'Nice dream.'

'Even if we lost, isn't it better to go down fighting, trying to make a difference?'

'Maybe. But in case you hadn't noticed, I'm just a captain, not a general. I'm not the one to do it.'

'You really can't see how things are shaping up, can you?' she seethed. 'You can't see the nose on your face sometimes!'

'I've enough to do leading this band. Somebody else can fight the world.'

Infuriated by his obstinacy, she fell silent.

Alfray took on the argument. 'If there's really a lot of disgruntled orcs deserting Jennesta, there's a chance to build an army here. The way things are going in this land there's something to be said for safety in numbers Greater numbers, greater safety.'

'And the more attention we'd draw,' Stryke countered. 'We're a warband. We've got mobility, we can hit and run. That suits me better than an army.'

'Doesn't alter the fact that orcs always get the raw end of the deal. Could be a chance to change that.'

'Yeah,' Haskeer agreed, 'we're everybody's punchbags. Even human kids are told we're monsters. They think we're built like brick shithouses with tusks.'

'You want to fight for the whole orc race, go ahead,' Stryke told him. 'We'll concentrate on the last star, even if we die trying.'

'So what's new?' Jup said.

A distant sound cut through their conversation, keening, doleful, uncanny. It prickled the back of their necks and goosebumped their flesh. The horses shied.

'What the hell . . .?' Coilla whispered.

Alfray had his head cocked, listening intently. To him it was unmistakable. 'Banshee. Was a time when you could go your whole life and never hear one.'

'First time I have,' Jup admitted, suppressing a shudder. 'I can see why they're supposed to foretell disaster.'

'I heard it once before, years back. On the eve of one of the big battles with the humans, down Carascrag way. It earned its reputation then. Thousands slaughtered. You don't forget.'

'They're not so rare anymore,' Stryke added. 'If you believe what's said, they're heard all over now.'

After what seemed an impossibly long time the noise trailed off and died. It left them sobered.

Then it started to rain. Large drops the size of pearls came down, rust-coloured and rank-smelling.

'Shit,' Jup complained. He turned up his collar and gathered in his jerkin.

'Something else to thank the fucking humans for,' Haskeer said, following his example.

Several heads turned in the direction of the ice sheet to the north at their rear, out of sight but omnipresent. The band rode on miserably.

A sodden hour passed. When conversation eventually stirred again, somebody mentioned Adpar and the lot of tyrants. That jogged Coilla's memory. 'There's something I've been meaning to ask you, Stryke. I completely forgot until now. When we were in Adpar's realm, at her deathbed, you told her she was dying because of Jennesta. How did you *know* that?'

'She's right,' Alfray agreed. 'We don't know what killed her.'

Stryke was taken aback. He hadn't thought about it. 'I . . . I just said it to get a reaction from her, I suppose.'

'But it did the trick, didn't it? It goaded her back.'

'Doesn't mean to say I was right. Maybe Jennesta's name was enough to rouse her.'

'Maybe.'

'Perhaps you're developing farsight, chief,' Jup suggested, not entirely seriously. 'Hope it works better than mine.'

Stryke wasn't amused. 'Orcs don't—'

An arrow zinged past his ear. His horse tried bolting and he struggled with the reins.

'*To the rear!*' Jup bellowed.

The band wheeled about, drawing weapons.

A group twice their size was galloping all out in their direction, mounted on dwarf yaks, shaggy furred and malevolent eyed. The riders were about a third shorter than orcs and chunkily built. Their spherical heads were disproportionately large, with jutting ears and attenuated, fleshy-lidded eyes. They were hairless, save for bushy sideburns, and their rugged hides had a green tint.

'Gremlins?' Haskeer exclaimed. 'What the fuck we done to upset *them?*'

'Wanna go and ask?' Stryke retorted.

'*They're coming in!*' Alfray yelled.

Some in the gremlin first rank had miniature curved bows. They unleashed bolts as they rode. Several flew over the Wolverines' heads. One embedded itself in Haskeer's saddle. Another nicked a grunt's arm. A couple of Wolverines replied in kind.

'To hell with this,' Stryke growled. '*Engage!*'

He spurred hard and took the lead, the band at his heels. Pounded by torrential rain, mud-splattered, they headed for the enemy ranks.

The two sides flowed into each other with cries and colliding steel. A mêlée of swinging swords, lunging spears and clashing shields broke out.

Stryke made short work of the first gremlin he met. Dodging the creature's misjudged stroke, he ribboned his chest and sent him flying. The next to jostle in laid his blade across Stryke's with startling fury. They chopped and hacked, steel beating steel in a primitive, shrill melody. Brute force got Stryke through his foe's guard. A further blow punctured the gremlin's lung. Without halt, another duel commenced.

Charging between two enemies, Alfray flipped his banner spar to the horizontal. It struck both of them, high enough and hard enough to unhorse the pair. A twist of the spar brought it to a defensive position in time to block a further opponent. Evading the raider's sword, Alfray rammed home the lance, turfing the eviscerated creature from its saddle.

An overhand lob delivered one of Coilla's knives to a gremlin's eye. He disappeared screeching in the rabble. Beading another target, she was about to throw again when a gremlin sideswiped her. His blade was already moving, and near lopped off her nose. She seized his sword wrist, her grip like a bear cub's jaw, then set about stabbing. A triad of strikes settled it, fast and deep. The corpse toppled.

One of the fallen's comrades moved in, shield up, scimitar gashing the air. She flattened back in her saddle and slammed her boot into the shield. Writhing to avoid his sword, grunting with effort, she pushed hard enough to tumble the gremlin from his mount. He fell to the mercies of pawing horses and yaks. No sooner was she up than another gremlin tried to make a name for himself. She ripped her sword free.

Haskeer's sword was buried in the guts of a previous victim and lost with him, several killings ago. His dagger had been spent in similar fashion. Now he ducked and weaved through the attackers seeking a weapon.

He saw his chance as he rode alongside a gremlin crossing swords with a grunt. The distracted creature was easy pickings for a blood frenzied orc. Haskeer reached out and hoisted him bodily from his mount. He swung the kicking foe over to his horse and brought the gremlin's back down onto the saddle's pommel, snapping his spine. Prising the sword from twitching fingers, he dumped the body.

An opponent rushed towards him with a levelled spear. Haskeer swerved and brought his sword down on the passing heft, slicing it in two. Turning quickly, he was in time to send a second blow to the back of his opponent's sinewy neck, dropping him. Then two more foes closed in. Bellowing a war cry, he powered into them.

In a fleeting lull, Stryke quickly scanned the scene. He reckoned they'd downed about half the enemy. The grunts were giving a good account of themselves and it looked like none of the band had taken serious wounds. One more push and they could end it. He bowled into the reeling scrum and commenced hacking.

Another ten minutes of furious combat decided the matter. The gremlins who were able began withdrawing, leaving the bodies of their comrades, and the odd dead yak, scattered across the muddy swarth.

Coilla struck down a fleeing gremlin by pitching a knife between his shoulder-blades. Stryke galloped to her.

'Do we go after them?' she said.

He peered through the rain at the retreating raiders. 'No. We haven't got time for games.' He cupped his hands around his mouth and yelled, '*No pursuit! Hold back!*'

Several grunts who'd given chase quit and turned, spraying mud. The others took to checking the enemy corpses, wary for shamming.

Jup, Alfray and then Haskeer joined Stryke and Coilla.

'What the hell was that about?' Alfray wondered.

Stryke shook his head. 'The gods know. Casualties?'

'Nothing serious, first look. I'll set to binding what we've got.'

'I reckon it was bounty,' Coilla volunteered.

'Or more of Jennesta's mercenaries,' Jup suggested.

'You wouldn't hire gremlins for the job,' Stryke said. 'The bounty, maybe.'

A grunt called to them.

'What is it, Hystykk?' Stryke bawled back.

'We've got a live one here, sir!'

They dismounted and sloshed over to see. Alfray was already there, kneeling in the slime next to a gremlin who could have been young, for all they knew. He had a bad chest wound, crusting his robe with gore. Rivulets of blood mixed with the drumming rain.

He was taking deep breaths. His eyes were open and he constantly licked his lips.

Jup got close and to the point. 'What is it, the reward?' The gremlin focused, but didn't comprehend. 'The bounty or what? Why the attack?'

Alfray started fussing at the wound. The gremlin coughed. A little scarlet trickle crept from the corner of his mouth. But he spoke.

'Retribution,' he whispered.

Stryke was puzzled. 'What do you mean?'

'Vendetta . . . revenge.'

'For what? How have we wronged you?'

'Murder. A kinslin.'

'You're saying we murdered your kin?'

'We killed any other gremlins lately?' Haskeer wondered out loud. Coilla shushed him.

'Who are we supposed to have murdered?' Stryke asked, his words deliberate.

'My clan . . . uncle,' the gremlin stumbled, his breathing more laboured. 'Just an . . . old, harmless . . . scholar. Didn't . . . deserve it.'

An uncomfortable feeling grew from the pit of Stryke's stomach. 'His name?'

The gremlin stared at him for a moment, then managed, 'Mobbs.'

Stryke flashed his dream and remembered thinking he'd visited the afterlife. His veins chilled.

'The bookworm?' Haskeer said.

Coilla bent to the gremlin. 'You're wrong. We met Mobbs, that's all. He was fine when we left him.' She wasn't sure if she was getting through.

Alfray's efforts with the wound were brisker. Blood still flowed. He dabbed his patient's face with a cloth to soak up some of the rain.

Stryke gathered himself. 'I'm sorry about Mobbs' death. We all are. He wasn't our enemy. In a way, we have reason to be grateful to him.'

Haskeer gave a small derisive snort.

'What makes you think it was us?' Stryke went on.

The gremlin's breathing was shallow now. 'Our own kind . . . found him. Group of . . . orcs . . . in area. Black Rock.' He achieved a look of contempt through the pain. 'You know this.'

'No!' Coilla exclaimed. 'We *rescued* him, for the gods' sake!'

'And you've been tracking us all this time?' Stryke marvelled. 'Your efforts were in vain, my friend.'

'Delorran,' Coilla said.

'Of course. Had to be.' Stryke sighed. 'And I'd wager Jennesta's not been slow in spreading this story to further blacken our names.' He turned back to the gremlin. 'It wasn't us. Believe that.'

The creature seemed oblivious. 'You have many . . . enemies. You'll . . . only last . . . so long.'

'This has been a senseless waste of life,' Stryke told him. 'Isn't there enough killing without adding to it?'

'Rich talk . . . coming . . . from . . . an orc.'

'We're not crazed animals. But attack orcs and you have to expect us to fight back. It's what we do. As for Mobbs, I'm telling you—'

Alfray laid a hand on his arm and slowly shook his head. Then he leaned forward and gently thumbed shut the gremlin's eyes.

Stryke got up. 'Shit. All we do is bring death and suffering.'

'And get blamed for everything,' Jup added.

'Poor Mobbs,' Coilla said.

'We *are* liable for his death,' Stryke told her. 'Not directly, but it's down to us.'

'That's not so.'

'Tell me how it isn't.'

She didn't answer. None of them did.

For a split second, the thought occurred to Stryke that at least Delorran had paid. Then he realised he'd learnt that in a dream. Hadn't he?

It rained harder.

8

Rain drummed on the canvas tent.

Jennesta paced. Patience wasn't a virtue with her, and she had never seen the gain in cultivating it. Her creed was that the rabble waited while leaders took. Seizing what you wanted got things done. But what she wanted was just beyond her grasp.

She brooded too, on the depletion of the earth energies that made her sorcery erratic, and the lengths she had to go to in replenishing it.

Frustration and uncertainty made her more than usually dangerous. Which, in Jennesta's case, was saying a lot.

She was toying with the idea of issuing some capricious order. Something that would achieve nothing beyond the needless wasting of a few lives and her pleasure at the smell of blood. But then the flaps of the tent were parted and Mersadion deferentially entered.

He bowed and was about to speak.

'Are we ready to leave?' she demanded, eschewing formalities.

'Almost, Majesty.'

'I hate this unnecessary waste of time.'

'The army needed resting, ma'am, and the livestock had to be fed.'

Jennesta knew the reasons well enough and waved aside his explanations. 'If you didn't come to tell me you were ready, then what?'

His reply was hesitant. 'News, ma'am.'

'And from your face, not good.'

'It concerns your Dragon Dam. Glozellan.'

'I know her name, General. What about her?'

He tried to break it carefully. 'She and ... two other handlers, along with their charges, have ... They've ... left your service, Majesty.'

As she took it in, tiny supernovas flared in her remarkable eyes. Darkly. '*Left my service.*' She mouthed the sentence slowly and deliberately. 'By which you mean they've deserted. Correct?'

She seemed to him for all the world like a coiled viper, ready to strike. Not trusting words, he nodded.

'You're sure of this?' She checked herself. 'Of course you are. Else you wouldn't risk telling me.'

Mersadion knew how true that was. 'We have no reason to doubt the loyalty of the other handlers,' he offered.

'As we had none concerning Glozellan.' She was seething, building up to something.

He trod gingerly, hoping to placate her. 'If you have misgivings, we can replace the handlers. And we still have sufficient dragons, ma'am, despite losing three. As to a new dam, there are several candidates for promotion who—'

'All the handlers are brownies. How can I trust *any* of them? There will be a purge in the dragon squadrons.'

'Majesty.'

'First the Wolverines, then the bounty hunters I sent after them; now the Mistress of Dragons has abandoned my cause.' She fixed him with her wintry gaze. 'And all the while a steady bleeding from my army. How do I come to be surrounded by so many cowards and traitors?

It was a question he would never dare answer. He thought to avoid it by shifting her view. 'You could see it as the ranks purifying themselves, ma'am. Those left are bound to be the most loyal to Your Majesty.'

She laughed. Head back, raven hair tumbling. A flash of sharp, white teeth. Her eyes glittering with mirth.

He adopted a nervous closed-mouth grin.

Jennesta gulped back her composure and, still smiling, said, 'Don't think I see anything funny, Mersadion, this is pure derision.'

His face resumed its wary slump.

'You have a politic way of putting things. You'd have me believe the flagon's half full.' She leaned in to him, her laughter already a fading memory. 'But you're just an orc. When it comes to thinking, you punch above your weight. Let me tell *you* why treachery decays the ranks. It's because the officers aren't harsh enough in their discipline. And the line of command stops at your door.'

Only when events went badly, Mersadion reflected.

Jennesta drew back. 'I won't tolerate laxity. This is your last warning.'

Whatever he expected her to say or do in no way prepared him for what happened next.

She spat at him.

The spray soaked his right cheek, below the eye and as far as the line of his ear. It was an action that shocked and bewildered him in equal part, and he had no idea how to react.

Then he felt warmth on his flesh. Prickly heat spread all over the side of his face. He winced with discomfort and raised a hand, but touching the affected area made it worse. In seconds it grew hotter, like myriad fiery needles piercing his skin.

Jennesta stood and watched, rapt and faintly amused.

The sensation moved to scalding, as though vitriol had been splashed on him. He abandoned composure and cried out. His face blistered. He smelt the tissue burning. Pain became torment, then went beyond that. He screamed.

'Last warning,' she repeated, weighting the words. 'Ponder it.' She discarded him with an indolent gesture.

Doubled in agony, effluvium rising from his ravaged features, he blundered his way out. Through the whipping flaps Jennesta caught a glimpse of him stumbling to a water butt. She heard him howl.

Her action was a scintilla of the rage she could have shown at his news. She'd had enough of reversals, and if he brought her more the price would be his life. But for now she was content to brand him a failure. Literally.

An unmeasured span of time passed as she reflected on events. It came to an end when several of her orc personal guard arrived, making an awkward show of subservience. They brought her a captive, bound with chains; an offering to revitalise her powers, if only temporarily. Despite her mood, the sight of the vessel stirred Jennesta's curiosity.

So many races, so large an appetite, so little time.

She had never had the chance to savour a nappee before. Nymphs of pastures and forests, they were a scarce, coy race, not often seen. This was a particularly fine example. The creature was tall for her kind at about three feet in height. She was slender, with sparkly, near luminous skin, and delicately beautiful.

Some said nappees had two hearts. Finding out would take Jennesta's mind off her travails for a while.

The rain had finally stopped.

Stryke allowed a short rest break, the band settling at a point where Norentellia's shore had partially eroded the inlet. Twilight thickened the sky, and the view was of frowning clouds over a black, wind-driven ocean.

After eating, Coilla and Stryke moved away from the others. Sitting on horse blankets, sharing a canteen of wine gifted by the centaurs, for a while they talked about the gremlin attack. But tiredness, the warmth of the alcohol and, above all, the desire to share his burden overtook Stryke. He steered the conversation to his bizarre dreams. Before long, Coilla knew all.

'Are you sure this place you dream about isn't somewhere you know?' she asked. 'Somewhere in the . . . real world, I mean.'

'No. The climate alone marks it out. When have we ever seen Maras-Dantia as it truly should be, as it was?'

'Then perhaps you've made it up for yourself,' she ventured. 'Your mind's somehow created what you *want* to be.'

'Which sounds like another way of saying I'm mad.'

'No! That's not what I meant. You aren't mad, Stryke. But with the world going to hell in a pisspot, it's natural to want—'

'I don't think it's that. Like I said, these dreams, or whatever they are, they're as real as being awake. Well, almost.'

'And you always see this same female each time?'

'Yes. It's more than seeing her, too. I . . . *meet* her, talk with her, like I would with somebody when I'm awake. Except not everything she says makes sense.'

Coilla frowned. 'That's unusual for dreams. She's not somebody you've ever known?'

'I would have remembered, believe me.'

'You say that like she's real. These are just dreams, Stryke.'

'Are they? I only call them dreams because it's the nearest I can think of.'

'They happen when you're asleep, don't they? What else does that make them except dreams?'

'It's the feeling I get, the . . .' He shook his head, frustrated with words. 'I can't put it over. You'd have to go through it yourself.'

'Let's get this clear,' she stated matter-of-factly. 'What are you saying's happening to you if they aren't dreams?'

'It's like . . . maybe when I sleep my guard's down, and that . . . lets something in.'

'Listen to yourself. You're not making sense.'

'I'm not, am I? But I know it's getting to where I don't want to sleep.'

'You have these . . . dreams every time you sleep?'

'No, not every time. And that sort of makes it worse. It's like throwing dice whenever I need to sleep.'

She weighed her next remark carefully. 'If they aren't dreams, there's one possibility to think about. Could they be some sort of magical attack?'

'By Jennesta, you mean?'

Coilla nodded.

'I've thought of that, of course I have. Do you think it's something she could do?'

'Who knows?'

'But why would she want to? I mean, what's the point?'

'To make you think you're insane. To sow the kind of doubts you're talking about and lay siege to your mind.'

'That occurred to me, but somehow I don't believe it. As I said, in many ways the dreams are . . . pleasant. They've even strengthened my will once or twice. How would that serve Jennesta's plan?'

'I'm not saying it is her, just that it's a possibility. And who knows how her twisted reasoning works?'

'I grant you that. I still think she'd go for something more direct though.' He studied Coilla's face, and what he saw there told him it was safe to lay everything out for her. 'That isn't all.'

'Uhm?'

'The dreams aren't the only strange thing. There's something else.'

She looked puzzled, and apprehensive. 'What do you mean?'

Stryke took a breath. 'That business with Haskeer and the stars. Him saying they . . . sang to him.'

'That was the fever.'

'I had no fever.'

It took a moment for that to soak in. Finally she said, 'You too?' Her tone was incredulous.

'Me too.'

'Gods, you've been bottling a lot up, haven't you?'

'Still think I'm sane?'

'If you're mad, Haskeer is too. Mind you . . .' They exchanged dry smiles. 'What do you mean by singing?' she asked. 'Can you put it better than he did?'

'Not really. It's like the dreams, hard to explain. But singing's as good a word as any.' His hand went to the pouch at his belt. It had become an unconscious action, like the fingering of a fetish object. If asked, he would have said it was because he so feared losing them.

'I owe Haskeer an apology,' she said. 'I doubted him. We all did.'

'It's changed the way I look at what he did.' Stryke admitted. 'But don't tell him. Don't tell anybody about any of this.'

'Why not?'

'Wouldn't exactly inspire them, would it? Having a leader plagued by odd dreams and singing stars.'

'But you've told me. Why?'

'I figured you'd hear me out. And I reckon that if you think I'm some kind of lunatic, you'd say so.'

'As I said, I don't think you are. Something's happening to you, that's for sure, but it doesn't look like madness from where I'm standing.'

'I hope you're right,' he sighed. 'So you'll keep this to yourself? For the sake of band discipline?'

'If that's what you want, yes. But I think they'd understand. The officers anyway. Even Haskeer. Hell, *especially* Haskeer. This isn't the kind of thing you can keep secret forever though.'

'If it really starts getting in the way of commanding the Wolverines, I'll tell them.'

'Then what?'

'We'll see.'

She didn't press him on the point. 'If you want to talk again,' she offered, 'you know I'm here.'

'Thanks, Coilla.' He felt better for unburdening himself, but also just a little shamed for confessing something he thought of as a weakness. Though it made some difference that she didn't seem to see it that way.

The rest of the band were packing away their gear and rolling up blankets. One or two were looking Stryke's way, expecting orders.

He passed the canteen to Coilla. 'Warm yourself on this. We'll have to move again.'

She took a swig and handed back the bottle. As they got to their feet, she asked, 'What do you think our chances are at Ruffetts View?'

'Could be promising. That's what I feel anyway.'

'Well, most of your hunches have paid off up to now. The longer the odds, you still come up. Maybe there's something in what Jup said about you getting farsight.'

She meant it light-heartedly. They both knew orcs had never had magical powers. But it hinted at another layer of complexity, and mystery, neither found particularly amusing.

'Let's get out of here,' Stryke said.

They rode on through the evening, alert for further trouble.

Coilla found herself at the back of the band, just forward of the rear lookouts, with Alfray at her side.

After some trivial exchanges he glanced ahead and behind, then confided, 'I'm worried about Stryke.'

She was taken aback, given her earlier conversation with Stryke, but didn't show it, and replied with a simple, 'Why?'

'You must have noticed how he seems so buried in himself.'

'He has been a bit distant at times,' she conceded.

He looked at her sceptically. 'More than that, I'd say.'

'He's under great strain, you know that. Anyway, it's not as if he's leading us badly, is it?'

'There might be one or two in our ranks who disagree.' He glanced her way. 'You know I'm not one of them. I've seen a lot of leaders in my time,' he added, 'and served under quite a few. He's the best.'

She nodded agreement, although her own experience was nothing against his. And in that second she realised how old Alfray was. At least, how old compared to the rest of them. It was something she always took for granted, and she was surprised at the impact the awareness had on her, at how unequal it was to the smallness of her observation. The danger they faced was drawing them all closer together, making them truly see each other for the first time.

'We've got to support him,' Alfray said.

'Of course we will, we're a warband. The *finest* damned warband. Even those few dissenters you mentioned, they'll stand fast for Stryke.' She didn't say it just because she thought that was what he wanted to hear.

He smiled approval, satisfied.

They rode on, preoccupied with their own thoughts and a mite drowsy from lack of sleep. Finally Coilla came out with, 'That battle you mentioned, at Carascrag . . .'

'What about it?'

'It made me think how little history we know. It's being lost, like everything else. But you've seen so *much* . . .' She stopped, afraid he'd see that as a reference to his age, a subject he'd been touchy about lately. But his expression showed no affront.

'Yes, I have,' he agreed. 'I've seen Maras–Dantia in a better state, when I was a hatchling and a young orc. Not like it was in our forebears' times, but better than now. The humans weren't as numerous, and the magic had only just started to fail.'

'But the elder races fought against the incomers.'

'Eventually. The trouble is that what made this land great is also its biggest weakness. We're too diverse. The old suspicions and hostilities delayed the races uniting. Some didn't even see a threat until it was almost too late. Hell, maybe until it *was* too late.'

'And things have gone downhill ever since.'

'Which is why it's so important to keep the ancient customs alive.' He slapped his palm against his heart. 'Here, if nowhere else. The first place we respect the traditions is in each of us.'

'That's becoming a bygone way of looking at it.'

'Perhaps. But think of the comrades we've lost. Slettal,

Wrelbyd, Meklun, Darig, and now Kestix. We couldn't give one of them a decent sending off, and that cheapens their lives.'

'We weren't able to. You know it's not always possible in combat.'

'There was a time when it would have been. A time when the traditions were upheld.'

She was surprised by his passion. 'I didn't know you felt this strongly about it.'

'Tradition is what's held us together, and we throw that away at our peril. It's one thing that keeps us different, keeps us . . . *us*. I mean, look at how the Square's disregarded these days, even scorned by some of the younger ones.'

'I have to admit I sometimes wonder if religion's served us that well myself.'

'Don't take this the wrong way, Coilla, but there was a time when no decent orc would say something like that.'

'I honour the gods. But what have they done to shield us from our troubles lately? And what about the Unis and their single god? What has that brought but misery?'

'What do you expect of a false deity? As to our gods, perhaps they ignore us the more we ignore them.'

She had no answer to that.

In any event their conversation was interrupted by cries from up and down the line. Grunts pointed to the west.

It was just possible to make out, far over the ocean, a blacker shape against the sable sky, travelling north. Its bulk obscured the stars as it moved, and its great saw-toothed wings could be seen flapping. A tiny burst of orange flame from the creature's head wiped away any doubts.

'Do you think we can be seen?' Alfray wondered.

'It's a long way off, and it's dark, so we'd be hard to spot. More to the point, is it one of Jennesta's or Glozellan's?'

'If it's hostile I reckon we'll know soon enough.'

They watched until the dragon was swallowed by distance.

9

Blaan sat cross-legged, tongue curling from the corner of his mouth, as he scraped his shining pate with the edge of a knife.

Nearby, Lekmann used a branch to poke at the contents of a blackened pot hanging over a lively fire. Aulay was stretched out on a blanket, his head resting on his saddle, scowling one-eyed at the brightening sky.

Dew still whitened the grass. The inlet coursed sluggishly beside them, mist rising in the dawn chill. Drogan Forest was in sight, but far enough behind for them not to be spotted by centaur scouting parties.

'When the hell we moving?' Aulay grumbled, his breath visible in the frigid air. He was rubbing the spot where his wrist joined the plug that replaced his hand.

'When I'm good and ready,' Lekmann told him. 'We're close, I reckon, and we can't just go charging in. We got to be careful going against them orcs.'

'I *know* that, Micah. I just want to know *when*.'

'Soon. Now save your puff to cool your grub.' He prodded at the concoction. It bubbled, releasing a disagreeable aroma.

'We eating now, Micah?' Blaan piped up, eyeing the pot.

'Watch out, pumpkin head's spotted fodder,' Aulay muttered caustically.

Lekmann ignored him. 'Yeah, Jabeez. Bring your bowl.' He commenced dishing.

A platter was handed to Aulay. He sat with it on his knees, picking at the offering with his knife. 'Slop,' he complained, routinely.

Blaan noisily wolfed his down using his fingers, which he licked wetly between mouthfuls.

Aulay made a face. 'Ugh.'

'You're glad of him in a scrap,' Lekmann reminded him.

'Don't mean I have watch him eat.' He turned his back and faced the forest.

Blaan finally realised they were talking about him. 'Hey!' he protested, full-mouthed and greasy-chinned.

'*Company!*' Greever barked. He dumped his plate on the ground.

The others did the same. They quickly got to their feet, weapons ready.

A party of riders came along the trail from Drogan. They were humans and there were seven of them.

'Who'd you reckon they are?'

'They ain't them custodians, that's for sure, Greever. Unless their usual clothes are in the wash.'

The riders were dressed not unlike the bounty hunters themselves. They favoured leather breeches, high boots and thick wool jerkins, uniformly shabby. Most wore skins against the cold. Their heads were topped with skull helmets and chain-mail caps. They were lean, bearded, weather-bruised men toting a variety of arms.

'Could be reavers,' Lekmann decided as they got nearer. 'Hadn't heard there were any in these parts though.'

Aulay spat. 'All we need, fucking brigands.'

'What do we do?' Blaan wanted to know.

'Play it peaceful,' Lekmann replied. 'Remember that we can get more by pouring honey than cutting throats. Besides, the odds are in their favour.'

'You think so?' Aulay said.

'You stay calm, Greever, and let me do the talking. If it comes to force, follow my lead, and keep those blades out of sight. Got me?'

They agreed, Aulay reluctantly.

The riders had seen them by this time, and slowed. They were watchful but approached without guile.

When they reached the trio, Lekmann beamed and hailed them. 'Well met!'

Two or three of the men nodded. A burly individual with a full beard and lengthy, unkempt hair was the only one to talk. 'And you.' He spoke gruffly and a little offhand.

'What do we owe this pleasure to?'

'Nothing in particular. Just going about our business.'

'And what might that be?' Lekmann asked, the smile still plastered to his face.

'We're trailing renegades.'

'Is that so?'

Aulay glowered but said nothing. Blaan looked on with his normal semi-vacant expression.

'Yeah,' the leader said. 'You?'

'Farmers. We're heading to buy some livestock up beyond Drogan.'

The reaver looked them up and down, as did several of the others. Lekmann hoped they didn't know too much about farming.

'You ain't into that Mani or Uni crap, are you?' the leader said.

'Not us, friend. A plague on both. We just want a quiet life. On our farm,' he added helpfully.

'Good.' He stared Aulay and Blaan's way. 'Your friends don't say much.'

'They're just simple farm boys,' Lekmann explained. He held his hand to one side of his face so Blaan couldn't see, winked conspiratorially, and added in a whisper, 'The big one's simple-minded, but pay him no heed.'

'He looks like he could knock down a door with his head.'

'Nah, he's harmless.' He cleared his throat. 'So, you're renegade hunters. Don't suppose there's much the likes of us can do to help speed you.'

'Only if you've seen any orcs in these parts.'

Aulay and Blaan stiffened. Lekmann kept down his reaction. 'Orcs? No. But if it's them murdering bastards you're after, you're all right by us.' He made an expansive gesture towards the way of the camp fire. 'You're welcome to share our food. We got fresh water and some wine too.'

The reavers exchanged glances. Their leader made the decision, emboldened perhaps by their greater numbers. 'That's neighbourly. We'll join you.'

They dismounted. Lekmann offered canteens and told them to help themselves to food. They took him up on the former, were less eager about the latter once they looked in the pot. Aulay and Blaan stayed where they were. None of the reavers paid them much attention.

'Tell us more about these orcs you're tracking,' Lekmann said, trying to sound casual.

'They're a desperate, bloodthirsty bunch by all accounts,' the leader told him. He took a gulp from his canteen. 'Warband. Call themselves the Wolverines.'

Lekmann prayed that neither of his partners would blurt out anything. He was in luck. 'You're going after a whole warband?'

'This is about half our force. The rest are searching over yonder.' He nodded across the inlet 'I reckon we're more than a match for 'em.'

'Them orcs got a fearsome reputation when it comes to fighting.'

'Overrated, if you ask me.'

'Had any sign of them?'

'Not yet. Thought we did last night. Turned out to be a pack of gremlins, riding like their arses were on fire.'

'You seem sure those orcs are around here.'

'They've been spotted, more than once.'

'Big reward?'

'Pretty big.' The reaver chief eyed him with what might have been a hint of suspicion. 'Why? Thinking of trying for it yourselves?'

Lekmann managed a laugh. 'What, *us*? You reckon we're the sort to tangle with orcs?'

The chief looked them over. 'Now you come to mention it, no.' Then he began laughing himself. 'Not exactly bounty hunter types, eh boys?'

His men found the idea so risible they joined in with the laughter. They pointed at the trio and rocked with crude, good natured mockery. Lekmann laughed. Even Aulay made an effort, showing his rank teeth in the rictus of a patently false smile. Last in, Blaan started, great shoulders heaving, jowls aquiver, eyes watering.

Dawn broke on ten human males laughing in each other's faces.

Then something shook out of Blaan's jerkin, bounced and came to rest at the reaver chief's feet. Still laughing, he looked down at it.

The dark brown, shrivelled object was a shrunken orc's head. A sober cloud darkened the leader's face.

Lekmann swiftly drew his sword.

'What?' the leader said.

The blade slipped smoothly between his ribs. He gasped, the whites of his eyes showing. Then he went down, choking on blood. Some of his men hadn't finished laughing when realisation dawned.

Lekmann made straight for another reaver, slashing at him. Blaan lurched into the group, striking out with his fists. Aulay quickly snapped a blade attachment into his arm plug and filled his other hand with a dagger. The reavers struggled to defend themselves, in a confused scrabble for weapons.

Downing his second man, Lekmann moved in on the third. Now he met resistance. The target had his sword drawn, and intended butchery became a fight. They swapped blows, the reaver defending himself with fury, but it was immediately obvious that Lekmann was the superior fencer.

Having crushed his first victim's spine with a bear hug, Blaan discarded the corpse. Another reaver immediately charged and smashed his fist into the side of Blaan's head. It had as much effect as gentle rain on granite. The attacker staggered back, nursing his knuckles. Blaan moved in, enormous hands clasped together, and slammed them into his chest, audibly cracking bones. Face twisted in agony, the man collapsed like a puppet with slashed strings. Blaan began stomping him.

Riled by the commotion, the reavers' horses first milled in panic and then bolted, scattering across the inlet.

Aulay tugged his blade from his opponent's stomach and let him drop. The next reaver took his place, snarling with wrath and hefting an axe. It may have been a fearsome weapon but it gave Aulay the reach advantage. Ducking a swing, he lashed out and laid open the man's forearm. Bellowing, the reaver swung again. Aulay retreated fast, blundering into the cooking pot and sending it flying. Then he went straight in again, evaded the other's guard and spiked his heart.

Lekmann blocked the last feeble passes of the foe he'd already bettered. A second later he dashed the sword from the man's grasp and sliced his throat. The reaver sunk to his knees gushing blood, rocked and fell face downward.

Aulay and Lekmann coldly surveyed their work, the bodies sprawled in the kind of grotesque postures only death accorded. Then they looked to Blaan. He was on his knees with the head of the last living reaver in an armlock. A powerful jerk snapped the man's neck. Blaan got up and lumbered over to them.

Aulay eyed him murderously but said nothing.

'Did you *hear* that?' Lekmann seethed indignantly. 'Did you hear what that son of a bitch said?' He scowled at the dead reaver chief. 'What a nerve, going after the Wolverines. They're *our* orcs.'

Aulay was wiping clean his blade. 'Told you we should've moved sooner.'

'Don't you start, Greever. Now let's get this sorted.'

They set to plundering the corpses. Coins, baubles and weapons were filched. Blaan found a stale crust of bread in one of the dead men's pockets. He crammed chunks into his mouth as he ferreted through layers of clothing. Aulay discovered a pair of boots his size, and in better condition than his own, and tugged them roughly from their late owner.

Lekmann accompanied his scavengery with muttered complaints about the standard of modern morality.

'Look at this,' Blaan exclaimed, spraying crumbs. He held up a rolled parchment.

'What's it say?' Then Lekmann remembered Blaan couldn't read. 'Give it here,' he said, snapping his fingers. He snatched the scroll and unfurled it. After a few seconds' lip moving and brow furrowing, he got the gist. 'It's a copy of that proclamation of Jennesta's, saying how the Wolverines are outlaws and the big reward and all.' He crushed the parchment into a ball and flung it away.

'Word's spreading, fuck it,' Aulay grumbled.

'Yeah. Come on, they've got friends and we've got competition. We can't afford lingering here.'

They began rolling the bodies into the river. The languid flow carried them slowly away in billowing red clouds.

What the trio didn't notice as they laboured was that they were being watched by a motionless figure, way back on the trail to Drogan. He was tall and straight, with lengthy auburn hair and a fluttering blue cloak. His horse was purest white.

But had they looked, he wouldn't have been there.

All she had found was chaos.

It was no more than Jennesta expected, having used her sorcery to slay her sister and throw her realm into confusion. But she had allowed herself to hope that the Wolverines might still be here, and it was becoming obvious they weren't.

She watched from her chariot on the edge of Scarrock Marsh as the last of her infantry trudged back after scouring the nyadd domain. A soupy haze clung to the marsh, and it stank of rotting vegetation. The more distant rugged peaks of the Mallowtor Islands were swathed in a greater fog and barely visible.

Jennesta didn't anticipate any differing reports from the returning troops to the ones she'd had earlier. All they had to tell was of skirmishes with the remainder of Adpar's warrior swarm and odd sightings of the elusive merz.

Unless she was brought some positive news soon she would let her anger have its head.

She turned to look at the scene behind her, where the bulk of the army was billeted. Between their massed ranks and her chariot a dragon had landed. Astride his horse, General Mersadion talked with the beast's handler. Eventually he broke off and galloped back to her.

On arrival he gave a brisk salute and reported. 'We may have word on them, ma'am.'

'Indeed?' She stared at him. The right side of his face was covered by a padded field dressing secured with ties. A hole had been cut in the bandages for his eye. Here and there, at the edges of the dressing, the beginnings of raw, scalded flesh could be seen. 'Explain.'

'A group fitting the Wolverines' description was seen past Drogan, going south along the inlet.' There was an understandable frigidity in the tone he used with her, but also a greater deference.

'How reliable is this information?'

'It was a night sighting, Majesty, so there is some room for error. But the odds seem good, and it fits in with other reports from that area.'

She glanced the way of the dragon. It was spreading its wings, ready to take off again. 'Can we trust the handler?'

'After the threats I applied, I think so. Anyway, if rebellion was in their minds presumably they simply wouldn't have returned. You do have loyal followers, ma'am.'

'How touching.' There was unalloyed sarcasm in her reply.

'But if it really was them,' she mused, 'where would they be going?'

'There are a few settlements down at the tip of the inlet, ma'am, mostly small. The biggest is Ruffetts View. All Mani, I believe. So your Majesty would be welcomed.'

'I don't give a damn if they welcome me or not. They can ally themselves with me if they choose. If it turns out that anybody there harbours the band they're my enemies. Alliances are made to be broken, if it serves my interests.'

'There are Manis in our own ranks, ma'am,' he reminded her.

'Then it will be a testing time for them, won't it? Organise the rabble, General. We march to Ruffetts View.'

Well back from the army's rump stood what was little more than a copse, although it was dignified by being named a wood. A clandestine party inhabited it, watchful for patrols whose sole job was rounding up deserters. They numbered about two dozen and they were all orcs.

The highest ranking soldier present, as attested by the tattoos patterning his cheeks, was a corporal, and he had a plan.

'Even taking a loop round the army we can get to the inlet first, providing we travel light and fast. Then we stick to the coast most of the way to Ruffetts.'

'Are we *sure* the Wolverines are there?' a troubled looking grunt asked.

'So they reckon. One of the dragon handlers reported as much, a couple of hours ago. I was there, I heard it myself.'

'Desertion, it's a big move,' another waverer said. 'Leaving Jennesta's downright dangerous.'

'More dangerous than staying with her?' the corporal came back.

That got a broad murmur of agreement.

'Right!' somebody called out, 'Look what she did to the General!'

Others took up the list of grievances.

'The executions!'

'Dumb orders and crazy suicide missions!'

'And the floggings!'

'All right, all right!' The corporal waved them silent. 'We all know her crimes. Question is, what we going to do about it? Stay here and waste our lives for her cause or join Stryke?'

'What do we really know about this Stryke?' the first grunt shouted. 'How do we know he'll be any better a leader?'

'Talk sense. Because he's one of our own, and he's been running circles round her lackeys. If you don't want to come, that's fine. The way I look at it, the life we got now ain't no life at all for an orc. Die here, die there, it's all the same.' Most of them were nodding. 'This way at least we get a chance to hit back!'

'At Jennesta *and* the humans!' an orc cried.

'That's right!' the corporal agreed. 'And we won't be the last to rally to his banner. You know how many others are whispering about going over to him. Well, the time for talking's done!'

'Do you think it's true that the gods sent him to liberate us?' a voice piped up.

The corporal scanned their faces. 'I don't know about that. But I reckon he's heaven sent however he came to us. Let's stand with him!'

It was enough to tip the balance. They were decided.

'Follow Stryke!' the corporal yelled at them, and they yelled back.

'*Follow Stryke!*'

10

Total darkness. Nothing to hear, to touch, to smell. An utter void.

A pinprick of light. It grew rapidly. So rapidly it was like flying out of a well, and the rush gave him vertigo.

Sensation flooded in.

Brightness, a soft breeze against his skin, the scent of grass after rain, the sound of lapping water.

He realised he was clutching something. Looking down, he found he had a staff in his hands. And he saw that his feet were planted on robust timber planks. Uncomprehending, he lifted his head.

He was near the far end of a wooden jetty extending out into a vast tract of lucent water. Sunlight dappled its rippling surface, glinting intensely. The lake's farther shore was lined with trees in full leaf. Behind them rose gentle hills, then far off blue mountains with their crests in downy clouds. Fragile birdsong attended the perfect day.

'Come back, dreamer.'

He turned quickly.

She was there. Straight, proud, magnificent. Wearing a shimmering black feather headdress and clasping her own staff. Directing a steel smile at him.

He started to say something.

Instantly she snapped into a combat stance. She had the staff pointing at him, holding it shoulder-height like a spear, hands well apart. Her body was primed, ready.

The blow came so fast he hardly saw it.

Pure instinct brought up his stave, thrust out to take the tremendous crack she delivered.

He was shocked.

She drew back, flipped her staff so she held it level and attacked again. Once more he blocked her hit with the shank, feeling its impact soak into his taut arm muscles. Ducking, she tried a low stroke, aimed at his waist, but he was quick enough to deflect it.

'Wake up!' she scalded, dancing out of reach. She was grinning and her eyes shined.

Then it dawned on him that this was no unprovoked attack. The female was paying him the compliment, high in orc terms, of a mock duel. Although to any other race the idea that there might be anything complimentary or sham about it would ring hollow. It wasn't unusual for orc sparring to result in broken bones and even the occasional fatality.

'Stop resisting and start fighting!' she cried, confirming it. 'It's no fun you just parrying!'

In responding defensively he'd risked insulting her. Now he entered into the spirit.

He leapt forward and swept at her legs. Had he connected she would have toppled. But she jumped nimbly, clearing the shaft, and immediately returned a shot of her own. It missed more by luck than any design of his.

They circled each other, knees bent, stooping to offer less of a target.

She lashed out with a high swipe to his head. He countered it with one end of his staff, chancing it snapping, and her pole bounced off at the impact. His follow-up targeted her midriff, and would have knocked the air out of her if she hadn't batted it away.

Her comeback was a rain of heavy blows that had him swirling his staff like a juggler's club to avoid them. A second's let-up allowed him to seize the offensive again but hammering at her with a will only saw his blows fended off with swift dexterity.

They skipped apart.

He was enjoying it. The exhilaration of combat coursed through him, quickening his mind and springing his step. As to the female, she was a dazzling combatant; all an orc could hope for in a sparring partner.

They set to again. He swiped. She dodged and spun. Their staffs clacked with blow and counter blow. He weaved, attacked, withdrew. She melted from his sorties like liquid, then gave back as good as she got. Up and down the jetty they fought, rapping their woods, powering forward, being forced back.

Then she put out a downward stroke to his shoulder. He veered. Her staff smashed onto one of the jetty's timber uprights and snapped.

He caught her wrist and they laughed.

She cast her broken staff aside. It clattered on the boards. 'Shall we call it a stand-off?'

He nodded, discarding his own weapon.

'You're a master in the profession of arms,' she panted.

He returned the tribute. 'And you're well versed in the way of the warrior.'

They regarded each other with heightened respect. He found her glistening muscles, her moist sweatiness, particularly fetching.

The moment went by. She asked, 'Have you yet achieved your goal? The task you spoke of, that means so much?'

'No. There are many blocks on my path Too many, I think.'

'You can get round them.'

He didn't see it like that. 'The orc way is to go through them.'

'True. But sometimes a feather outweighs a sword.'

His confusion was obvious.

There was a tiny splash close by. A fish, orange and gold with black whiskers, swam into view. It nosed at the reeds growing from under the jetty.

She nodded at it. 'There's a creature that doesn't know the limits of its world, and in its ignorance has happiness of a sort.' She knelt and skimmed her hand through the water. The fish darted away. 'Be like a fish, and what stands in your way will be no more than water.'

'I can't swim.'

She laughed aloud, but there was no trace of derision in it. 'I mean only this: think on how much better you are than a fish.' While he pondered that, she stood and added, 'Why is it that when we meet I feel there's something almost . . . ethereal about you?'

'What do you mean?'

'Other-worldly. As though you're here but not quite. I remember our encounters as being more like dreams than reality.'

He wanted to know what she meant, and to tell her that's how it was for him, literally.

But he fell back into the void.

He came round with a start.

There were reins in his hands. He was riding with the band on the trail to Ruffetts View.

It was mid-morning. The day was overcast and drizzly.

He shook his head, then rubbed the bridge of his nose with forefinger and thumb.

'You all right, Stryke?'

Coilla rode beside him. She looked concerned.

'Yes. Just a bit—'

'Another dream?'

He nodded.

'But you only closed your eyes for half a minute.'

He was confounded. 'You're sure?'

'Maybe less than that. Just a few seconds.'

'It seemed . . . so much longer.'

'What was it about?' she asked tentatively.

'The female was . . . there.' He was still muzzy-headed. 'She told me things I sort of understood, but . . . not quite.' He caught her eye. 'Don't look at me like that.'

She held up her hands to mollify him. 'Just a little puzzled, that's all. What else?'

Stryke creased his brow, perplexed by the memory. 'She said I seemed kind of . . . *unreal* to her.'

For want of anything better to say, Coilla replied, 'Well, why shouldn't a dream have dreams?'

That was too deep for him. 'And we had a mock duel,' he added.

She raised an eyebrow, aware that in certain circumstances a mock duel could be the orc equivalent of flirting.

'I know what you're thinking,' he said. 'But this is somebody in a dream!'

'Maybe,' Coilla ventured cautiously, 'you've created your perfect female. In your mind.'

'Oh, that makes me sound really sane,' he came back sarcastically.

'No, no, no, I didn't mean that. It's understandable, in a way. You've never mated. Few of us have, given the life we lead. But you can't deny your . . . natural urges forever. So it comes out in dreams.'

'How can I think about having an alliance with somebody who doesn't exist? Unless I really am halfway to madness.'

'You're not, trust me. I mean, perhaps this dream female is what you want, not what you can have.'

'It doesn't feel like that. Then again . . .' He couldn't explain. 'I'll tell you one thing that really pisses me off though. I never get to learn her damn *name*.'

Several hours passed uneventfully.

By the afternoon Stryke had to order another halt to replenish their food and water before the final push to Ruffetts. Groups were sent off to hunt and fish. Others were assigned to gather wood, roots and berries.

Stryke left Coilla out of the foraging parties. He steered her well away from the others, and they settled by a thicket on the inlet's ocean side.

'What is it?' she asked, thinking that perhaps he wanted to talk about his troubling dreams again.

'Something I noticed earlier. I don't know what to make of it.' He reached into his belt pouch and brought out the stars, then laid them next to each other on the grass between them. 'I was looking at these and . . . Well, let's see if I can do it again.'

She was puzzled, and not a little intrigued.

He selected the sandy-coloured seven-spiked star they got from Homefield, followed by the dark blue one with four spikes from Scratch. An intense look on his face, he brought the two artifacts together. A minute or two's fiddling ensued. 'I don't know if . . .' There was a dull click. 'Ah! There.'

The stars had melded together, held fast by several of their spikes, although it was hard to see how they could.

'How did you *do* that?' she said

'I'm not really sure, to be honest.' He passed the coupled stars to her.

Even close up she couldn't quite grasp what the mechanism was that united the two objects. Yet they fitted together so perfectly they now looked like they were designed as a single piece 'This can't be right,' she muttered, turning the thing over in her hands.

'I know. It's almost as though it shouldn't be possible, isn't it?'

She nodded abstractly, engrossed by the mystery. 'I guess whoever made them was very clever.' That didn't convince even her. She had never come across a craftsbeing this smart. Tugging at them, she asked, 'Do they come apart again as easily?'

'Takes a bit of jiggling and some force. But maybe that's because I'm not doing it quite right.' He held out his hand and she gave them back. 'Thing is, they look right, don't they? As though they were meant to do this. It's not just a fluke, is it?'

'No, I don't think it is.' She couldn't take her eyes off them. 'You found this out by chance?'

'Sort of. Like I said, I was looking at them, and suddenly I . . . *knew*. It seemed obvious somehow.'

'You've hidden talents. It never would have occurred to me.' Her gaze was still on the linked stars. There was something about their union that seemed to defy logic. 'But what does it mean?'

He shrugged. 'I don't know.'

'Of course, you've realised that if two go together—'

'The others might as well, yes. There was no time to try it.'

'There is now.'

He reached for one of the other stars. Then checked himself. What stopped him was a rustling in the undergrowth beside them. They stood up.

Bushes parted and a figure stepped out, no more than two yards away.

'*You!*' Coilla exclaimed, hand flying to her sword.

'What the *hell*?' Stryke thundered.

'I promised we'd see each other again,' Micah Lekmann reminded them.

'Good,' Coilla seethed, regaining her poise. 'Now I can finish the job properly.'

The bounty hunter disregarded her threat and looked down at the stars. 'Very considerate of you, having these ready for me.'

'You want them, you come and take them,' Stryke replied coldly.

'Hear that, Greever?' Lekmann called out.

A second human emerged from the thicket on Stryke and Coilla's other side. His false hand had a saw-toothed blade projecting from it; his real hand held a knife.

'What is this,' Coilla sneered, 'an assembly of bastards?'

Aulay glared at her, radiating pure hatred.

'See, Greever?' Lekmann said. 'Divide and conquer.'

Pointing his sword attachment at Coilla, Aulay growled, 'It's time for payback, bitch.'

'Whenever you're ready, one-eye. Or should that be one-hand? Or ear?'

His face boiled with rage.

'Where's the stupid one?' Stryke wondered.

'The *other* stupid one,' she corrected.

Another clump of scrub was breached and Blaan erupted in a shower of leaves. He carried a hefty club of seasoned wood, topped with sharpened studs.

There was no sign of any of the other Wolverines.

'All we want is your heads,' Lekmann stated matter-of-factly, 'and them.' He indicated the scattered stars. 'So let's not make too much of a fuss, eh?'

'In your wildest dreams, poxbag,' Coilla told him.

Weapons slid from greased sheaths.

Stryke and Coilla moved back to back. She faced Aulay, by preference. He took Lekmann and Blaan.

The bounty hunters moved in.

Stryke hit out at Lekmann's probing sword. Once, twice, three times their blades met, briskly clattering. A small retreat by Lekmann gave Stryke the chance to turn swiftly and kick Blaan hard in the stomach. The big man half doubled and almost stopped coming. Stryke returned to beating metal with the leader.

On Coilla's side a four-bladed storm raged. To match her adversary she had armed herself with sword and knife. Now she engaged in a blurring round of strokes and counter-strokes. Swipes glided over heads and just short of guts. Jabs were sidestepped, chops deflected. Their blades locked and she booted his shin like a mule to part them. He hobbled back, fury bursting. His quick recovery almost had her throat, but she swatted aside his pass and repaid it with her own.

Blaan was crowding Stryke again. Dodging Lekmann's blade, Stryke spun and whipped his sword the big man's way. It was a close miss, but enough to repel him for a moment. Then it was back to hacking at the swordsman.

Aulay braved Coilla's flashing blades and got himself through. A backhand swipe of his dagger barely missed her face, and she was lucky to escape a thrust to her chest. Rallying, she sent out a combination of blows that forced him to retreat. While he was still off-balance she leapt forward and took a swing with her sword that by rights should have split his trunk. Instead it glanced off his artificial hand, striking blue sparks and adding to his frenzy.

Stryke had to make a choice. Both his opponents were near

enough to cause real grief, and it was a question of who to deal with first. Blaan decided it. His club came down in an arc that would have crushed Stryke's skull if his footwork hadn't defied it. Stryke's blade whipped out like a viper and laid open Blaan's arm. The human roared, rage outweighing his pain.

Coilla and Aulay had fought to something like a stand-off. They fell into pure slog, each battering away to breach the other's guard, both possessed by stubborn bloodlust.

Taking advantage of Stryke's diversion with Blaan, Lekmann charged in, speed hazing his blade. Stryke stood his ground, repulsing every stroke. Then he went on the attack, powering into the human, driving him back pace by pace. The chance of a kill was good. Blaan spoilt it. Blood streaming from his wound, club swinging, he barged into the fray again. Stryke directed a side-sweep at him. It didn't strike home, but it did send him reeling back to crash against the bushes.

Blaan was about to rejoin the fight when a great shudder ran through him. He moved away from the bushes, walking stiffly, eyes glazed. A further step revealed his fate.

He had an axe buried in his back.

The spectacle stopped the duellists in their tracks. Coilla and Aulay, Stryke and Lekmann backed off and gaped as Blaan shambled, the club still in his hand.

Haskeer exploding from the thicket broke the spell. Jup and two or three grunts were close behind.

Lekmann and Aulay turned and fled, plunging into the copse several yards distant. Jup and the grunts belted after them. Coilla joined the chase.

Stryke and Haskeer stayed were they were, mesmerised by Blaan. The axe head was sunk deep between his shoulder blades, with rivulets of blood running down his back, yet he kept on walking. His ire was aimed at Haskeer. Somehow he lifted his club. Lurching forward, he made to brain the orc with it.

Haskeer and Stryke acted simultaneously. One planted his

sword in Blaan's chest, the other in his side. Tugging their blades free they watched the giant sway, then fall heavily, face first. The ground shook.

There was a commotion in the thicket. Mounted on horses, Aulay and Lekmann tore out, swiping at the orcs chasing them on foot. Stryke and Haskeer threw themselves aside and the riders thundered through. Coilla ran up and lobbed a knife. It whistled over Aulay's shoulder. The bounty hunters put on a burst and rode hell for leather along the inlet.

'Do we go after them?' Coilla said. She was panting.

'By the time we got to our horses there'd be no point,' Stryke judged. 'Let 'em go. They'll be another time.'

'Bet on it,' she replied.

Stryke gathered the stars, then turned to Haskeer. 'Good work, Sergeant.'

'My pleasure. Anyway, I owed him.' He walked to Blaan's corpse, put his foot on its back and pulled out the axe. Stooping, he began to wipe its head with handfuls of grass.

Jup wandered over and stared down at the mountainous body. 'Well, at least the carrion's going to feed well today.'

'This is getting to be one hell of a crowded inlet,' Coilla complained.

'Yes,' Stryke agreed, 'we do seem to have a lot of unwanted suitors at the moment.'

'Don't expect it to get any better,' Jup told them.

11

It was early evening when the band arrived at Ruffetts View.

Their first sign of the settlement came when they spotted a hillside with an acutely angled slope. Chalk figures had been cut into the surface: a stylised dragon, an eagle with spread wings and a simple representation of a building fronted with pillars. The markings were fresh, their lines almost luminously bright in the gathering dusk.

The settlement was in a small valley close to the shore. A tributary snaked past it, and a wooden landing-stage had been built on the encampment-side bank. Several canoes and dugouts were tied up by it.

A vigilant approach took the band to a hill overlooking the colony. Stryke assigned a couple of grunts to tend the horses, then led the rest of the Wolverines to the hill's peak.

Ruffetts View had grown over the years to occupy a fair portion of the valley. It was a walled settlement. Tall timber uprights surrounded the whole sprawling community. Here and there, watchtowers poked above the walls, like modest cabins elevated beyond their status. There were several pairs of gates, and they were open.

'They don't seem to think they're under any threat,' Coilla remarked, indicating the gates.

'But it's obviously designed to be defended,' Stryke said. 'They're not complete fools.'

'That's one hell of a weird-looking place,' Jup decided.

What they saw inside the perimeter bore out his opinion. A track of compacted shard ran just inside the walls, following their lines. On the other side of that was a jumble of shacks and humble lodges, mostly built of wood, though some were stone, slate and even wattle-walled. Others seemed to be dwellings, but on a finer scale than those in the outer rim.

The centre of the settlement held the most bizarre sights. It was made up of three enormous adjoining clearings. In the one on the left stood Ruffetts' second highest structure; a stone pyramid taller than the outer walls. Rather than having a pointed tip, it was crowned with a plateau and low ramparts. Recent light rain had made its surfaces shine.

In the levelled space on the right stood a building still under construction. Through scaffolding, the upper part of its timber skeleton could be seen. The area below had been faced with what might have been grey and white marble. Pillars were being erected. It was obvious that the chalk etching they had seen earlier was a crude likeness of this structure. They took it to be the temple mentioned by Katz.

But what was in the centre clearing, by far the biggest, awed them most.

This area was surrounded by a circle of huge, blue-tinted standing stones. Most were in pairs, tall as houses, supporting a third, horizontal stone. The impression was of a series of high, narrow arches.

'The amount of work that must have taken,' Alfray marvelled.

'Humans are mad,' Haskeer stated. 'What a *waste*.'

Other lower stones, equally massive, were scattered within the circle in no obvious pattern.

Coilla gazed at what was in the circle's core. 'That's amazing,' she whispered.

'You've not seen one before?' Alfray asked.

She shook her head.

'Me neither,' Jup added.

'I've seen one or two,' Alfray said. 'But never this big.'

At the centre of the circle was a further set of the blue stones, ten of them, laid to form a pentangle.

From its heart erupted a geyser of magic.

It was silent and shimmering, like a vertical rainbow, but with a quality resembling steam that made it waver and dance. Its fluctuating edges were marked with a slightly darker, constantly changing palette of primary colours. The air around the energy spout was distorted, as though it was a hot day.

The peculiarity of it struck them dumb.

At length, Jup remarked, 'The magic must be strong here, with so much escaping to soak the land.'

'But it has to be constantly replenished,' Alfray reminded him. 'It belongs in the earth, *feeding* the land, not bleeding from it.'

There were plenty of people about in the settlement, and they all seemed to be moving with purpose. They thronged the streets, leading horses, driving carts, running errands. More swarmed over the temple, working on stone and wood, the sound of their labours just audible.

Coilla turned to Stryke. 'So what do we do?'

He was distracted by the incredible sight of the magic flow, but drew his eyes away. 'Well, these are Manis. They should be more welcoming of elder races.'

'You're talking about humans,' Haskeer reminded him. 'You can't rely on anything they do.'

'Haskeer's right,' Alfray agreed. 'Suppose they decide to be hostile?'

'We've got two choices here,' Stryke judged. 'Either they're going to be friendly and maybe we can trade for the star. Else they're hostile and there's nothing we can do against that number. So we might as well be open and go in under a flag of truce.'

Coilla nodded. 'I agree. After all, we know Katz got in there. So they're welcoming of pixies at least.'

'But remember what Katz said,' Jup put in. 'They're building that temple to house the star. If they'd go to that much trouble they're unlikely to part with it easily.'

'Yes,' Alfray said. 'A few bags of crystal aren't going to sway them.'

'Here's another thought,' Coilla ventured. 'If they prize their star so highly, how wise is it walking in there with four more of them?'

'We wouldn't exactly shout about it,' Stryke assured her.

'No, but what's to stop them forcibly searching us?'

'You could leave the stars with a couple of the band out here, Stryke,' Alfray suggested.

'I'm not happy with that. Not that I don't trust any member of the band. It's just that would make whoever we left vulnerable to attack by a larger force. I'd prefer to hang on to them.'

Coilla thought that wasn't the whole reason, and that he simply couldn't be parted from the things, but kept the opinion to herself. 'You really want all or nothing at all, don't you?'

He didn't answer.

Haskeer spoke up. 'This is just like what happened at Trinity, ain't it? Why can't we go about it a similar way?'

'No,' Stryke replied, 'it's different. There were dwarfs there that Jup could mingle with. Can anybody see any dwarfs down below?' They couldn't. 'Right. No other fish to swim amongst.'

If they thought that was an odd analogy they kept it to themselves.

'So what's the plan?'

'I reckon that, given the gates are open and they're being no patrols, they're trying to live peaceably. I say we get down there. Spy out things. See what the humans are like.'

'And try to steal their star,' Jup finished for him.

'If we have to. If they won't trade for it, or listen to reason.'

'We have *reason* on our side?' the dwarf came back sardonically.

'I want to think on this,' Stryke told them. He looked at the sky. 'We either go in right now, before it gets too dark, or wait for daybreak. I vote for daybreak.'

The others could see his mind was set. They agreed.

Though Alfray cautioned, 'You said yourself there's a lot of activity in these parts. It won't do to linger too long here. We might have unwanted company breathing down our necks.'

'I know. We'll have double guards, and any sleep's going to be done with an eye open.'

On another hill, not that far away, Kimball Hobrow was moved by the spirit and in full flow.

' . . . *marching under the banner of our Lord God Almighty!*' he bellowed.

The roar of many throats answered his words.

He stood next to Mercy, bathed in the eerie, flickering light of stands of torches burning on either side. Before them stretched a vast army, an ocean of human faces, holding aloft their own myriad brands. His custodians made up the front ranks, in pride of place.

'*Our hour of deliverance is near!*' he promised them. '*We need only the will, my brethren, to go forth and smash the heathens! To grind the bones of the dissenter Manis and the godless elder races! And I have that will!*'

Another avalanche of roars urged him on. Pikes and pennons jabbed the air.

'*I have that will and I have the broad shoulders of the God of creation to back it!*' As they cheered he scanned them, making a theatrical show of it. His was a ragtag horde, with custodians, Unis from farther afield who heeded the call, and a smattering of dwarf clans. But they had the Holy Spirit moving in them. Except for the dwarves, who were here for coin. '*We have many foes,*' he warned, '*for the black affliction of wickedness is everywhere! As I speak, one such is ahead of us in our crusade to Ruffetts! You know her! She is the Whore of the scriptures, the viper in God's earthly Kingdom! But together we shall rout her!*'

Approval rang out like thunder.

'*We are many and we will be more! We march for the future of our races!*' He had to include the wretched dwarf element, for now. '*For the children!*' Hobrow thrust a hand out to direct their gaze at Mercy's forlorn expression. '*For our immortal souls!*'

His army's clamour was fit to raise the dead.

Three to four hundred human corpses littered the killing field, along with an uncounted number of horses and beasts of burden. Overturned wagons and carts, some burning, formed islands in the slaughter.

Jennesta watched, uninterested, as her troopers moved through the fallen by torchlight, pillaging and killing the wounded.

Mersadion, his face swathed, invited her to celebrate the small victory.

She was in no mood to. 'I *curse* it. Having those fools blunder into us means more delay. Nothing is as important as the band and the instrumentality.'

Forgetting herself, she had used a word she had never used to him before. He had some small idea of its weight, but fought not to show it. 'The dying words of one of the enemy, ma'am, were that this force was on its way to join a greater Uni army.'

'Where?'

'That we couldn't discover, my Lady. But we think not far.'

'Then increase security, strengthen the guard. Do what you have to. Don't bother me with these matters.' Her temper rose sharply. 'Just get us to Ruffetts View!' She flicked her hand to dismiss him.

He went back into the night, nursing his growing canker of resentment.

There was a rivulet flowing nearby. She plucked a torch from its bracket, and went over to settle on the low bank and brood.

Her brand, thrust into the earth beside her, cast its flickering light on the dark waters. After a while she became aware that the reflection had taken on a more distinct tone. The pattern of its movement on the surface subtly changed, its brightness grew. Fire and water united and swirled.

More in weary resignation than surprise, Jennesta watched as the likeness of a face coalesced. A result of Adpar's death was that an elaborate medium was no longer necessary should Jennesta and her surviving sibling want to communicate. The trouble was it worked both ways.

'You're all I need, Sanara.'

'*You cannot hide from the consequences of your actions.*'

'What would you know about my actions, you . . . prodnose?'

'*I know the wickedness you practised on our sister.*'

Jennesta thought that given the chance she'd happily do it again. And intended to. 'You should be glad of what I did. It made for one less tyrant in the land. That's the sort of thing to please you, isn't it?'

'*Your hypocrisy's breathtaking. Don't you realise that many consider you the greatest tyrant of all?*'

Jennesta put on a flattered expression. 'Oh, really?'

'*You know full well that your despotism is blacker than most.*'

'Worse than the tyranny of the Unis' absurd sole deity? Harder than the followers of that unforgiving god?'

'*You're likening yourself to a god now, are you?*'

'You know what I mean. Anyway, where is the evidence that the accursed Uni god even exists?'

'*You could say the same of the elder races' gods.*'

'Who's setting herself above the gods now?' Jennesta sneered. 'Anyway, was this visitation only to berate me? Or do you have something useful to say? I am busy, you know.'

'*You drive away even those who try to help you. You drive everybody away.*'

'I'm still strong enough to achieve what I must.'

'*Perhaps. And I suppose I should be content that your support will in time bleed dry.*'

'I'll have what I want long before that, and then they'll be no need of corporeal followers.'

'*There are other, powerful, players in this game. And perhaps they include someone you need fear.*'

'Who?' Jennesta snapped. 'Who would dare? Unis, Manis, religious fanatics? Or those orcs I pursue? A band that runs and won't even stand to fight me? Those stupid savages?'

'*You mock them but they've proved more successful than you in this enterprise.*'

'What do you mean?'

'*I've said enough.*'

'They have more than one of the instrumentalities now, is that it?' She did little to disguise the eagerness in her voice.

Sanara didn't reply.

'Your silence is eloquent, sister. Well, I should thank you for that. Now I know that catching this band promises even more riches than I suspected. They've done the work for me.'

'*You're courting death and damnation.*'

'Is *that* all? I am the mistress of both, Sanara, and neither holds any fears for me.'

'*We shall see. But why cause so much grief? There's still time to mend your ways.*'

'Oh, fiddle me another air, you pathetic little whinger!'

'*Don't say you weren't warned.*'

'You plucked the words from my mouth,' Jennesta intoned menacingly, then slashed her hand through the water, breaking their connection.

She conceded to herself that dealing Sanara a similar fate to Adpar wouldn't be as easy. Sanara's protection was so much stronger. But she resolved to put the task near the top of her list.

Stryke and the band were still on their hill when dawn broke.

Shafts from the rising sun glanced off the structures below. Birds were singing.

Those of the band on sleep rota started to wake. Stryke had hardly slept at all. Coilla hadn't much either.

'Are they never still?' she wondered, nodding at the settlement.

People moved around purposefully, even at this hour. Materials were being carted to the temple and hoisted up the scaffolding.

'They're a busy lot,' Stryke replied. 'They worked on the building all night.'

There were humans outside the gates too. Some on foot, some riding along the front of the walls on horses.

Yawning, Jup said, 'They do seem to have patrols then.'

'They'd be fools not to,' Haskeer muttered.

Alfray stretched. 'Decided what we're going to do yet, Stryke?'

'Go in, I reckon, open and peaceable.'

'If you say so.'

'You seem doubtful.'

'We all are, a bit,' Coilla told him. 'We'd be hostages to fortune if things go wrong.'

'What else can we do? Like I said—' He looked over his shoulder, downhill, away from the settlement, an attentive expression on his face.

'What? What is it?' Coilla said.

Alfray joined in. 'Stryke?'

'Something's coming,' Stryke declared.

Haskeer stared at him. 'Huh?'

Then they saw them. A group of riders on the trail into the valley.

'Gods!' Jup exclaimed. 'They must be a couple of hundred strong.'

Coilla shaded her eyes with a hand. 'And they're orcs.'

'By the Square, they *are*,' Alfray confirmed. 'What do you reckon this is, Stryke?'

If our luck's out, it's another of Jennesta's hunting parties.'

'They've seen us,' Haskeer informed them.

Some of the mounted figures were waving shields and spears.

'They don't look hostile,' Jup said.

'Unless it's a trap,' Haskeer warned.

'I told you so, Stryke!' the dwarf blurted out. 'Farsight!'

'What do you mean?' Stryke was uncomfortable.

'You knew they were coming before we saw them. They made no noise. So how?'

'Just a . . . hunch.' He was aware of them looking at him strangely. 'What's the matter, don't any of you ever trust to instinct?'

Alfray nodded towards the riders. 'This isn't the time. What are we going to do about them?'

Stryke sighed. 'I'm going down to them. You and Coilla come with me, along with four grunts.'

He turned to Jup and Haskeer. 'You two assume command until we get back.'

If any of them thought this was a bad idea they didn't say it.

Stryke, Coilla and Alfray started down the hill, mustering Orbon, Prooq, Vobe and Finje on the way.

They arrived on the level at the same time as the mounted orcs. They looked peaceable. Many were smiling. Stryke thought that a couple of them were among Katz's bodyguard back in Drogan.

A corporal in the front rank seemed to be in charge. He hailed them. 'I'm Krenad. Well met! You're Stryke, right?'

'What of it?'

'It's you we've come to join.'

'I'm not recruiting.'

Corporal Krenad's face lost some of its shine.

'Hear him out, Stryke,' Coilla whispered.

When Stryke spoke again it was more placatingly. 'Where you from?'

'All over, Captain. Most of us deserted Jennesta's horde. The rest we picked up on the way here. And there's others coming, no doubt of that.'

'Why? Why do so many of you persist in following me?'

'I would have thought that was obvious, sir.' the corporal responded in a baffled tone.

'How did you know where to find us?' Alfray interrupted.

'From Jennesta, in a way.'

'What?' Coilla said.

'She's coming here, with an army. Big one. And not all the warriors she leads feel disloyalty the way we did. Far from it. Travelling light, we outpaced her. She's been trailing you for a while now, and one of her dragon handlers spotted you.'

'Well, we knew she was heading for Drogan,' Alfray conceded.

'Once you were spotted moving down the inlet she decided to skirt the forest,' Krenad explained.

'At least the centaurs should be spared her attention,' Coilla said.

'Oh, it's you she wants. Badly. But that ain't all.'

She raised an eyebrow. 'It gets worse?'

'There's another army ahead of her, coming this way too. Unis, we reckon. Both should be here in a day or so.'

'Shit, it does,' Coilla murmured. She turned to Stryke. 'You can't send them away. Not with Jennesta and the gods know who else on our heels.'

Stryke looked doubtful.

'We're on the end of a peninsula, if you hadn't noticed,' Alfray put in. 'If we have to fight our way out of this box some extra help's going to be useful.'

Stryke considered that.

'Come on,' Coilla urged. 'Military logic alone tells you it makes sense.'

'All right,' Stryke relented. 'For now. But until we get things sorted you're under my command, right, Corporal?'

'Yes, sir! That's just what we want.'

Somebody in the ranks shouted, 'When do we start fighting?'

'I've no plans for that!' he returned. Then he addressed the four Wolverine grunts. 'Get these soldiers billeted.' To the corporal he added, 'You'll take your orders from these troopers as though they were mine. Understood?'

Krenad nodded.

Stryke turned and began trudging back up the hill, Coilla and Alfray in tow.

'*Damn*,' he breathed. 'A force this large is going to make the Manis think we're here to attack.'

Coilla shook her head. 'Not necessarily. Not if we get in there now and explain things. An open-handed approach, as you said.'

'Maybe it's providential that these orcs have come,' Alfray pronounced.

Stryke glared at him.

Coilla smiled. 'Looks like you're being cast as a leader whether you like it or not, Stryke.'

He glanced back at the expectant warriors. 'I don't want this.'

'You've got it. Cope.'

12

Holding aloft a flag of truce, and on foot, Stryke marched to the settlement's gates. Coilla, Alfray and Jup went with him. Haskeer had been left in charge of the forces outside.

A group of Mani guards, half a dozen strong, appeared at the gates as Stryke's party reached them. They were dressed uniformly in dark brown jerkins and black trews with high leather boots. All wore swords, and two or three had bows looped over their arms.

'Well met,' Stryke said. 'We come in peace.'

One of the guards wore a green arm sash that seemed to indicate his seniority. 'Approach in peace and we accept you in that spirit,' he responded, apparently reciting a protocol. He departed from it to add, '*Why* have you come?'

'To speak with your leader.'

'We have no one leader. There's a council made up of the people's elders, the military and the priesthood. Decisions are taken communally.'

'Fine. Can we see somebody from the council then?'

'We don't refuse audiences unreasonably, but tell me the nature of your business.'

'We simply seek the protection of your walls while we rest before moving on.'

'You have a large force with you, and you're orcs. Is our protection necessary?'

'Even orcs need to sleep, and these are anxious times. And we're no threat, you have my word on that. We'd even be prepared to give up our weapons.'

That seemed to tilt the balance.

'That's not an easy offer for an orc to make, I think,' the officer said. 'You can keep your weapons. But be warned that trickery will be met by force.' He pointed up at one of the watchtowers, then another on the opposite side of the gates. Several archers stood in each, bows notched. 'Your movements will be shadowed, and they have orders to cut you down at any sign of violence.' He gave a light, almost apologetic smile. 'You'll understand the need for our caution.'

'Of course. Like I said, anxious times.'

The officer nodded. Then he lead them into the settlement.

'That's a promising start,' Coilla whispered.

Before Stryke could answer, they were facing another welcoming committee. It consisted of two humans they took to be elders, and a straight-backed military type whose triple green arm patches implied high rank.

One of the elders stepped forward. 'I'm Councilman Traylor, this is Councilman Yandell. Greetings. And Commander Rellston here leads our armed forces.'

The Commander didn't speak or even break a smile. He was in his prime, as far as the orcs could tell when it came to humans, with the beginnings of grey in his hair and full blond beard. His bearing, manner and weathered features spoke of a life as a soldier. He surveyed them with hard eyes.

Stryke remembered himself and responded. 'Greetings. I'm Stryke. These are some of my officers. Thank you for making us welcome.'

Rellston snorted. 'You're the Wolverines, right?' It wasn't really a question.

There seemed no point denying it. 'Yes.'

'I've heard you've been causing trouble in various parts.'

'We don't go looking for it, and any we've caused has been with Unis.' That wasn't entirely true, but it wouldn't have done to be totally honest.

'Maybe so,' Rellston replied sceptically. 'Let me tell you that trouble isn't something we encourage here. We try to live peaceable, and regard our neighbours, but at the end of the day we just want to be left alone. Anybody bringing us strife, particularly if they're of another . . . race, gets dealt with.'

Stryke was glad Haskeer wasn't with them. The gods knew how he'd react to the Commander's pomposity and attitude. 'We're here with no bad designs,' he assured him. Thinking of the star he knew that to be at least half a lie.

'What do you want of us?'

'Nothing that will do you harm.'

'To be specific?'

'We only need to rest in a safe place. We won't even ask for provisions or water.'

'Nevertheless, this isn't a haven for charity cases.'

'Remember we fight for the same cause.'

'That's debatable.'

Stryke didn't take the hook. In any event the Commander was more or less right.

Before anything else could be said they were joined by two more humans, an adult female and a boy child.

She was tall and slim, with long black hair, its glossy locks enfolded by a headband studded with discreet opalescent gems. Her complexion was peachy, her eyes cobalt blue. They matched her golden corded robe and the patterning on her soft suede boots. Her face was open and seemed kindly. In so far as orcs and dwarfs could judge such things, she would be considered handsome by her kind.

Traylor said, 'This is Krista Galby, our High Priestess.'

Stryke named himself for her. She held out a hand. The gesture almost startled him, unused as he was to human customs. But he took it, careful not to squeeze her slender, elegant fingers too hard, and shook. The hand was soft and warm, and quite unlike the healthy, rough clamminess of an orc's touch. Diplomatically he hid his distaste.

'These are some of the famous Wolverines,' Traylor informed her.

'Indeed?' the priestess responded. 'You have bloodied a few noses in recent times.'

'Only ones we found stuck in our business,' Coilla said.

Krista laughed. It sounded genuine, unforced. 'Well said! Although of course I do not approve of violent behaviour.' She added, 'Unless strictly justified.'

Coilla, Alfray and Jup were introduced as Rellston looked on disapprovingly. Then Krista laid a tender hand on the boy's head, ruffling his ebony hair and drawing a shy smile from him. 'This is my son, Aidan.'

There was no mistaking that he was her offspring, even to orc eyes. He shared his mother's likeness and her comely features. Stryke reckoned him to be seven or eight seasons old.

He noticed also that Krista Galby obviously had authority here. The others, even the Commander in his surly way, acted deferentially to her.

'What is the purpose of your visit?' she asked.

Stryke didn't get the chance to explain as Councilman Yandell spoke then, for the first time. 'Stryke and his company wish our protection.' He glanced Rellston's way. 'The Commander has some reservations on the matter.'

'He is right to be prudent about our security,' she replied tactfully, 'and as ever we are all grateful for his vigilance.'

Stryke suspected he was witnessing a play-off between the spiritual and temporal powers in this place. He thought she was handling it well.

'But I see no reason to doubt the good intentions of our guests,' she went on, 'and it is a principle of our community that we welcome all who come without malice.'

The pair of elders nodded in agreement.

'You would have them stay without limit?' Rellston queried.

'I would have them benefit from the usual custom, Commander, and enjoy our hospitality for a day. I'll take responsibility for them. Is that acceptable to you, Captain?'

'It's all we need,' Stryke confirmed.

The elders made their excuses, stating that there was much work to be overseen, and left.

Rellston lingered. 'Do you require an escort, ma'am?' he asked pointedly.

'No, Commander, that won't be necessary.'

With a parting glare he moved off.

'You must forgive him,' she told the Wolverines. 'Rellston is a good military man but he lacks . . . shall we say a rapport with other races. We aren't all like that.'

Coilla changed the subject. 'There seems to be so much activity here. Can we ask what's going on?'

The High Priestess pointed in the direction of the magic geyser, its upper plume visible above the rooftops. 'All we do revolves around that.'

'When did it start?' Alfray wanted to know.

'There was a small escape when the community was established some years ago, when I was no older than Aidan here. It's the reason the founders chose this place. Just lately the cleft has grown to what you see now.'

'The escape of so much energy must be bad for the land,' Jup remarked.

'Very bad. But we've never found a way to cap it. So we've turned to another solution.'

'What might that be?'

She looked at them for a moment, seeming to weigh things in her mind. 'I'll show you,' she decided. To her son, she said, 'Aidan, back to your studies.' It was obvious he would have preferred to stay, but under her beaming gaze he obeyed. They watched as he ran into the settlement's jumble of streets.

Krista headed the Wolverines in a different direction.

As they walked, Jup, in an undertone, said, 'Just a day . . .'

Stryke gave a small nod. He knew full well they needed to work fast to achieve their aim in that short a time.

The High Priestess lead them toward the heart of the settlement. On the way they were the object of curiosity, but no overt hostility. Then they took a path that fetched up at the half-built temple.

It was an imposing structure, even unfinished. The material being used for facing was marble, as they'd suspected, and the pillars on either side of the entrance, six in all, were as tall as mature oaks. A flight of broad steps swept up to the great double door entrance, which was guarded by troopers with pikes. The interior was lit by lamps and brands, and there was a hint of that most precious material, stained glass. Hundreds of men and women swarmed in and out of the building, and over the wooden scaffolding encasing it. Wagons lined up to deliver their loads.

'I'm sorry,' Krista apologised, 'but we aren't allowing anyone in unless engaged in the construction work. Visitors would only slow things down.'

Stryke suspected that wasn't the main reason.

'It's an amazing achievement,' Alfray marvelled, straining his neck to take in the uncompleted domed roof.

'We're very proud of it,' she answered. 'Do you know anything about our system here?'

Jup spoke for all of them. 'Nothing beyond you being Manis and sharing our loyalty to the true gods, and a respect for Nature.'

'Yes, that's right. But here in Ruffetts we've melded some of our own traditions to that. Our belief is that creation functions as a triad. On a secular level, that's how we govern ourselves, with major decisions made by a board of Citizenry, Military and Priesthood. The dictum of a trinity upholds our spiritual life too. We call them Harmony, Knowledge and Power.' She nodded at the temple. 'This is Knowledge. Come and see Harmony and Power.'

Intrigued, they followed her, taking a southward avenue.

At length they came to the middle clearing and its circle of blue stones. Up close, their true enormity came home to them.

But the magic geyser at the circle's centre was much more impressive.

'The energy's strong here,' Jup said. 'Very strong. I can almost *taste* it.'

Stryke thought he could too, like he'd been sucking a chunk of metal. He had goosebumps all over his flesh, and was aware of a faint ringing in his ears. But orcs weren't supposed to be susceptible to the magic, and neither Alfray nor Coilla commented on any effects, so he kept his counsel.

'This is Harmony,' Krista explained. 'These particular stones have a certain . . . property. I admit we don't really understand what it is. We do know they can attract and direct the earth energy.' She indicated the pyramid. 'Then it goes there, to Power, to be stored.'

'And you've done this?' Jup asked.

A slightly downcast expression passed across the Priestess' face. 'Not yet. But we think we're close. The earth energy is a mysterious force. We know so little about it.'

'Perhaps that's all the more reason not to mess with it.'

'I agree, and I know it was us incomers who have caused the problem. Or the Unis, rather, and their meddling with the power lines.'

'I meant no offence.'

'I take none. But believe me, here at least we are trying to heal the land and restore its power. We feel responsible for what humans generally have done.'

'Then this is an enterprise to be supported,' Alfray reckoned.

'We believe that all races can live together, and work harmoniously with Nature. I know this seems an absurd dream in the present climate.'

'That it does, ma'am,' the dwarf agreed.

'But it's no reason not to try,' Coilla butted in. 'We all have a dream to chase.'

Krista picked up the implication in her words. 'Well, I hope you catch whatever dreams you're after.' Her tone was sincere.

For the Wolverines, a sympathetic human was a rare experience. None of them knew quite how to react.

'What's life without a dream?' Coilla said.

Krista smiled at her. 'That's how we see it.'

Outside, the rest of the Wolverines and the orc deserters were growing restive. It helped when some Mani guardsmen, along with a few citizens, came out to pass the time of day and distribute a little food and ale. But the troopers were still frustrated by having to kick their heels.

The end of their hiatus was at hand, had they known it.

One of several lookouts on top of the adjacent hill began shouting and frantically waving his arms. Then the others joined in. They were just a bit too far away, and the wind was just a bit too intrusive, for their words to be clear.

Haskeer turned to one of the grunts standing nearby. 'What they saying, Eldo?'

He shrugged. 'Dunno, sir.'

Cupping an ear, Haskeer tried listening again. None the wiser, he started bellowing back. The lookouts gave up and began pelting down the hill.

The first to arrive was gasping for breath. '*Riders. Lots . . . of . . . riders. Coming . . . valley.*'

'What are they?' Haskeer barked.

'Black . . . shirts. Hundreds.'

'Shit! Hobrow's men! *Krenad!* Get over here!'

The corporal dashed to him.

'I thought you said they were behind Jennesta!'

'So they were, Sergeant!'

'You're saying Unis are coming?' a Mani guard caught on.

'Yes,' Haskeer told him. 'Custodians, out of Trinity.'

'*Hell.* We have to get everybody inside and raise the alarm.'

'Right! Eldo, Vobe, Orbon! Get everybody through those gates, on the double!'

As the grunts ran to spread the word, the Mani said, 'We've got to go in on foot! If we ride in, we'll spread panic!'

'What?'

'My people will think you're attacking!' he explained impatiently.

'Got it.' He put his hands to his mouth. '*Walk the horses! No riding in! Walk your horses!*'

There was a rush for the gates.

Stryke and Krista were discussing how best to bring in their waiting troopers when they were interrupted by a distant commotion. Then a bell began ringing. One by one, others took up the peal all over the settlement.

'The alarm!' she exclaimed. 'We're under attack!'

'But who—?' Coilla began. The arrival of the Commander on horseback cut her short.

'What is it, Rellston?' Krista called out. 'What's happening?'

'*Unis!* Approaching at speed!' He scowled at the band. 'Looks like treachery to me!'

'No!' Stryke protested. 'Why would we be plotting with Unis? This has nothing to do with us.'

'So you say.'

'Use your head, Commander!' Krista intervened. 'If our guests were hostile they'd hardly present themselves as hostages.'

'Are these humans black clad?' Alfray asked.

'Yes,' Rellston replied.

'Custodians. Kimball Hobrow's followers.'

'Hobrow?' Krista mouthed.

'You know of him?' Coilla said.

'Of course. One of the more implacable of the Unis. And his followers are fanatical.'

'Tell us about it,' Jup contributed.

'Come on!' Stryke snapped. 'To the gates!'

'Hold it!' Rellston bellowed. '*I'm* in charge of security here!'

'We're professional fighters. We can help!'

'There's no time to argue!' Krista reminded them. 'Let the orcs help, Commander. I must be at the temple!' She ran off.

Looking disgusted, Rellston wheeled about his horse and galloped away.

The band ran for the gates.

Arriving minutes later, they found most of the orcs had got in, although a few stragglers were still on their way. A crowd of Manis had gathered, handing out weapons. Humans and orcs stood ready to close the gates. Haskeer was in the middle of the tide, mustering a defence.

Prooq came out of the mob and reported to Stryke. 'Sir! Force of Hobrow's men. Four, maybe five hundred. Right behind us.'

Orcs were still streaming through the gates, which had begun to shut.

Krenad arrived.

'Didn't you say Jennesta would arrive first?' Stryke shouted at him.

'She's either been held up or this is some breakaway group sent ahead by the Unis.'

'Does it *matter*?' Coilla complained. 'They're still attacking!'

Stryke took the point and started shouting orders. Between times he told Krenad how to deploy the deserter force.

Through the part-open gates they saw the remaining late-comers racing home. A large force of custodians was close behind. Once the orcs were safely through, many hands strained to close the doors.

Before they could, the first twenty or thirty custodians forced their way through. Defenders scattered. The Unis set about the crowd with swords and spears.

'Let's get 'em!' Stryke yelled.

They flowed into the scrum as the gates were finally closed on a mass of Unis trying to get in. The defenders, mostly on foot, had their work cut out dealing with those that had made it through.

Haskeer adopted a typically direct solution. He lifted a barrel and hurled it at the next passing rider. It struck the man squarely, crashing him to the ground. The barrel shattered in an explosion of broken wood and metal hasps. Red wine showered everybody in reach.

'What a waste,' Jup sneered. He clamped a knife in his teeth and clambered to the top of the barrel's mate. A custodian came close. Jup leapt at him. They plunged to the ground together in a battling tangle. The dwarf finished it with his knife. Then he was up and looking for another mark.

Coilla grabbed the reins of a riderless horse and quickly gained its saddle. Drawing her blade, she made for a Uni busy hacking at a couple of men with pikes. He turned to engage her. They swapped three or four passes before she inflicted a wound. The custodian fell and the pikemen rushed in to deal with him. Coilla quickly snatched the vacant horse's bridle and held it until Stryke climbed on. Then they went hunting separately.

He made a first easy kill by chopping a Uni low to his back, freeing another horse. The next human put on a better fight. They hacked at each other as their mounts spun and reared. At last Stryke buried his sword in the enemy's chest. This time the steed bolted, carrying the dead weight into a knot of Manis who unceremoniously pulled off the corpse. One of their number vaulted aboard and went looking for prey.

Alfray found himself the quarry. A Uni bore down on him, jabbing with a spear. He batted it away, backing to the wall. Suddenly a pair of orcs appeared and threw themselves at the rider. They tugged at him, dodging his flailing spear. His balance was ruined. He came to grief on the compacted earth, a grunt's sword across his throat.

Jup downed a Uni with a lucky knife throw. Haskeer dragged one free of his horse and pummelled him senseless.

Greater numbers told, and in minutes the invaders were dead or dying.

Stryke and his offcers gathered.

'That would have been just the opening salvo,' he told them. 'Opportunistic, probably. We have to make this place secure before the rest get themselves organised.'

The bells took on a new urgency. They heard a distant roar.

A grunt they didn't know ran up to pass on the word. 'There's trouble at the west gates! They couldn't shut 'em in time!'

'Krenad!' Stryke shouted. 'Half your group with me! You stay with the rest and guard these gates!'

Manis were already running west. A greater uproar rose from that direction. More bells rang out.

'This is going to get out of hand if we don't act quickly!' Alfray bawled, climbing onto a commandeered horse.

Haskeer and Jup had rides too. The orc foot-soldiers moved to them *en masse*.

'All speed!' Stryke ordered, spurring hard.

He took his troops to the source of the turmoil.

13

The small army of orcs thundered through the streets, picking up citizenry as they went. Stryke and his officers rode. Bar a handful, the others ran.

Their passing added further confusion because many of Ruffetts View's inhabitants had no idea who this unknown force was. Every few yards they had to be vouched for by Manis jogging with them who knew the score.

When they got to the west gates they were wide open.

A huge fight was boiling around the entrance, with many more custodians inside than at the other gates. Most of the defenders were on foot, though some mounted Manis swam through the sea of bodies. Commander Rellston was one of them. They could see his sword working up and down above the crowd.

More of the enemy were spilling in. The humans trying to close the doors had a hopeless task. As things stood, with their numbers almost equalling the defenders in the area, the raiders were near having the upper hand.

'What's the plan, chief?' Jup asked.

'Take half the strength and engage the Unis in here. I'll lead the other half for command of those gates.' Then he had the best orc riders brought to him, and told them, 'Take our horses.

What we need to do has to be on foot. Your targets are the Uni cavalry. Got that?'

The grunts mounted and stood ready.

'Coilla! Haskeer!' Stryke called out. 'You're with me for the gates! Alfray, follow Jup! Now get those troops mustered!'

A custodian was laying about the humans trying to close one of the gates. An arrow flew across the top of the crowd and downed him. A tattered cheer went up from those who saw it.

With a much larger number of orcs, many unused to their new commanders and band discipline, it took precious minutes to organise things. But Jup finally got his sixty or so grunts divided into five groups. He would lead one, Alfray another. Experienced grunts were given command of the remaining three.

The dwarf confided to the old warrior that he was worried about working with unknown soldiers.

'But they're orcs! You can rely on them.'

'I never doubted that. But I don't *know* them. Suppose there's a bunch of dwarf haters in their ranks?'

Alfray almost laughed. 'Don't worry. They're new, anxious to please. They'll jump the right way.'

Stryke's sixty were formed into a battle wedge. All the while he drummed into them that their only focus was the gates.

When everything was ready, Stryke yelled, 'Hold until I give the word!' He elbowed himself into the prow of the wedge, sword and dagger drawn. Haskeer and Coilla stood beside him.

He bawled the order and a two-stage operation began.

The first required Jup and Alfray to soften up the opposition.

Their five groups went in, entering the fray from as many different directions. From the start they found they were expending as much energy on clearing Manis from their paths as engaging with their targets.

The squad Alfray fronted met little resistance at first. That was mostly due to spending several minutes reaching the first knot of wildly battling Unis. And once he got there, Alfray saw that beyond them, at the gates proper, Uni footsoldiers were spilling in. The enemy was dangerously near to establishing a foothold. Alfray began the work of thwarting that.

A custodian's horse waded over and its rider picked Alfray to shower with blows. He could do little more than deflect them with his shield. While he looked for an opening to counter-attack another Uni joined in, battering at the raised swords of the troopers beside him.

Determination and seasoned skill got Alfray through his opponent's guard. His blade raked the man's outstretched arm. It was enough. Almost immediately another of Alfray's squad rushed in to skewer the man on a pike, clearing him off his horse. The second rider was overcome by the sheer weight of half a dozen frenzied grunts.

Then there were no more horsemen ahead. But there were footmen aplenty. Alfray preferred that. It put things on a level.

He was about to pick a target from the plentiful supply when one chose him. A well-built and particularly mean-looking individual dashed in, howling, armed with a sword and hatchet.

Alfray blocked the first blow from the axe. He parried the sword and returned a swipe. All the while he was aware of the rest of his group engaging in vicious hand-to-hand combat. Over the racket he could hear Unis shouting praise and en-treaties to their god.

There wasn't much finesse in his duel with the Uni. It was a battering contest, down to the basics of strength and stamina. But Alfray had equipped himself with a shield, and in those conditions that gave him leverage. They chopped and hacked, pummelling each other's blades, trying to do down the other by sheer slog.

Alfray felt his age, something he didn't welcome this early in a conflict. But no sooner did he have the thought than it energised him. He began hitting out with greater force and wider swipes. The Uni started backing. Alfray blocked a cross with his shield. Then he sent out a blow of his own and it connected, gashing the man's side. It wasn't a profound wound, but pain had its way of wrecking a fighter's concentration.

The Uni tried to rally, and did a reasonable job of fighting back, but it was downhill for him from there. Alfray found it easier to dodge the man's subsequent passes as he waited for an opening. His chance came when the human put out a swipe too wide and too high. Alfray darted in and clashed his shield against the hatchet, neutralising it.

Then his sword flashed into the custodian's heart.

Fights boiled all around. As Alfray withdrew from his kill, a grunt went down next to him with his skull shattered. He wasn't a Wolverine.

Alfray faced another incomer's blade.

A bird, or a watchtower lookout, might have discerned some pattern in the anarchy below. They would have seen Alfray's group well into the mêlée, with Jup's almost parallel. The other three squads would show as having eaten through the fighting mob to a lesser extent. But all were inexorably working their way to the heart of infection.

Stryke held his contingent back, awaiting the opportune moment.

Jup's group was having no easier a time of it than any of the others. He saw comrades fall. Every step forward had to be paid for dearly, every kill was hard fought.

In unison with two of his squad, he managed to avoid the probing spear of a mounted Uni and help pull him from his saddle. The dwarf's companions killed the spilt custodian. Jup made a snatch for the horse's reins but the spooked animal bolted, trampling Manis and Unis alike. Confronted by a human looking for a mount, it reared and brought down his hooves on the unfortunate's chest. Then the beast was lost in the scrum.

There was no time to worry about the loss. Jup's detachment was embroiled in fights with more riders, and now Uni foot-soldiers had joined the quarrel.

Two black-uniformed, sword-toting fanatics closed in on him. His comrades were more than fully occupied; he would have to deal with the threat alone. He didn't wait for the first of his foes to arrive. Yelling a battle cry, he powered into the man, slashing maniacally. The custodian immediately went on the defensive. All the while his companion weaved on the periphery, looking for a way through Jup's fury.

He almost found it when the dwarf, swerving away from a thrust, stumbled and nearly fell. The second Uni rushed at him, sword levelled, with the intention of running him through. Jup deflected the blade and with swift instinct swiped his own across the man's throat.

The first custodian wasn't slow in trying to exact revenge. He took a chop at the dwarf's legs, intending to hamstring him. Jup skipped aside and narrowly escaped the injury. Then he forced himself back on the man, windmilling his sword, giving his bloodlust its head. The Uni stood his ground, Jup gave him that, but it might have gone better with him if he hadn't. A blur of muscle-aching swordplay turned the tide against him. At last, Jup laid his blade across the man's face, cutting deep. He howled and his head went down. He was seen off with a hefty downward chop to the nape of his neck.

There was barely time for Jup to take a breath before a new contender stepped in to bait him.

Stryke judged the moment right to take in the wedge. He bellowed an order. Shields were raised. With Haskeer to his right and Coilla on his left, he plunged them into the mob. They bulldozed and booted aside Mani allies when they obstructed their course. Any Unis in reach were butchered. The wedge had the hardest job of all. They had to get to the very heart of the enemy breach, clear it and master the gates. Stryke wondered if a sixty-strong force would be enough.

He headed for the goal like a blinkered horse, cutting down anybody in black who got in the way. Haskeer and Coilla worked alongside, hacking, slashing, stabbing. A prickly, unstoppable leviathan, the wedge cut a swathe through the barrier of flesh, depositing a toll of dead and maimed in its wake. Stryke couldn't say with honesty that its only casualties were from the enemy side.

They were about halfway, and the going was even harder, when something significant swam into view.

Commander Rellston.

He was on his horse but only just, stranded in the middle of a pack of Unis about to overwhelm him.

Stryke came to a swift decision that in truth he wouldn't have otherwise made. But he knew the value of a commander, even a bigoted one. His plan meant a slight change of direction, taking them more toward the centre of the gates. This he conveyed with a snapped order.

He was glad he had two trusted officers up front with him, and that he'd positioned other Wolverines at crucial points in the wedge. They could be relied on to carry out the change and make sure the others complied.

Like a great ship tossed on an ocean of blood and tormented flesh, the wedge slowly turned to a new course. It might already have been too late for Rellston. He was besieged by more invaders than he could sensibly engage, and only luck had stopped him succumbing.

The wedge ploughed on, barrelling aside friends and enemies. At last it arrived at the Commander and began chewing his antagonists. At that moment his horse went down, slain by a hatchet blow to its head. Rellston all but disappeared in the chaotic struggle. Stryke, Haskeer and Coilla began carving through the Unis, the others covering their backs.

Rellston was half crouching, doing no more than warding off his foes with a shield.

Quickly felling the would-be murderers, Stryke and Coilla made room for Haskeer. He reached down, grabbed the Commander by the scruff and hoisted him to his feet. Half dragging him, they pulled Rellston into the relative protection of the wedge. He was bloodied and pale, but nodded his gratitude as the wedge resumed its journey.

Within six torturous paces the second worst thing that can happen to somebody in a flying wedge befell Coilla.

A second's inattention had her missing an incoming blade

until it almost hit. She ducked, jabbed back and lost her footing.
Reality whirled and she was separated from her comrades, alone
in the scrum. The wedge, unstoppable, rolled on. It moved
slowly, but still she couldn't get back to it.

Then three Unis closed in, fresh from a kill.

Coilla didn't fool with the first. She knocked his sword aside
and riddled his breast with rapid cross-strokes. The other two
came at her with murderous speed. She glanced away the blade
of one, delivered a blow to the other's shield.

A frantic exchange of swordplay ended with one Uni down,
coughing blood. The remaining custodian tried to pay her back.
She spun to him, averting his blade with a ringing impact. Their
next exchange wound up with his abdomen lacerated. He sank
to his knees, clutching his flowing stomach.

Coilla looked around. The end of the wedge was moving
out of reach. It was close, but separated from her by layers of
people. And other Unis were coming her way. Too many of
them.

She had a crazy idea, thought *What the hell*, and went for it.

Running the few paces between her and the disembowelled
human, she used his drooping shoulder as a springboard. He
cried out as she left him to his fate. The added height gave her
enough clearance to get over the heads of the crowd. She
landed on the wedge, miraculously missing up-thrust swords
and spears, thumping heavily on a shield. Helping hands lowered her, and she worked her way to the nose, breathless.

'Glad you could drop in,' Stryke remarked sardonically.

Shortly after, the prow of the wedge met Jup's squad battling
in from their left. They melded, and together attacked the final,
clotted knot of Unis fighting to get in the gates. Aid came from
arrows directed from a nearby watchtower. But bolts were
winging in from the outside too. The danger of their position
was underlined when a grunt caught one in his head and
collapsed lifeless.

Stryke peeled off twenty troopers and assigned ten to each
gate. Once they joined the Manis already struggling with them,

the great doors began to inch shut. With a supreme effort, the last of the fresh invaders were forced back. The gap between the gates narrowed. Then they met with an echoing crash. A massive wooden crossbar was hurriedly passed through iron loops to secure it. Numerous fists and sword hilts could be heard pounding against the other side.

There were still invaders within the walls, but they were isolated and outnumbered now. It didn't take long to quell them.

Jup slumped against the gate, sweat pouring down his face. 'That was too close,' he panted.

An hour or two later, Stryke and Coilla climbed to a walkway at the top of Ruffetts' outer wall. There were other Manis on it, standing apart from them. gazing over the fortifications. The orcs stared too, trying to estimate the size of the army laying siege. It occupied a vast area. Hundreds of humans topped the surrounding hills too, including the one which just hours before the orcs had occupied. Stryke and Coilla agreed that they numbered fifteen to twenty thousand, which would match the settlement's population, if not actually outstrip it.

Down in the township some kind of Mani religious ceremony was going on. It centred around the geyser, which could just be seen through gaps in the buildings, and above them. Figures were outlined by the eerie glow, with hands linked and robes billowing. Beyond stood the temple, bathed in the soft radiance.

Stryke wasn't happy. 'The defence of those gates was a shambles,' he complained. 'We lost seventeen. The gods know how many Manis went down. Plus injuries. It shouldn't have happened.'

'These people aren't fighters,' Coilla said. 'The military contingent here's probably no more than ten per cent. They're not like us. Warfare doesn't come naturally to them. You can't blame them.'

'I'm not. I'm just saying that you need the right tools for the job. You can't cut butter with a club.'

'They've got their dream.' She wondered if that was an appropriate word to use to him, all things considered. But he didn't react. 'It seems to be all that matters to them.'

'They should learn that dreams have to be defended.' He looked out at the army again. 'If it isn't already too late.'

'So how do we get out of this mess?'

'We could just cut and run. We might make it.'

'Without the star? And leaving these humans to fight alone?'

'Is that really our problem?'

'They offered us hospitality, Stryke.'

He sighed. 'The other option is to throw in our lot with them and help get a proper defence sorted.'

'Post orcs throughout the settlement,' she speculated. 'Maybe divide our force into five or six units and command one each.'

He nodded.

'You'll have Rellston to convince,' she told him.

'He may be pig-headed but I hope he's not a fool. If he's got any military blood at all, he'll see the necessity.'

'And saving him should count for something.'

'Maybe. But he's a human, isn't he?'

'I kind of like Krista,' she admitted. 'And that isn't something you'll hear me say about a human very often. We've come across worse specimens of their race. Take a look outside.'

'What a mess. Getting stuck in a siege wasn't part of the plan.'

'We had a *plan*? Look, we have to make our alliances where we can. At least we're locked in with the star.'

'How do we know that? We haven't seen it.' He did his instinctive thing of absently reaching for the belt pouch.

'I believed Katz. And they're building that temple to house something.'

'They might have moved the star somewhere else since he was here.'

'We'll never know unless we take the trouble to find out.'

'How? Walk into the temple and ask?'

'I want your permission to try getting into that place to check.'

'It's risky.'

'I know that. But when did risk figure too highly in what we've done lately?'

'All right,' he replied warily. 'But only when the time's right, and only a look. Now's obviously not the time to steal it.'

'Obviously,' she returned dryly. She allowed herself a little petulance at what she considered an unnecessary comment and fell silent.

They returned to staring at the army.

Outside Ruffetts, in the broadest part of the valley, Kimball Hobrow walked through the massed ranks of his army with Mercy at his side. Men called out good wishes to them, and godly supplications.

'The failure of the first onslaught is a disappointment,' he confessed to his daughter, 'but at least it did the heathens some damage. Generally God has been good. He got us here before the Whore.'

'And the Wolverines are inside. He delivered them to our justice, Daddy.'

'*His* justice, Mercy. As it's *His* will that we expunge this nest of vermin from His good earth. When we burn this place it'll be the first beacon, letting the whole land know that the righteous are on the move. Then let the sub-humans beware.'

She gave an excited little clap of her hands, taking an almost childlike delight at the prospect.

'If need be we'll build siege engines to get us in there.'

They came to a crowd of custodians, gathered around a punishment detail. The men parted at sight of them. A man was spread and tied, face forward, on a whipping frame. His bare back was bloody and lined with red weals.

'What's this man's crime?' Hobrow asked of the custodian with the whip.

'Cowardice, Master. He ran from the fight at the settlement.'

'Then he is fortunate to keep his life.' He raised his voice for the benefit of them all. 'Heed this well! The same fate awaits any who defy the Lord's will! Proceed with the punishment.'

The whip-man resumed his lashing.

Mercy wanted to linger and watch. Her father didn't like to deny her.

14

The more Stryke saw of the settlement's defences, the more he realised how tenuously protected the place was.

He was walking the streets of Ruffetts View with Commander Rellston. The human's surly nature had hardly improved, but at least he was now amenable to the orcs helping with the defences. And Stryke admitted to himself that he had some admiration for the man, as far as he could have for any human. They saw eye to eye on military matters.

What shocked Stryke was that Coilla's estimate of ten per cent under arms was probably optimistic. Seasoned warriors were in a definite minority here.

They came to a group of citizens, twenty or thirty strong, practising in pairs with staffs. A soldier was drilling them. It took no more than a minute to realise they were at best raw, at worst useless.

'You see what I have to work with?' Rellston complained.

'It's been obvious since we got here, with the exception of your crew. How did the settlement come to this?'

'It's never really been any different. A legacy of the founders. This colony was established on the principle of harmony, and even those of us who chose the martial life agree with that. But times have changed. It's always been hard, but in recent years it's become a lot more dangerous. Our military force hasn't grown to match the threat And so much goes into the new temple: manpower, coin. Now I fear we're paying for it.'

It was the longest speech Stryke had heard him make. 'The land grows more perilous daily,' he agreed. 'But right now we have to see what we can do to shorten our odds on getting through this. I wanted to suggest that I break down my force into five or six more manageable groups. That way we spread their expertise around.'

'It would give the citizens a bit of backbone, yes. Hmm. All right. Let me know what I can do to help.'

'There's something you can help me with now.'

'What's that?'

'Tell me where to find the High Priestess.'

'It's no secret. Go to the back of the temple. You'll find just two houses in the roadway directly opposite. She occupies the first.'

Stryke thanked him and they parted.

He followed the directions and found the house easily. It was large and built well of durable materials, but he guessed that reflected her rank. He had no need to approach the door. The building had a small, low-walled garden to one side, and Krista Galby was working in it. Her child played nearby.

She saw Stryke coming and greeted him.

'Well met,' he returned. 'Am I troubling you?'

'No.' She dusted her hands. 'I tend the plants as much for spiritual reasons as anything else. It's good to have contact with the earth at a time like this. Is there news?'

'Not really. The Unis are getting themselves organised out there. Just biding their time for the attack, I reckon.'

'There's no chance they'll go away?'

'Unlikely.'

'Are they here because of you?'

The question took him by surprise. 'I . . . If they are, I'm sorry. It wasn't our plan, I promise you that.'

'I believe you. I'm not blaming you for anything, Captain. It's just . . .' Her gaze went to the boy. 'It's just that I hate warfare. Oh, I know it's necessary sometimes. I'm not so naive as to think we shouldn't defend ourselves. But war is usually stupid, wanton and pointless. I hope you'll forgive me for insulting your trade.'

'Some call it an art.' He smiled thinly. 'I take no offence. We orcs are born to war, but we take no pride in suffering or injustice. Though most won't believe it.'

'I do. You know, you're the first member of your race I've actually spoken to. Orcs follow the Tetrad, don't they? The Square?'

'Many do.'

'Excuse my curiosity. But I am after all a High Priestess of the Followers of the Manifold Path. Naturally the topic interests me. Do you follow the Square?'

It was another question that threw him. 'I . . . suppose I do. It's the way I was brought up. All of us were. I haven't given these things much thought lately.'

'Perhaps you should. The gods can comfort us in troubled times.'

'Mine have done precious little of that for a while.' There was an edge of bitterness in his voice that startled even him. He tried changing the subject. 'What happened to Aidan's father?'

'Should something have?'

'I don't see him here.'

'He's dead. In one of the endless conflicts with the Unis. Over something so trivial it would be amusing if it weren't . . .' She gave up on the memory.

'I'm sorry if I caused you pain.'

'That's all right. It was a while ago. I should be over it by now.'

He thought of why he was there and felt a pang of guilt. 'Loss is always with us,' he said. Then despite himself he shivered.

She noticed. 'You're cold?'

'No. Just . . .'

'Like somebody walked over your grave, to coin a phrase?'

'Sort of.'

'Has this happened to you before, while you've been here in Ruffetts?'

'Why the questions? I just shivered.'

'I do it too, quite often. It's the escaping earth energy. I feel it like goosebumps, or liquid trickling on my skin.'

That was a fair description of what he'd just felt.

'But it doesn't happen to everybody,' she went on, 'just the attuned. The energy flows through me, I'm aware of it all the time. For most people, most of the elder races too, I think, it isn't like that.'

'You're saying that I'm . . . *attuned*?'

'It can't be. Orcs don't have any affinity with the magic, do they? No magical skills. Which we believe comes from you not absorbing the energy somehow, the way many of the other elder races do Unless . . .'

'Unless what?'

'Do you ever have sudden flashes of perception? Farsight, perhaps? Or prophetic dreams?'

She was sharply intuitive and it troubled him.

'You do, don't you?' Krista gently insisted. 'Your face betrays you, for all its inscrutable qualities.'

He wrinkled his craggy brow. 'What are you getting at?'

'You could be a sport, like me. There are many different kinds. In my case, quaintness, as my people sometimes call it, means I can feel the flow. Of magic.'

'I don't understand.'

'From time to time all races seem to throw up a very small number of special individuals. They have a sort of . . . *twist*, compared to everybody else. Usually their twist has something to do with the earth energies. Sometimes it's a completely wild talent. These special types are known as sports. Many wise beings have pondered their mystery. Some think they're rare deviations from the racial norm. Mutations.'

'Doesn't that mean a freak?'

'Only to the ignorant who want conformity. Like the Unis,

Hobrow's brand in particular, who would see it as some kind of abomination to be persecuted.'

'You've made a lot out of a shiver.'

She smiled. 'There are other signs. Sports are said to be characterised by a higher than normal intelligence, for instance. Not always – there have been idiot savant sports – but usually.'

'What cause have I given you to think that of me?'

'Your actions.'

'I'm just a simple soldier.'

'I think you could be much more than that, Captain. You already have a reputation, you know. Even we've heard of it, and how there are many who would follow you. Sports are often leaders. Or messiahs.'

'I'm neither. I want no followers.'

'It seems to me you've already attracted some. Either that or warbands have grown considerably bigger.'

'That wasn't of my choosing. I didn't ask them to dog me.'

'Perhaps the gods desire it. You should learn to bend to their will, Stryke.'

'What of *my* will? Do I have no say in it?'

'Our will is as important as the gods', because we use it to carry out their design.' Krista thought for a moment. 'These strange experiences you've been having . . .' She saw the attempted denial in his face. ' . . . that you imply haven't happened; did they begin recently?'

'There might have been one or two . . . odd dreams.' Stryke was amazed hearing himself admit it to her. 'But I think you're wrong about all this,' he added hurriedly. 'As I said, I'm a soldier, not a mystic.'

'If it *has* started recently,' she ploughed on, ignoring him, 'and you had no hint of sport before, something must have triggered it. Or rather, boosted what was already there, what was innate.' Smiling, she added, 'Of course, I could be wrong.'

'I have to go,' he told her.

'Not for anything I've said, I hope. Because, even if I'm

right, it shouldn't be seen as a bad thing. It can be a very rocky road or a blessing; it's up to you.'

'It's nothing you've said,' he assured her. 'I have to help with the defences.'

'We should speak about this again.' When he made no reply to that, she asked, 'Why did you come?'

'No reason. Just passing.'

Stryke left suffering another twinge of guilt. But at least he should have given Coilla enough time to check the temple without the High Priestess being there.

Coilla should have been in and out by now. She hadn't even got in. The guards had seen to that.

Stryke had agreed that this was the best opportunity. For the first time, work had been suspended on the temple due to the siege and there were no workers smothering the place. He had gone off to distract Krista Galby, to prevent her turning up unexpectedly. It might be Coilla's only chance. But for those damned guards.

There were four of them and they took turns patrolling. One pair stayed at the gates while the other did the rounds, then it was turnabout and off again. She'd crouched miserably in a clump of bushes opposite for nearly an hour, watching the guards and keeping an eye on passing citizenry. If she didn't see a way in soon she'd have to abandon the mission.

No sooner had the thought occurred than her break came. Four relief guards arrived. They mustered at the bottom of the temple's steps, and the old guards walked down to greet them. The doors were unprotected. If Coilla moved very fast, hugging the shadows, she might just get herself up the side of the steps and in. But it would take only one of the gossiping soldiers to turn and see her for the game to be up. A big risk, that had to be taken now or never.

She took it. Stooping low, running fast, she rushed from her hiding place and got across the avenue. She scaled the steps two or three at a time. Then she was at the doors, which were conveniently in a pool of gloom. There was a moment's anxiety when she thought the place might be locked. But obviously no one saw the necessity with guards about. The round iron handle, big as her hand, turned freely. Pushing the door just enough to sidle in, she carefully closed it behind her.

Standing absolutely still and silent, she listened, just in case there was somebody inside. Detecting nothing, she looked around. There were no lamps or candles burning. But light came in from the open roof, lofty windows and a high section of uncompleted wall. It was dull but enough to see by.

There were some internal furnishings, including rows of benches and the beginnings of an altar. Several pillars had been erected, taller and slimmer than the ones outside, presumably as roof supports. A single, shorter pillar, the circumference of a wagon wheel, stood beside the altar, near to a boarded window. She went over and saw that something was sitting on its flat top, arranged so that people on the benches could gaze up at it. Not being able to make out what it was, she climbed on to the altar to see better.

It looked as though she had found the star. Details were hard to make out, but she reckoned it was red, and it certainly had more spikes than the others.

That was all Coilla needed to know for now. She clambered down and padded back to the door. Very carefully and quietly she eased it open a crack. Then froze. Two sentries stood a couple of feet away, their backs to her. Worse, at the bottom of the steps the other guards were talking with the High Priestess and Commander Rellston. Praying she wouldn't be seen, she gently closed the door and retreated.

It was time to think fast. She scanned the massive building. Only one possibility presented itself, and it didn't look easy.

Creeping back to the altar, she scaled it again. Even standing on the edge, the stout pillar was just beyond reach. But she thought she might be able to jump to it if she took a short run. Her hands would have to connect with the flat top, and the pillar's fluting would have to be pronounced enough to give her feet purchase. Two big ifs.

She moved to the far side of the altar, beaded the target, took a breath and ran. As she leapt, it occurred to her that the pillar might be free-standing and go down when she hit it. In which case every guard in the settlement would be in here.

Luck was with her. Her hands came down on the pillar's top, painfully, and she held on. Her boots gripped on the fluting. The whole thing didn't collapse, as she'd feared. Then it was a case of scrabbling her way up until she was able to perch unsteadily on the plateau, crowding the star. And it was the star, she saw that clearly now. As she thought, it was red, and she counted no less than nine projecting spikes.

For a second she was tempted to take it. Good sense prevailed.

She hadn't finished yet. The next step was to get from the pillar to the boarded window, which fortunately had a deep sill. It was as long a jump as the one she'd just taken, and of course she couldn't have a run at it. There was no point delaying. Tensing her muscles, she launched herself. She made it to the sill, but only just. For a dizzying second she thought she was going to fall. Clamping her palms on the sides of the window's alcove saved her.

Drawing a knife, she set to work on the nails holding one of the boards. It was fortunate that they'd been hammered in from her side. What seemed an eternity went by as Coilla prised them loose. She expected the guards to burst in at any moment, or the Priestess to enter. At last she got the board off, and was relieved to see scaffolding outside. The plank she passed out through the gap. Next she began squeezing through herself. That proved tense too; the space was only just wide enough.

She kept low on the scaffolding, trusting she wouldn't be seen. Then the board had to be wedged back in place behind her, lest it be thought someone had broken in. Finally she scanned the street, saw no one, and swiftly descended to ground level.

Sighing with relief as she melted into the shadows, Coilla promised herself she'd never take up burglary as a profession.

Jennesta tossed scraps of raw meat to the flock as she rode.

The dozen or so scavengers swooped and screeched, catching the titbits in the air and gulping them whole.

'Aren't they delightful?' she enthused.

Mersadion grunted a platitude and gazed at the harpies. He found their black leathery skin, bat-like crinkly wings and razor-toothed maws far from adorable. But it never did to gainsay his mistress.

His bandages were off now, and he was depressingly self-conscious about the wound. Angry blisters pockmarked the whole of the right side of his face, leaving his cheek a ruin. He looked like a partially melted candle.

For her part, Jennesta took pride in her handiwork, and had insisted that he rode on the left side of her chariot in order to admire it.

'You know,' she mused, 'I was a little peaked about that run-in earlier, letting Hobrow and the Unis beat us to Ruffetts View.'

He could have laughed at her choice of words to describe the wrath she'd displayed at the time. Had he not valued his life.

'But I'm beginning to see the positive side of it,' she finished.

'Ma'am?'

'Ever heard the expression rats in a trap, General? Having the main forces of our enemy trapped at the end of that peninsula does hold certain advantages for us.'

'And by rights, the Manis in Ruffetts View should ally with us against them.'

'Only if it suits me. I'm in no mood to put up with nonsense from any source.'

He wondered when she ever was.

'Another bonus,' she continued, 'is you telling me that deserters from my ranks may be there. We will shortly lop the head from more than one serpent, Mersadion. How does our strength compare with what we will meet?'

'Bigger than the Unis, Majesty. Should you require us to engage the Manis too, we might be able to match their combined forces.' He hoped to the gods it didn't come to that.

She fell silent, contemplating a gratifying slaughter. Maybe even the final battle that would confirm her mastery. Most of all, she relished the thought of catching up with the Wolverines.

The last of her scraps had gone. Putting up a greater racket, the harpies clamoured for more.

'They're boring me,' she decided, 'Call for archers.'

Coilla met up with Stryke in one of the row of shacks Rellston had allotted the orcs as billets. Jup, Alfray and Haskeer were there too. Stryke wanted to tell her what Krista had said to him, but not with an audience, so it would have to wait.

She wasted no time reporting. 'You were right, it's there. I had a hell of a time finding out though.'

'Tell me about that later. What does it look like?'

'Red, with nine spikes.'

'Easy to get out?' Alfray asked.

'Well, once you're inside the temple, yes. It's just sitting on top of a pillar. But the place is guarded. And as to getting it out of the settlement—'

'What we gonna do about that, Stryke?' Haskeer interrupted.

'I don't know. We need to think this through.'

'I reckon the humans here won't hold off the Unis for too long. I say we grab the star and fight our way out with it.'

'Taking on both the whole of Ruffetts *and* the army outside? Talk sense.'

'Besides,' Coilla said, 'the humans in this place deserve better than that. They've done nothing against us.'

Haskeer gave her a dirty look, but said no more.

'For now, our survival depends on riding out the siege,' Stryke judged, 'and we're going to have to help with that. If and when we can get our hands on the star, we will.'

'That seems right,' Alfray agreed.

'Is there anything else, chief?' Jup wondered. 'We're going to be missed if we're much longer.'

'There's one thing,' Stryke replied. His face wore a curious expression, part apprehensive, part something that might have been excitement. They were intrigued.

He dug out the stars one by one and placed them on the table. Finally, he brought out the two he'd somehow fused together and put them down too.

'What the hell?' the dwarf said. He reached out and hefted the united pair.

They gathered round and examined them. There was universal bafflement.

'Coilla already knew about this,' Stryke admitted. 'I was waiting for the right time to show the rest of you.'

'How did you manage to do it?' Alfray wanted to know.

'That's not easy to explain. But watch this.'

He took the coupled stars back, then selected the grey, two-spiked instrumentality they got at Drogan. Concentrating hard, he began fiddling with them.

'What's he doing?' Haskeer muttered.

'*Ssshhh!*' Coilla hissed.

They watched him wrestling with the things in uncomprehending silence for over a minute.

'There,' he declared at last, holding up the result.

All three stars were joined, looking like one seamless artifact. They passed it round.

'I don't get this,' Jup confessed. 'I can't see how they connect, yet . . .'

Stryke nodded. 'Strange, isn't it?'

'How *do* you do it?' Alfray repeated.

'Just playing around with them at first. Then I kind of . . . *saw* how they went together. Any of you probably would too, if you worked on it long enough.'

Alfray stared at the newly constructed object. 'I'm not so sure about that. I certainly can't make out the trick.'

'It's not a trick. They must have been designed to do this.'

'Why?' Haskeer asked, eyeing the stars suspiciously.

'Your guess is as good as mine.'

'It stands to reason that they'll all fit like this,' Jup surmised. 'Have you tried, Stryke?'

'Yes, when I've had the time. I can't do it beyond those three. The other one just won't go. Maybe we need the last star to make it work.'

'But what does it mean? Once it's together, what's it *for*?'

If Stryke had an opinion, they were destined not to hear it.

The alarm bells rang out.

'Shit,' the dwarf cursed. 'They're back.'

15

The township was full of running people and galloping horses. Wagons careened around corners, platoons of defenders jogged to defensive positions, civilians doled out weapons from handcarts.

Stryke and his officers, along with several score grunts, raced to their mustering point in the shadow of the pyramid. The rest of the orcs were already there, or close to arriving. Bellowing over the commotion, Stryke ordered them into their six designated squads of approximately forty troopers each. He, Alfray, Coilla, Haskeer and Jup headed groups one to five. Corporal Krenad had been given command of group six.

With Rellston's agreement, the squads had been designated areas to fortify, alongside the Mani defenders but independent of them. But they also had a roving brief. They could go where needed to help strengthen the defences.

'Keep an eye on the watchtowers!' Stryke reminded them. 'They'll signal where you might be needed! The alarm bells are a signal too, remember!' It was a far from perfect system, but the best they could do. 'You don't move from your positions unless your leaders say so!' he added.

One by one, the commanders raised an arm to indicate they were ready.

'To your places!' Stryke roared.

Coilla's squad passed his on its way out. 'Good luck,' she mouthed.

The six groups set off for their scattered posts. Stryke's was on the south wall. That pleased him. He'd be facing the main bulk of the attacking army.

He got there in minutes, and immediately started urging the grunts up the many ladders to the walkway. Then he scaled a ladder himself, and spent a moment ordering his squad into position. There were hundreds of Mani militia on the gangway already. Stryke was careful to mix his force in with them.

He spotted a young Mani officer. 'What's happening?'

'You can see for yourself. They've been grouping themselves for a couple of hours. Now this.' He nodded at the landscape.

What Stryke saw was not one army but at least four. The Unis had divided into segments, thousands strong, and each was moving towards the settlement. There were covered wagons at the rear of each segment. The divisions on the flanks were going off at tangents, Stryke guessed in order to surround Ruffetts.

'They're going to hit us on several sides at once,' he told the officer.

'And they've held back reserves.' The human pointed.

Thousands more troopers had stayed in the enemy camp's staging area at the far end of the valley.

'It's the smart thing to do,' Stryke said. He looked up and down the battlements. 'Do we have water wagons nearby?'

'I'm not sure.'

'I think you should. Fire's one of the biggest hazards in this kind of situation.'

The officer went off to sort it out.

Down below, the miniature armies approached. Each consisted of about two-thirds infantry and the balance cavalry. The footsoldiers dictated the pace of advance, which was consequently slow. But there was something about their ponderous movement that made them seem the more inexorable and threatening.

Stryke walked the gangway, checking that his command was in order. He came to a pair of Wolverine grunts, and felt glad they were there.

'Noskaa. Finje.'

They returned the greeting.

'What do you reckon they'll try, sir?' Finje asked.

'If you don't count that little skirmish last night, this is the first really determined assault. I reckon they'll stick by the book. Strong contingents to the gates and ladders for the walls.'

'But they're religious fanatics, sir,' Noskaa remarked. 'There's no telling what they'll do.'

'It does you credit to realise it, trooper. Always expect the unexpected. But in a siege both sides' options are limited. We're in here, they're out there. Our job's to keep it that way.'

'Yes, sir,' they chorused.

'Keep an eye on the watchtowers,' he reminded them, 'and help out the Manis wherever you can. Providing that doesn't contravene any order of mine,' he added.

They nodded.

Stryke resumed his inspection. That done, like thousands of others all he could do was watch the attackers nearing.

As the next hour or two stretched out, the four divisions of the Uni army moved into position, facing the settlement from each point of the compass. That meant Stryke and his comrades were looking down on a mass of troops. Those on the battlements and those on the ground jeered at each other and slung insults.

Stryke paced the walkway, dealing out encouraging back-slaps and cheering words. 'Steady, lads . . . hold your fire . . . stand solid . . . watch each other's backs . . .'

Then it went very quiet.

A series of high-pitched piping notes rose from the besieging armies, made by reed whistles.

'That's their signal!' Stryke barked. 'Prepare to repel!'

A deafening roar went up from the attackers and they flooded in on all sides. The defenders sent up their own answering cries and the siege proper commenced.

The first priority was to stop the attackers reaching the walls. Mani archers took the brunt of that, loosing arrows by the hundred down on the charging infantry. Shields went up below and bolts rattled off them. But many found their fleshy targets. Soldiers fell with pierced eyes, throats, chests. Some unfortunates in the front ranks were peppered by numerous arrows and went down to be trampled by the troops behind. Horses fell, spilling their riders, and they too succumbed to the rain of spikes.

A party of enemy archers, hundreds strong, tilted their bows skyward and loosed their own swarm over the walls.

'*Incoming!*' Stryke bellowed.

Everybody who could, took cover. Scores of arrows showered on the walkway, killing and wounding, but most overshot and fell into the settlement itself. Reservists and civilian auxiliaries caught the storm. Men, women and pack animals collapsed under the downrush. People ran for cover, some screaming. Field surgeon teams began dashing to the wounded.

Stryke heard the blasted bells ringing everywhere. He looked up to the nearest watchtower, but none of the lookouts was trying to signal. Then again they had their own problems, with dozens of enemy archers trying to pick them off. He stayed put.

He realised he was crouching next to the young Mani officer. He looked scared.

'First siege?' Stryke asked.

The white-faced officer nodded, too nervous to speak.

'They're just as frightened as we are, if it's any help,' Stryke told him. 'And remember that your men's lives depend on you.'

The young man nodded again, with more resolve, Stryke thought.

'We're likely to see nothing more than an arrow exchange for some minutes yet,' he explained. 'They're trying to keep us pinned down so they can get close enough to start scaling.'

The Mani archers knew that. They were popping up at random to fire their arrows, then ducking to reload.

'Can we hold them off?' the officer said.

'No. Not unless both sides have an endless supply of arrows. Even if they did, their offcers are going to be urging them to the walls soon.'

Stryke looked down into the settlement and saw a water wagon drawing up, pulled by oxen. It was essentially a huge barrel on wheels, with rows of wooden buckets swinging on its sides. Arrows clattered on and around it. A couple pierced the oxen's backs and they lowed pitifully.

A shout went up from the battlements, not just Stryke's but all around.

'They're bringing in the ladders!' somebody yelled.

Stryke braved the fusillade and peeked over the wall. Hundreds of ladder carriers, working in pairs, were racing towards the fortifications. As he watched, at least three of them went down. But their numbers, and the covering fire, meant a goodly portion would get through.

He turned to the officer and held his gaze. 'Our best chance is to make sure as few of them as possible get over. Just a handful can cause mayhem if they're determined enough.' He heard the blood-chilling war cries of the besiegers. 'And this lot are determined if nothing else.'

The tops of ladders showed above the battlements, swaying as the men holding them below struggled to get them against the walls. The Mani archers, and spear-throwers too now, began targeting the holders. They were particularly vulnerable and succumbed in droves.

But inevitably more than half the ladders slapped against the walls, their tops visible above the screen. Defenders moved to dislodge them.

One crashed into place next to the officer and Stryke.

'Come on!' he said.

They scrambled to it and grasped its uprights. With a mighty heave they pushed it away. There was nobody on it. They watched it fall back and the soldiers below scattering.

Other ladders were being climbed. Lines of Unis swarmed up them with swords drawn and raised shields. Stryke and the officer rushed to help topple them. The first one they reached had three or four of the enemy more than halfway up. With a couple of grunts aiding, they managed to push the ladder clear of the wall. It swayed for a second in an upright position, then went over with its screaming load.

There was no respite. Numerous ladders were clamping themselves to the wall now and the defenders who weren't hurling projectiles or firing arrows dashed from one to the other. Stryke knew this was happening all around the settlement. He just hoped there was no weak point that would allow a major breach.

As he had the thought, the first Uni got to the top of the wall and began scrambling over. Stryke bounded over to him and slashed his face to ribbons. The howling man fell, striking his fellows on the lower rungs and they all plunged together.

Now another Uni head appeared, and another, and several more. In the space of a few seconds a couple of dozen made the top and many got on to the walkway. They had to be dealt with. Stryke barrelled into one, blocked his cross and gutted him. The man fell into the settlement. A sword swished over Stryke's head. He turned and felled the attacker, kicking his corpse over the side. The young officer was engaged in a fight himself, and giving a good account. He despatched his opponent and turned to face another. Stryke got involved with his own duel.

There were brawls all along the walkway, and bodies of Unis, Manis and orcs plunged screaming from the height. A ladder poked up at an unattended stretch of wall. A Mani defender, not much more than a boy, threw himself at the man who jumped over from it. He was outmatched. The officer saw what was happening and ran to help. A furious exchange with the invader showed that he was no match for him either. Three or four passes into the duel, the Uni buried his sword in the officer's chest. The Mani went down. The interloper returned his attention to the boy.

Stryke raced over and commenced battering at the invader. It took him half a minute to break through his defences and see him off. Kneeling by the fallen officer, Stryke immediately realised he was dead. 'Shit!' he hissed. The boy was looking at them. 'Do your duty!' Stryke yelled. The boy rejoined the fray. A grunt caught Stryke's eye and nodded. He went to shadow the youngster.

Stryke took up his sword again and cleaved the next head to show.

Coilla was on the other side of the settlement, helping defend the opposite wall.

The position was similar to Stryke's. Ladders were slamming against the battlements. Grappling hooks flew over. Perhaps ten Unis had made the walkway and they were being engaged with vigour.

Coilla ended combat with a foe by hewing deep into his neck. Then she went straight on to the next, hacking at his shield like a mad thing. That was finished for her when a grunt cut down her opponent from the rear.

As she backed off, a clay pot sailed over the wall and shattered on the gangway. The oil it contained immediately ignited, sending a sheet of flame over the boards. Another pot landed on the gangway behind her.

'Hell's teeth!' she exclaimed. '*Get some water up here!*'

Fights boiled on despite the flames. Some Manis and orcs tried beating out the flames with blankets while they dodged arrows. Then the colony's fire-fighters arrived and got a chain going. Slopping buckets of water were passed up the interior ladders to be emptied and thrown back.

Coilla left them to it and skirted the fires to engage a fresh batch of Unis. She downed one instantly as he straddled the wall. The next got over and put up a fight. He couldn't match her speed or fury and took a stroke to the heart. A third was sent howling back to the ground with her dagger in his chest.

She didn't know how much longer they could hold them off.

Over at the west gates, scene of the incursion the day before, Haskeer was in the eye of the storm. There was conflict all around on the walls, and he could hear the sound of battle at other gates, but nothing was happening here. The only sign of hostility was a pounding on the doors he guarded. Even that sounded more like individual hatchets and fists rather than a war engine.

He kept one eye on the watchtowers, hoping for a signal that would take him to the action. As yet, none had come.

'Just my luck to get stuck with the third tit, Liffin,' he grumbled.

'Yeah, it's not fair, Sarge,' the grunt agreed.

'What's the matter with those Uni bastards? Can't they knock down one pair of gates for a good fight?'

'Inconsiderate,' Liffin sniffed.

An object sailed high over the wall and fell towards them. They could see it was one of the enemy's fire canisters, its fuse smouldering.

Haskeer brightened. 'That's more like it!'

They followed the clay bottle's trajectory as the crowd scattered. It fell about five yards in front of them and didn't go off.

'Bull's bollocks,' Haskeer groaned.

'Better luck next time, eh, Sarge?' Liffin commiserated.

The bell in the watchtower above rang out. The lookouts were signalling.

'At *last*,' Haskeer sighed. 'Hive off half the strength, Liffin, and take command here. I'm needed at a hot spot.'

'Yes, Sarge,' Liffin replied glumly.

★

Alfray was on another wall. Apart from that, his experience was the same as Stryke and Coilla's. Raiders flowed over the ramparts and they did their best to kill them.

The object of Alfray's attention was a whiskered bully trying to part his head from his shoulders. He was using a two-handed axe to realise the ambition, but the orc had other ideas. He also had a nimbler weapon. His sword flashed beneath the axeman's guard not once but twice. The Uni staggered and went down. One of the grunts snatched up his axe and turned it on another interloper.

Alfray's limbs ached and he already felt exhausted. But he pushed that back and bowled into a new knot of custodians. Working in unison with a pair of grunts, he drove them back to the screen. One went over it. The other two were felled where they stood.

He turned, running the back of a hand over his brow, and saw black smoke rising from the direction of Coilla's wall.

Jup had been called to firefight on the seaward side.

There was a small gate there, falling within Krenad's remit, but things had got out of hand. The Unis had rammed it with a burning wagon. The gate was part open, part on fire, and the enemy were filing in through a gap.

The narrowness of the entrance helped. It meant the attackers couldn't establish a bridgehead of any size as long as the defenders kept striking them down on arrival. Heaps of dead, mostly Unis, surrounded the gate. But the flood of invaders was so strong it was hard to tackle them all.

Jup and half his squad upped the odds on re-sealing the fissure. He went about it by sending a wedge of thirty shielded troopers to the cleft with the aim of stopping the inflow. Thirty more were assigned to shove out the wagon and get the doors closed. The remainder of Jup and Krenad's squads were busied with dousing the fire and going after the loose Unis already inside.

It was touch and go for a while, but they staunched the flow.

He would have liked a breather. He didn't get it. The local watchtower's bell sounded and the guards frantically signalled his next destination.

Stryke had answered a call for help too.

In the event, the incident he had rushed to, on the north side, proved relatively easy to cope with. He was grumpy about being sent on a wild-goose chase, but glad he took only ten troopers with him. More than that he didn't dare spare from the wall.

Now he was returning at all speed, with the grunt Talag at his side, the others close behind. As they turned at a group of buildings and entered the stretch running to their post, they saw a commotion ahead.

A lone Uni on horseback was tearing towards them. An angry mob snapped at his heels. The man must have got in one of the breached gates and somehow evaded the welcoming committees. He was travelling all out, whipping the horse's flanks with his reins.

About halfway between the rider and Stryke's squad, somebody tried to run across the avenue. It was a child.

Stryke recognised him as Aidan Galby.

The orcs shouted at him, and the crowd did the same. For his part, the rider kept coming and didn't alter course.

He hit the boy, bowling him aside like a rag puppet. Aidan tumbled across the path and came to rest face down in front of a building.

The impact slowed the Uni, although it didn't deter his flight. As he was spurring again, half Stryke's squad rushed at him. Talag was one of the first to get there. He and two others snatched the horse's reins. But it was Talag who tasted the Uni's wrath. The man struck him down with his sword, cleaving his neck with a savage blow.

Stryke rushed forward and took hold of the rider's trailing

greatcoat, pulling him from the mount. Then he ran him through with his blade, piercing his heart. Letting the body drop, he turned to Talag. One look was enough.

He ran on and reached the boy. There was no doubt he was badly hurt. He was unconscious and breathing feebly. Stryke knew it was unwise to move anyone who was injured, but he needed to get the hatchling to a proper healer. Gently, he lifted the child's prone form.

Noskaa appeared on the gangway above and called down.

'You're in charge until I get back!' Stryke shouted at him.

He ran with the boy in his arms.

16

Stryke ran through the chaos, clutching the injured child. Sounds of the siege still raged on every side. Bodies continued to plunge from the ramparts. Fires blackened the sky. He turned away from the outer rim and headed to the settlement's core, weaving through narrow streets, side-stepping or barging aside the bustling humans.

Finally he came to Krista's house. It was being used as a makeshift field hospital. Stretcher-bearers queued to carry in the injured and walking wounded jammed the entrance. But when they saw his burden they moved aside.

He crashed into the building and found it overflowing with the stricken. Scores of makeshift beds filled every room and lined the corridors. Less seriously damaged individuals sat and leaned as their hurts were tended. The nursing was undertaken by female acolytes of the Mani order.

'The High Priestess!' he demanded forcefully. 'Where is she?'

Shocked novices pointed to a room packed with occupied beds. He rushed into it. Krista stood at the far end, ministering to a wounded soldier. She looked up and saw him. Her face contorted with shock and dread, her eyes widened.

'What's happened?' she cried, rushing to take the child.

Stryke hastily explained.

She gently laid the boy on a vacant straw mattress and called to him. 'Aidan. *Aidan!*' She turned to Stryke. The colour was draining from her features. 'He was supposed to be here. I don't understand. He—'

'I reckon he got caught up in the chaos and was hurrying back to you when it happened. How bad is he?'

'I'm not skilled enough to know. But it doesn't look good.'

Physicians arrived, homing in on the commotion. They were Mani healers with incense swingers and poultices. Clustering around the patient they commenced prodding and conferring. They didn't look hopeful. And to Stryke's eyes, very competent. But he didn't voice that opinion.

He glanced at Krista. She was beginning to be swallowed by quiet despair.

Unnoticed, he slipped away. Once out of the house and through the press at its door he started running.

He went to the wall Alfray was helping defend. Sections of it were smouldering from recent fires, and there was still a measure of chaos. But there seemed to be fewer attackers coming over. Stryke thought the onslaught might be abating. Pushing through the mob of defenders, he eventually found his corporal at one end of the walkway, wiping blood from his sword. His clothes were spattered with it too. So were Stryke's, now he came to notice.

'Stryke?' Alfray said. 'What is it?'

'Krista Galby's child. Aidan. He's been hurt.'

'How so?'

'Hit by a horse. A runaway Uni in the settlement. He's in a bad way, I reckon.'

'What are his injuries?'

'He was out cold when I just saw him. I think he took the blow to his chest and side mostly.'

'Any bleeding? Wounds? Broken skin?'

'I'm pretty sure not. There was no sign of blood anyway. He was having a hard time breathing.'

'Hmm. What treatment's he getting?'

'I don't know. Well, a bunch of Mani healers were around him when I left. You know the sort. Chanting and incense.'

'They must be doing more than *that* for him.'

'Whether they are or not they didn't fill me with confidence,' Stryke confided. 'You've dealt with injuries like that before, haven't you?'

'Plenty of times. From falls and combat. Maybe half who get 'em pull through. Of course, I can't say how bad it might be without seeing him.'

'I'm thinking they need a decent combat physician over there.'

'Surely he'll get the best of care, being the High Priestess' son?'

'Maybe he will. But in this chaos? I'm doubtful. Will you come now and look at him?'

'How are they going to feel about an outsider, and an orc at that, sticking his nose in?'

'I should think Krista would be glad of any help. And I reckon you've had more experience of real healing than most here. The treatment many of the wounded are getting seems very basic; you must have noticed that.'

Alfray mulled things over for a minute. 'This has nothing to do with the star, does it?'

'What do you mean?'

'Could you be thinking, perhaps, that if we can help her son, the High Priestess might be grateful enough to . . . I can see that wasn't on your mind. I'm sorry. It was unworthy of me.'

'It really isn't that. He's just a hatchling. This war wasn't of his making. Like the orc hatchlings and the innocent young of the other races who've suffered.'

'Many of them at the hands of humans,' Alfray replied cynically.

'Not these humans. Will you come?'

'Yes.' He surveyed the scene along the wall. 'Things are quietening a bit here. I think they can spare me.'

He handed over control to a capable orc trooper. Then they commandeered a couple of horses for the return journey.

Krista's house was just as congested. If anything, more wounded were being delivered. The pair of orcs elbowed through, ignoring protests of the kind Stryke didn't get when he took in the human child earlier. They made their way to the far room, stepping over the injured, standing aside as sheet-wrapped bodies were carried out.

The assembly of Mani healers and holy men around Aidan's bed had grown to four. They were muttering charms and burning herbs. Krista herself was kneeling on the floor next to the boy, head slumped in her hands, obviously desperate. The arrival of the orcs had them all turning to look. Their blood-stained clothes and grimy faces were the object of scrutiny.

Stryke and Alfray strode to the bed.

'How is he?' Stryke asked.

'No change,' Krista reported.

'You know my corporal here, Alfray. He's had a lot of experience with these kinds of injuries, in the field. Would you mind him asking some questions?'

Her eyes were glistening. 'No. No, of course not.'

The healers seemed less than pleased, but they didn't contradict their High Priestess.

'What's your judgement?' Alfray wanted to know.

The physicians exchanged meaningful glances. For a moment it looked as though nobody was going to reply. Then one, the oldest and most whiskery, spoke for them all. 'The boy is injured inside. His innards are crushed.' It came out like he was talking to a backward infant.

'What's your treatment?'

The ageing healer looked affronted at being asked. 'The application of compresses, the burning of certain herbs so that he may inhale their goodness,' he replied with slight indignation. 'And entreaties to the gods, naturally.'

'Herbs and prayers? That's all right as far as it goes. But something more practical might be better.'

'Are you a healer? Have you studied the art?'

'Yes. On the battlefield. If you mean from books and sitting at an old man's feet, no.'

The old man puffed himself up. 'Age brings wisdom.'

'With respect,' Alfray responded, although it was obvious to Stryke at least that he felt little, 'it can also bring a rigid way of looking at things. I speak from some knowledge of the subject. In orc terms I am not in the first flush of youth. Like you.'

The healer looked affronted. His colleagues were evidently scandalised. Seeking higher authority, the elderly one appealed to Krista. '*Really*, ma'am, this is too much. How do you expect us—'

'Let Alfray look at the boy, High Priestess,' Stryke interrupted. 'What have you to lose?'

The old healer persisted. 'But, ma'am—'

She overruled him. 'This is my son we're talking about. If what Corporal Alfray has to say can help, I want to hear it. If not, you can continue with your ministrations. Please stand aside.'

With resentful glances at the orcs and some under the breath comments, the four healers stepped away. They went off to the end of the room and conversed darkly in undertones.

'I need to examine him first,' Alfray said.

The priestess nodded consent.

He bent to the boy and pulled back the blanket covering him. He was still wearing his shirt. Alfray drew a knife.

Krista gave a sharp intake of breath, a hand to her mouth.

Alfray gave her a reassuring smile. 'It's just to expose the afflicted area. Don't be concerned. It's something I would expect to have been done already,' he added, directing a pointed glance at the huddled physicians.

He used the blade to cut away Aidan's shirt and reveal his torso. The knife returned to its sheath, he gently probed the lad's chest and side with his hands. He indicated black and blue patches that were starting to colour the skin. 'There's some bruising coming up. A good sign. There are no open wounds or blood flows. That can also be to the good.' He felt around the area of the ribs. 'There might be a break here. His breathing's shallow but regular. The pulse is regular too, though faint.' He lifted the child's lids. 'The eyes tell us much about the body's humours,' he explained.

'What do my son's tell you?'

'That his injury is bad. But perhaps not so bad that he need pay for it with his life.'

'Can you help?'

'With your permission I can try.'

'You have it. What will you do?'

'The proper binding of his hurt is the first priority, to put right the shock his system took in the impact. But before that the affected area should be washed, lest any infections creep in. The gentle application of some balms I carry should also help.'

'I can do that.'

'It would be fitting. When he's able I'd also like him to take an infusion of herbs. The ones I use for *practical* purposes.' It was another dig at the disgruntled healers. 'That and rest are what I advise.'

His manner impressed her. 'I welcome your advice. Let's get started.'

'Anything I can do?' Stryke said.

Alfray waved a distracted hand at him. 'Leave us.'

Peremptorily dismissed, Stryke crept out. He got back into the street and took a deep breath to clear his head of the odour of death and suffering.

People were running by, spreading word that the latest attack was dying down.

'The enemy are pulling back!' a passing youth shouted at him.

For now, Stryke thought.

There were no more offensives in the following hours. By early evening the defenders had fallen into a kind of tense apathy, overlaid with exhaustion. Outside, the army was regrouping. Nobody thought they wouldn't try another assault.

Stryke, Alfray, Coilla, Jup and Haskeer were on a wall together, watching, just like thousands of others.

Haskeer was in the middle of a familiar diatribe. 'I mean, it's not as though it's our fight anyway, is it?' He jerked a thumb at the settlement below. 'When all's said and done, these are still humans, ain't they? What have they done for us, apart from losing us Talag?'

Regret at the loss of their fallen comrade was something they could all share.

'One of the band's longest-serving members,' Alfray reminded them.

'We're lucky not to have lost more,' Haskeer said.

'They've done plenty for us,' Coilla responded. 'I do wish you wouldn't see other races the way so many of them see us.'

'You've changed your tune,' he came back. 'You didn't care for humans more than I did last time you spoke about it.'

'That's not altogether true and you know it. Anyway, I'm coming to see life's more complicated than that. Maybe it's just down to good beings versus bad beings, and to hell with races.'

'To an extent,' Alfray cautioned. 'But let's not lose our identities. They're too important.'

'There are some races who don't seem to mind handing over their identities to others,' Haskeer remarked, looking at Jup. It was a naked reference to dwarfs and their artifice.

'Gods, not that again!' Jup complained. 'Will you stop blaming me for everything my race does? As though *I* was personally responsible.'

'Yes, leave it, Haskeer,' Stryke warned. 'We've enough of a fight on our hands without you starting more.'

'We won't be able to fight off another attack like the last one, I know that much,' Haskeer grumbled. 'Not with the humans here.'

'They have spirit,' Coilla reckoned. 'That stands for a lot.'

'Fighting spirit stands for more.'

'You're too hard on them.'

'Like I said, they're humans.'

The exchange halted when someone appeared at the top of the ladder leading from the settlement. It was Krista Galby. She stepped onto the walkway holding the hem of her gown up slightly to avoid it snagging.

They greeted her, though Haskeer's welcome was subdued. She seemed in better spirits.

'I've come to tell you that Aidan's improved,' she told them. 'He's conscious and seems to recognise me. His breathing's better too.' She moved to Alfray and took his coarse hands in hers. 'I have you to thank for this. I don't know how I can ever repay you.'

'You have no need. I'm glad to hear the boy's mending. But he still needs doctoring, and will for a week or two yet. I'll come by and see him again later.'

'Thank you.' She was smiling. 'The gods have favoured my son, and you.'

'Perhaps Alfray deserves the lion's share of gratitude on this occasion,' Stryke said dryly.

'Don't mock the gods,' Alfray cautioned. 'It's unwise. My efforts would have come to nought without their approval.'

Stryke nodded at the besieging army. 'I wonder if they're thanking or cursing *their* deity?'

'You're a sceptic, Captain?' Krista asked.

'I don't know what I am these days, to be honest. Events tend to turn an orc's head.'

None of them knew how to respond to that.

'I said I could never repay you,' Krista repeated. 'But if it's in my power to grant you something you desire, just tell me.'

'What about the star?' Haskeer blurted.

The others gave him murderous looks.

'Star?' At first, she was mystified. Then her intuitive streak kicked in. 'Do you mean the instrumentality?'

'The . . . what?' Jup replied innocently.

'Instrumentality. It's a religious relic. I suppose it does rather look like a simple star. Is that what you meant?'

They could hardly deny it.

Coilla quickly stepped in. 'He meant, can we *see* it?'

'How did you know we had an instrumentality? We make no secret of it, but we don't boast of the fact either.'

'A merchant we met on the road told us about it. Katz. A pixie.'

'Ah, yes. I remember him.'

'He made it sound so interesting,' Coilla went on, hoping she wasn't digging an even bigger hole. 'We promised ourselves that if we were ever in Ruffetts we'd try to take a look,' she ended lamely.

'As I recall, Katz expressed little interest in it. In fact, he abused our hospitality by entering the temple when forbidden. We had to ask him to leave.'

'We didn't know that.'

'The instrumentality is very important to us. It means much to my people, and to the gods. But I'd be glad to show it to you whenever you want. Though with respect I wouldn't have thought a religious relic would be of interest to a warband.'

'Oh, it's not all fighting and mayhem with us,' Jup told her. 'We appreciate culture too. I mean, you really should hear Haskeer's poetry sometime.'

'Is that so? Well, you obviously have hidden depths. I'd rather like to.'

Haskeer gaped at her. 'What?'

For an awful moment they thought she meant now.

'So, the instrumentality and poetry,' she went on. 'That's something we can look forward to.'

'Yes. It would be . . . pleasant,' Stryke replied unconvincingly.

'There's much to be attended to,' the High Priestess said. 'I have to go. Thank you again, Alfray. All of you.'

They watched as she descended and moved off through the streets.

'You *idiot*, Haskeer!' Coilla stormed.

'Well, if you don't ask you don't get.'

Jup put in his oar too. 'You really are a prize fuckhead, Haskeer.'

'Go and suck a rock. And why did you have to tell her I write poetry, you little snot?'

'Oh, shut up.'

'Well, at least we know what she thinks about parting with the star,' Alfray said.

'Yes,' Coilla agreed. 'But thanks to gnat brain here—' she indicated Haskeer '—we might have shown our hand.'

'That bloody Katz could have told us he was kicked out,' Jup complained. 'Now what do we do?'

'Sleep, if you've got any sense,' Stryke advised. 'I'm going to. You should all do the same while you can.'

'And make the most of it,' Jup added sourly. 'It might be the last time.'

17

He was aware of her standing by his side. Together, they gazed out at the ocean.

A playful wind lightly whipped their clothes and faces. The sun was high and the day hot. Flocks of pure white birds winged above the distant islands. They gathered, too, at the tip of the peninsula to the south.

He felt no need to speak, and she seemed to feel the same. They simply let the vast, calm body of shining water cleanse and pacify their spirits.

At length, although their appetite for the scene had not been sated, and probably never could be, they turned away. Leaving behind their vantage point on the chalky cliffs, they began the gentle descent into rolling pastures. Soon, the grass was ankle-deep, its vivid emerald splashed here and there with clusters of flowers like golden nuggets.

'Is this not a fine place?' the female said.

'It outdoes any I've known,' he replied, 'and I've travelled far.'

'Then you must have seen many regions to match its charm. Our land is hardly bereft of nature's wonders.'

'Not where I come from.'

'You've said that before. I confess myself puzzled as to where that might be.'

'At times like this,' he admitted, 'so am I.'

'Ever the riddler,' she teased, her eyes flashing, amusement lighting her strong face.

'I don't mean to be.'

'No, I truly think you don't. But you have the power to remove yourself from the mystery that seems to dog you.'

'How?'

'Come and make a life here.'

As with the first time she mooted the notion, he felt a shiver of excitement and longing. It was partly the richness of the land, partly her and the implied role she would play in a new life. 'I'm sore tempted.'

'What's stopping you?'

'The two things that always stand in my way.'

'And they are?'

'The task I would leave undone in my . . . own land.'

'The other?'

'Perhaps the hardest to overcome. I have no understanding of how I come and go from this place. Nor control of it.'

'Accomplish the first and you will conquer the second. You have the power. Your will can triumph, if you just let it.'

'I can't see how.'

'But not for want of looking, I'll wager. Be minded of the ocean back there. Were you to fill your palm with water from it and dwell upon that, would it mean the rest of the ocean had ceased to exist? Sometimes we cannot see because we look too closely.'

'As ever, your words touch something in me, yet I can't quite grasp its shape.'

'You will. Honour your obligations, as a good orc should, and a way will open from your land to mine. Trust me.'

'I do.' He laughed. 'I don't know why, but you have my trust.'

She joined in the laughter. 'Is that so bad a thing?'

'No. Far from it.'

They fell silent again.

Now the pastures were on a keener slope, and he saw that they were making their way down into a valley, surrounded by gentle hills, although one fell at a more acute angle.

Nestled in the middle of the lush depths was a small encampment. It consisted of perhaps a dozen thatched round dwellings and half again that number of longhouses, along with stockpens. There were no defensive fortifications, fire ditches or any other protective barriers. Orcs could be seen, and horses and livestock.

He couldn't remember ever seeing the camp before, but somehow it stirred a recollection that wouldn't quite be brought to mind.

As they approached, he asked, 'Did this place ever have an outer wall?'

She seemed almost amused by the question. 'No. There has never been the need. Why do you ask?'

'I just felt . . . I don't know. Is it named?'

'Yes. They call it Galletons Outlook.'

'You're sure? Has it ever been called something else?'

'Of course I'm sure! What else could it be called?'

'I can't remember.'

The mention of names diverted his thoughts from the enigma for a moment. 'There's something I'm determined to know this time,' he told her resolutely.

'And what might that be?'

'Your name. You know mine. I've never discovered yours.'

'How did we allow that to happen?' She smiled. 'I am Thirzarr.'

He repeated it several times under his breath, then declared, 'I like it. It has strength, and attends your character well.'

'As does your own, Stryke. I'm glad you approve.'

That felt like some kind of victory to him, despite its seeming smallness, and for a moment he relished the feat. But when he glanced again at the valley floor and its settlement, something was once more roused in the recesses of his mind. He still couldn't bring it into focus.

They were on the level now and nearing the encampment. The feeling he couldn't name grew stronger. Before long they were entering the modest township. Nobody paid heed, except for one or two orcs who waved greetings at his female companion. At Thirzarr, he corrected himself.

Without let, they passed through the clearing, skirting huts and pens. Then, near the camp's southern end, Thirzarr stopped and pointed. He looked and saw she was indicating a pool, near perfectly round and filled with sparkling water. She went to it, and he followed.

They sat side by side on its rim. She ran her hand through the water, delighting in the liquid's sensuous caress. He was occupied with whatever it was that wouldn't yield to his recall.

'This pool . . .' he said.

'Isn't it lovely. It was why they founded this settlement.'

'There's something familiar about it. About all this.'

'You could make it more familiar still if you were to come here and settle. If you were to come to me.'

It should have been a moment of delight. Yet it was soured. For the first time in her company, he was troubled. Each element he had seen, could see now, tumbled through his mind. The ocean and peninsula. The valley with its hills. This pool. The steep bank yonder that should have been decorated with chalk figures.

Realisation hit him like a storm.

He leapt to his feet and cried, 'I know this place!'

He sat upright, instantly awake.

A few seconds passed before he adjusted to his surroundings. Slowly it dawned that he was in a shack in Ruffetts View, alone, waiting for a besieging army's next assault.

Half a dozen deep breaths were needed to shake off the dream and bring him back to reality.

What he couldn't free himself of was knowing where he had just visited, if visited was the right word.

It was here.

The sun crept wearily above the horizon but there was no birdsong to greet it.

Pale, chill light threw long shadows from the eastern hills but nothing could hide Hobrow's vast encampment. From tents and picket-lines rose the murmur of purposeful activity. Surgeons were still labouring over yesterday's wounded but the Unis were readying themselves for another assault, spurred on by the black-garbed custodians. They were everywhere, urging riders and foot-soldiers into formation. Never mind that many bore blood-soaked bandages and half of them had found no chance to eat.

Hobrow himself had no desire for food. He stood on a lightly wooded slope, well beyond bowshot of the heathens in Ruffetts. Though the breeze wafted delicious scents from the cook-fires, the only hunger he had was for the Lord's work.

Beside him, Mercy knelt, fervently whispering, 'Amen!'

Hobrow reached the end of his prayer and laid one hand on her shoulder. 'You see, my dear? See how fragile their defences are? How thinly their defenders are stretched? Today the Lord will give them into our grasp and they shall fall before our blades like wheat before a scythe.'

For a moment they stood side by side, ignoring the bustle of his thousands of soldiers. From here the Mani settlement seemed no more than a toy, the houses mere blocky shapes with threads of smoke from their chimneys drawing charcoal lines against the azure light of morning.

'They must know they're doomed, Father,' Mercy said. 'How can they possibly hold out against us?'

'They are blinded by their wickedness. See how that cesspool of evil throws its hideous vapours into the air?'

She could hardly avoid seeing. In the centre of the settlement the half-built dome of the temple glinted beneath its scaffolding, but she scarcely noticed the structure. Beside it, fountaining high above the little colony, the vent of earth power shimmered brightly with every colour Mercy could imagine.

Greatly daring, she answered, 'How fair the face of evil seems. I could almost believe that such beauty can only come from the Lord.'

'The Lord of Lies, perhaps. Do not be taken in, child. The Manis are a corruption before God and man. And today God will send them to the Hell they deserve.'

In the settlement they were scarcely holding chaos at bay.

The last flames were almost out now, though the stink of

burning was heavy and soot stained the exhausted firefighters. They'd worked all night to keep dozens of blazes under control as time and again the Unis had rained fire canisters down on the town. The pool in the square by the northern gate had shrunk under the assault of the bucket brigade. Now it was slowly filling again, its surface mirroring the dying fires in crimson and black. Manic hammering rang out from the stockade where new timbers were filling gaps. The clang of the blacksmiths answered as weapons were mended at the forge. Children were dashing about, their arms full of arrows for the watchmen on the walkway.

Still preoccupied with what he thought of as the revelation in his dream, Stryke trudged tiredly across a square to meet Rellston. He saw a family of humans standing, holding hands around a funeral pyre. The tiniest infant was bawling at the pain of her burnt and blistered face and the eldest lad, who couldn't have been more than ten seasons old, had his mouth set in a grim line though the effect was somewhat spoiled by the tracks of tears cutting through the dirt on his face. An old woman beside the widow couldn't stop coughing as the smoke eddied around the square.

Stryke saw Rellston, as weary as himself, jump aside as a cart rumbled around a corner. It was heaped high with more bodies for the pyre. He stopped for a word with a man who had a bloodied rag tied around his shoulder then came straight towards the Wolverines' leader. 'Join me for a drink, Stryke?' he asked, in an unusual show of openness. He didn't wait for an answer.

Stryke fell in beside him. 'Where are we going?'

'The seaward wall. I want to see how the repairs are going.' The human strode on, pushing his way through the crowded streets. He kept glancing at the orc then looking away as if he wasn't sure what to say.

Stryke wasn't about to help him.

Finally the man said awkwardly, 'You made the difference, you know. You and the rest of your band. We're just not used to warfare on this scale. If it hadn't been for you we wouldn't have made it this far. Thank you.'

Stryke nodded acknowledgement. 'But you're still wondering if the Unis would have attacked at all if we hadn't been here.'

'By the look of them they'd have come against us anyway sooner or later. That Hobrow's a fanatic.'

The sun was a finger's breadth above the horizon now, a malevolent orange orb. Rellston squinted at it through the drifts of smoke. 'How soon before they attack, d'you reckon?'

'Soon as they finish praying, I suppose. What plans have you got?'

They had reached the seaward wall now. The Mani commander ducked under a blanket hung across a blackened doorway. The door itself was a heap of ashes that squelched underfoot. He shrugged. 'Keep doing what we're doing. And pray ourselves.'

'That's all well and good,' Stryke said thoughtfully, 'but we have to do more than that. In the long run besiegers always have the advantage over the besieged.'

Rellston stepped over three or four of his command, who were sleeping on the floor, and helped himself to a bottle from a cupboard. Not bothering to look for glasses, he took a swig of the fiery liquor and passed the bottle to the orc.

'We have our own wells here. So long as we can keep from being overrun we'll make it.'

'Except you can't possibly have enough food to last forever.' The orc slumped on a chair and nodded at the wall of the stockade, just visible through a window. 'They do.'

The Uni commander couldn't hide his desperation. 'The gods know we can't keep taking losses like yesterday's! And they have enough men to come at us every night. What can we do?'

'I don't know yet. But something has to give. In the meantime, mind if I make a suggestion?'

'Help yourself. I don't have to follow your advice.'

'Have you got bucket brigades sorted for the next attack?'

'Of course.'

'Then get a team collecting cooking oil, axle grease, anything that'll burn. Put it in a pot with a rag for a wick and we can get our own back.'

Rellston grinned, his teeth white in the sooty stubble of his face. 'Fight fire with fire, you mean?'

'Exactly. After what they did to your township last night I don't think your people will have any moral objection. When they come again we can lob firepots of our own at the bastards.'

'Trouble is,' Rellston said, not grinning anymore, 'their fighters still outnumber ours. They don't have women and children eating their supplies either.' The commander hauled himself to his feet. 'Better get in position. They'll be here again soon enough.'

Stryke climbed the wall facing Hobrow's main encampment. He could see the Unis on their knees. Hobrow himself could be made out standing on a knoll, his arms upraised. But the light, salty breeze carried the man's words away and Stryke couldn't make out what he said. He knew it meant nothing good for orcs or Manis though.

From his vantage point, the Wolverine leader spotted his officers in a fierce conversation. Haskeer gestured and Coilla made damping motions, but when they spotted Stryke they surged towards him. Even now. some Manis gave them a wide berth.

He descended and met them. They all started speaking at once.

'Shut up!' he snapped. 'The last thing I need is you lot arguing.' He glanced at a tumbledown shack. 'In there. We need to talk.'

With Alfray keeping watch through a crack in the door, the rest of the Wolverine command squatted in the cobwebbed shadows.

'First off,' Stryke said quietly, 'it's pretty obvious this town won't make it. Half of them can't fight and Hobrow's got his followers stoked up. Any ideas?'

The Wolverines looked at each other. 'We fight,' said Coilla. 'What else?'

'Exactly. "What else?"' Stryke's words hung in the grimy air.

Jup asked slowly, 'What do you mean?'

'I mean we *could* just leave them to it. With the humans fighting each other, they'll be too busy to come after us.'

'You mean we just find a way out of here while they're occupied?' Haskeer said. 'Sounds good to me.'

Coilla hissed, 'You can't mean that! We'd have had no chance against Hobrow's men if it wasn't for them. We can't desert them now.'

'Think about it,' Stryke urged. 'I know the Manis are our allies now, sort of. But what do you think will happen if the last star falls into Hobrow's hands?'

Jup jumped to his feet. 'Who cares about the star?' he said angrily. 'We've got four of them, haven't we? Isn't that enough for you? Or do we have to throw our lives away too?'

Stryke glared at the dwarf. 'Sit down and shut your mouth. Isn't it obvious to you that the star's got power? It's something to do with the magic of the land. If Hobrow gets his hands on it, that power will be his.'

'Either that,' Alfray said from his post by the door, 'or he'll destroy it. But us getting killed is more likely out in the open against the whole Uni army. And I never was much for betraying people I've fought alongside.'

'Look,' Haskeer said as the dwarf sullenly resumed his place in the circle, 'they're only humans, ain't they? All right, they've been welcoming to us, given us food and shelter, but they need us more than we need them. If it was the other way round, they'd take from us and think nothing of it. You know they would. That's human nature.'

Coilla had been thinking about the implications behind Stryke's words. 'You mean you've decided we're going for the star and done with it?'

Stryke nodded. 'I say for the meantime we stay here and fight. Then, when we get a chance, we take the star and get out under cover of darkness.'

One by one they agreed, some with more reluctance than others. Alfray was the least happy, but even he could see that Ruffetts View didn't stand much chance of surviving.

Swallowing down his own guilt, Stryke said, 'Coilla? You've been in the temple. Do you think you could steal the star for us?'

'If I have to. It shouldn't be too difficult. After all, they haven't got time to guard the temple when there's a fucking siege going on, have they?'

'Look,' Alfray said, abandoning his post and coming to stare down at Stryke with a spark of anger in his eyes, 'if we're sneaking out of here, what are you planning on doing with the enlistees? You're not going to leave them behind just like that, are you? Because I'd find that hard to believe of the Stryke I know.'

'No, Alfray, I'm not. I'm an orc and we look after our own. We'll let them know, don't worry.'

'I'm not worried,' the old corporal said. 'I'm just not abandoning anybody, that's all.'

'Neither am I, Alfray. Neither am I. So what I—'

Alarms bells began to sound. From the wall of the stockade men were shouting.

The orcs sprang to their feet, heading for the door. At that moment a fire canister burst on the thatched roof above them. Burning pieces of straw and wood showered down, filling the hut with smoke.

Stryke jumped forward, pulling Coilla out of the way of a falling timber. 'Let's get out of here!'

The rain of fire continued, kept in check only by the archers Rellston had posted on the walls, and by the bucket brigades within. Sheltering under overhanging eaves where they could, the Wolverines pounded off to their respective posts. Dodging and ducking, they were just about to split up when a lookout called, 'They've stopped! They're pulling back!'

'Must be so they don't hit their own troops,' Stryke said. Then he shivered as something coursed through him.

Coilla hadn't noticed. 'See that?' she said.

In the middle of the tension, with battle about to be joined, the High Priestess was chanting around the geyser of magic. Still in her blue robes, though they were somewhat stained now, she was slowly circling the fountain of rainbow light, hand in hand with a chain of her followers. Around her, tattered and worn, a group of women of all ages were watching. Red, green and yellow gleamed on their faces as they took up the eerie chant.

'What are they doing?' Jup said.

'Trying to turn the magic on the Unis,' Stryke answered without thinking. Then wondered how he knew.

'Well, we need all the help we can get,' the dwarf muttered.

Stryke tried to pull out of the strange feelings that rippled around him. 'I'm all for calling on the gods,' he said with an attempt at his former cynicism, 'but there are times when a good sword is your best guide.'

Coilla put a hand on his arm. 'Why don't we tell them we have the other stars?'

He looked puzzled. 'Why would we do that?'

She shrugged, seeming almost embarrassed now, if that were possible. 'If they're as powerful as they're supposed to be, maybe the stars could help.'

'Do you think anybody around here would know what to do with them?'

Jup grimaced. 'We don't know what to do with them either.'

Stryke fought to control himself. The waves of vibration inside him made it hard to think. The others looked at him expectantly while Krista and her handmaidens continued to sing their invocation to the Trinity. He found himself wishing that he'd had the time to tell Coilla what the Priestess had said about the possibility of his being a sport.

Consciously anchoring himself in reality by straightening his shoulders, he took a deep breath and said, 'I still think the stars are better with us.'

'But why?' Coilla's words burst out louder than she'd meant. Some of the singers turned to glare at her. 'They've brought us nothing but trouble this far,' she ended more quietly.

'I just don't want to risk them falling into the Unis' hands,' Stryke said.

Coilla looked at him strangely. 'Are you sure you just don't want to share them? You're getting mighty possessive about the damn things if you ask me.'

'Yeah!' Haskeer said. 'You won't even let me touch them any more.'

Jup smirked. 'Not since you went crazy.'

'Shut up about that, will you? It was just the humans and their fucking plague, all right?'

Before anyone else could speak, Krista's chant reached such a high pitch that it was on the limits of hearing. The sound seemed to knife through Stryke. The Priestess and her acolytes were swaying backwards and forwards now, their faces alight with rapture.

'How can they stand that shrieking?' Jup whispered.

Alfray spoke, dispelling Stryke's mood. The old orc indicated Krista's unearthly hymn. 'Think it'll work?'

'I bloody hope so,' Jup said. 'A battle's a battle, and all that, but I'm sick to death of everybody being after us.'

For a moment an unusual sense of optimism held the band.

Then alarm bells sounded again and somebody shouted, 'There's another army out there!'

'Oh, *fuck*!'

In the sudden silence that filled the holy place, Jup's words rang out somewhat louder than he intended.

18

Dashing to the walls, the orcs swarmed up to the walkway. As far as the eye could see there were soldiers marching, horses trampling, banners rippling. But with the smoke from the fires still burning in Ruffetts, and perhaps five hundred bonfires on the enemy side, nobody could see clearly for more than a few feet. But they didn't have to be able to see clearly to realise that the army of the besiegers had more than doubled in size.

Squinting, cloths tied around their faces to keep out the choking fumes, the Wolverines watched the endless tide of men and horses rolling black across the crests of the hills. By the time the newcomers' vanguard had reached the Uni camp there was no sign of the rearguard. Just an endless swarm that covered the landscape from one side of the horizon to the other.

Stryke closed his eyes in despair.

Haskeer was the first to find his voice. 'Now the shit hits the windmill.'

But suddenly the Uni camp was filled with shrieks. Coughing, Coilla said, 'Doesn't sound much like a joyous reunion to me.'

Jup leapt up and down in uncharacteristic glee. 'They're *Manis*! Look, there are orcs up there, hundreds of 'em! The Manis have come to lift the siege!'

'You're right!' Coilla said. 'They're attacking the Unis from the rear.'

'There's dwarves!' Jup pointed excitedly at the first group of his own people he had seen in a while. 'A whole mass of 'em!'

Haskeer sneered, 'So what? They won't make a difference unless they're being paid well.'

Jup grabbed him by the throat. 'Says *who*, goat breath?'

Before Haskeer could reply Stryke pulled them apart. 'We don't have time for this. Can anybody see whose army it is?'

Batting windblown sparks out of the smoky air, the Wolverines peered through the shimmering waves of heat.

'Don't know,' Coilla decided. 'Don't care. There's more of them than there is of the Unis and that's good enough for me.'

Stryke rested his hands on the palisade. 'This is gods-sent. We've got to get out there and help.'

Inside Ruffetts View a frenzy of activity burst out, with Rellston snapping commands left, right and centre. Runners took his orders and within a short time forces were mustering. Foot-soldiers forced their way through the crowds to line the streets near the northern gate. Meanwhile, riders were saddling up and pushing their way from the stables so they could form up around the small pool in the square.

The Ruffetts commander had his work cut out, sending citizens to the walls while the townswomen were left to battle the fires still raging in the poorer quarters, where houses were built mostly of wood.

Stryke pushed his way through the throng, wishing he hadn't told the enlistees to also assemble by the landmark pool. The noise was appalling. He dodged as a horse shied at the din, and shouldered his way through to the edge of the muddy water.

He wasn't surprised to see that even in the crowded square the humans had left a space around Corporal Krenad. Two hundred orc warriors were enough to give most beings a sense of respect.

'Ready for the charge, Corporal?'

The deserter's face split in a grin. 'Much better than skulking around inside these poxy walls, sir. If you want a good sally, I'm your orc.'

They had to shout to make themselves heard. Now a strange quiet fell on the muster.

Climbing into the saddle of a horse Krenad had brought him, Stryke found out why. High Priestess Krista Galby was walking through the square. Despite it being so packed, the inhabitants of Ruffetts still found space to make way for her.

Serene, Krista had a brief word with Commander Rellston, then headed for the Wolverines. Stryke heeled his horse forward to meet her.

She rested a hand on his leg and looked up into his eyes. 'Once someone has felt the power of the land, it will grow in them,' she whispered. 'Sooner or later, the land won't be denied.'

Suddenly she wasn't serious at all. With a gleam of exaltation in her eye, she straightened. Though she hardly raised her voice, her next words rang through the square. 'Let each of you know that you fight for the land. So the land will strengthen you, bring the power of the earth into your hearts. Open yourselves to the power of the earth. Know that the wind is the earth's breath, and that we fight for the land's well-being. For the land will not be denied. Too long has it shed tears for its despoilers. Now, as the power of the earth soars above your heads—' from the geyser a plume of coruscating pseudo-flame leaped higher, by chance or by design '—your spirits will be renewed, in this life or the next, and the blessings of the Manifold Path will be above you and before you. They will be behind you and on either hand, to guard and guide and shield you as the land's own.' Her hands rose in a graceful gesture of benediction. Then she vanished into the crowd.

Rellston's command burst into the silence. 'Open the gates! At the trot!'

Flanked by Coilla, Jup, Alfray and Haskeer, Stryke held his restless horse in place by sheer muscular power.

Once more the square was filled with noise. Under its cover, Coilla said, 'If anything happens to you all the stars will be lost at once. Split them up between us, Stryke.'

'No chance.' His automatic refusal brought her chin up stubbornly. He added persuasively, 'They belong together, Coilla. I don't know why, they just do.'

Already the first columns of trotting men were at the gates.

'Either that or you're just too possessive to let them out of your grasp,' she said.

Secure in the centre of her army, Jennesta stared down from her chariot on the hilltop.

A seething battle was underway in front of the squalid, smoking settlement. Trapped by the steep sides of the valley, pinned down by her loyalists and those pathetic human and orcish renegades, Hobrow's Unis were grimly digging in.

She laughed. 'Pitiful, aren't they, Mersadion?'

'Yes, my Lady.' Unconsciously, the general's hand lifted to touch his scarred and blistered cheek. 'But there are still twenty thousand of them.'

The queen's eyes glittered. 'Your point?'

'That . . . that it will be a great victory for you, my Lady.'

'I like a great victory. And so should you, General. Because if I don't get one, you don't get to live. Do I make myself clear?'

Mersadion bowed to hide the hatred he could feel inside him. 'Indeed you do, my Lady.'

'Good. Then arrange for a three-pronged attack. I want our humans ready for a frontal charge. Yes? Were you about to question my orders?'

'No, my Lady. Never.'

'That's right. We mustn't let ourselves get carried away, must we? I want the orcs on that ridge over there, ready to attack from the cover of the trees. The dwarves can take that hilltop on the left. When my humans feint with a charge, those stupid Unis won't be able to spread out sideways to encircle the charge. But some will be lured forward and *that's* when our flanks will attack theirs. Simple, you see?'

He did indeed. 'It's brilliant, my Lady.'

'Of course it is.' She smiled down on the sea of glittering pikes and swords below her. 'And while we're at it, Mersadion, I want the harpies ready to fly once that Uni rabble has committed itself to a charge.'

What's left of them, the general thought, turning away to pass on his orders. Why the queen had chosen to pleasure herself by setting the harpies on each other the night before, he could not fathom. Although insanity couldn't be ruled out.

Fortunately Jennesta was happy. Excited. Girlish even, at the thought of the bloodletting to come. She flicked her reins and began trundling her scythe-wheeled chariot to the front ranks of her vanguard. Once she was in position, she had Mersadion give the signal for the charge.

Step by step the horses flung themselves forward, gaining momentum. Knowing she looked magnificent, all aglitter in the sun, Jennesta thundered down on her enemy, sweeping her army out around her like a jewelled cloak.

This was going to be easy.

Kimball Hobrow could scarcely believe it. Just moments ago, he had been in charge of a besieging force that outnumbered the heathen scum in that wretched little dump below. He couldn't lose. He could even pity the stupidity of those Manis, laid out before him like ninepins, waiting for the will of God to bowl them aside as a testament to His power.

And now he was facing not one but *two* armies. Armies that made his own forces look like a temple picnic.

'What'll we do, sir?' said the sweat-streaked custodian before him.

'The Lord's will,' Hobrow said, outwardly calm despite the first stirrings of panic in his breast.

'Is it a test, Father?' Mercy asked, turning her innocent-looking face up to his.

'It is, daughter.' He raked the trembling custodian with a glance as the ground began to shake beneath Jennesta's chariot charge. 'Why? Do you think the Lord has abandoned us? Is our faith so weak?'

'N . . . no, sir.'

'Indeed not. We shall slay these unbelievers. The Lord's name will ring down glorified through the ages. If He is with us, how can we lose?'

The custodian could not find words. He shook his head as Hobrow made a blessing in the hot, dusty air.

'Get back to your place, man! Do the Lord's will!' Hobrow had already dismissed him from his thoughts. He beckoned to two of his inner circle. They trotted obediently to him. 'I have bad news for you,' he told them. 'I know you long to take part in the glorious slaughter but the Lord has other plans for you.'

Both of them actually looked regretful. 'Tell us, master,' they chorused.

'Guard my daughter with your lives, for did not the Lord command us to protect the innocent?'

They nodded, awestruck at the responsibility.

'Then take her to safety.' Hobrow stooped, his angular body looking like some strange bird as he bent to kiss Mercy's brow. She bent her head in submission to his authority, but he had already gone.

One glance was enough to show him that the tatterdemalion force from Ruffetts View was no more than a few hundred beings. Already he could see the Whore, riding down on him in a glitter of gold and steel. Her front rank crashed into the Unis' pikemen with a shock that transmitted itself through the ground. For a moment he could even see the Queen, screaming in rage as one of her horses impaled itself on one of the deadly weapons.

Smiling to himself, Hobrow swung up into the saddle and galloped into the fray. How could she be so stupid? When had a cavalry charge ever broken through a solid line of pikemen? The Lord was with him indeed.

This was going to be easy.

As the dark mass of Jennesta's army shocked into the foremost rank of the Unis, Stryke spearheaded his orcish cavalry unit at their rear.

Although they were going uphill, not the best of tactics for a charge, their opponents were in confusion. Hobrow's soldiers had fired a single scant volley of arrows, most of which had fallen short. Firing downhill made it hard to judge distance.

'I guess the best of Hobrow's archers are up at the sharp end,' Coilla said, crouching low over the neck of her racing mount.

'I ain't complaining,' Haskeer replied.

The Wolverines thundered on. The smoke was thinner the further from Ruffetts they went, but the battle above was raising so much dust it might as well have been fog. The grass was grey with it, and even the sun was no more than a faint ball hanging halfway up the sky. It didn't stop the sounds of battle, though, and the very ground was trembling beneath the pounding hooves.

Stryke looked to his right. As agreed, Rellston's cavalry was sweeping down on Hobrow's flank from a gentle slope. The Unis' own horsemen were somewhere up ahead, out of sight behind the shifting mass of the fighting. The Wolverine already knew the enemy would keep their horses at the major battlefront against the unexpected Mani army.

To either side, having set off some minutes earlier, Rellston's foot-soldiers were beginning to form into lines. The front row wielded short stabbing swords while their comrades levelled long lances. From behind them whistled flight upon flight of javelins. They plunged into the Unis' flanks. Some clattered off shields, but others found their mark and a ragged chorus of shrieks had Stryke and Coilla grinning with maniacal pleasure.

Only fifty yards before the orcish cavalry punched through the Uni lines. Twenty . . . Ten . . .

From straight overhead came unholy screams of laughter. Confused, the Wolverines looked upwards and recoiled.

A dozen winged creatures came out of the dust cloud, stooping down on the dumbstruck Unis. Hobrow's archers never knew what hit them. From behind the harpies swooped on them, dragging struggling bodies up into the air then hurling them down upon their comrades. A grisly rain of blood spattered on men and earth alike.

Only a handful of bowmen realised what was happening. Caught completely off guard, they sent a few arrows upwards but for the most part the shots fell back down, doing more harm to the Unis' own troops than to the harpies, who hid cackling behind the cloud.

Too late to stop his headlong dash, Stryke found himself riding down a boy whose mouth was an O of astonishment. The boy fell beneath the plunging hooves, his scream abruptly cut off. Then it was hack and slash, duck and parry.

Now that the orcs had torn a hole in the Unis' defence, Rellston's troops were through. Hobrow's forces gathered in tight knots, fighting for their lives. And every now and then a harpy would dive down to seize another victim, scattering his ripped limbs onto his terrified comrades.

The outcome was inevitable.

'Like spearing fish in a barrel!' Haskeer cried, his blade a whirling circle of crimson.

'Yeah,' Jup panted, his own share of victims marking his path. 'It's almost a crime.'

At the battlefront above the narrowest part of the valley, Jennesta was incensed. True, her personal bodyguard had thrown themselves at the pikemen, their sheer ferocity driving back the Unis. But that still left her with an overturned chariot and a dead horse in the traces.

'Do something!' she screamed at Mersadion as she dragged herself to her feet.

'Yes, my Lady.' Cursing, the General ran after another chariot.

As soon as the driver slowed to hear his commander's orders, Mersadion leaped aboard and hurled the man out onto the trampled grass. Another team was right behind. With not so much as a backward glance Mersadion left the fallen charioteer to the mercy of spinning hub scythes.

He knew Jennesta in her turn would do the same to him. She bounced away across the rutted ground, whipping her horses to a headlong gallop.

The scent of blood was in her nostrils, singing through her whole being, filling her with a deep hunger. She drove straight at the gap where the pikemen had died and plunged into the battle. The remnants of her personal guard hurried to catch up with her.

Abruptly she slowed. It wouldn't do to get too far ahead of her men. And slewing the chariot to a stop, she opened her eyes wide in surprise.

A stray breeze had, for an instant, swept the dust aside. Clear as day, she saw that at the foot of the valley a force from the settlement had cleaved into the Unis' rear.

A force that included *orcs*.

It might mean nothing. After all, she had orcs of her own, and there were plenty of them scattered about Maras-Dantia.

But then again, it might mean something. It might mean she'd caught up with those thieving turncoats after all.

Jennesta's faint scaling gleamed as the sun lit up her flashing smile.

In the mêlée outside the north gate of Ruffetts View, the groups of Unis struggled on, unwilling to die without taking as many Manis with them as they could. There couldn't have been more than two or three thousand of them left at the bottom of the valley but they were selling themselves dear.

Weary beyond belief, Stryke stopped for a breather. It was bloody work, hot and sweaty despite the unnatural chill in the air. Happily, the harpies had gone now, either shot down by bowmen or fled back to wherever they had come from. Their appearance had bothered him. As far as Stryke knew, they hadn't touched one of the troops from Ruffetts View. How had they known to attack the Unis? Come to that, he had no idea why the other Mani army had turned up without warning.

Telling himself he was just reacting to Hobrow's fanaticism, Stryke reached for his water-flask. Then cursed as he realised it had been cut loose in the battle. Fortunately the stars were secure.

Coilla reined in beside him. 'Gods! I'd kill for a drink of ale,' she said, wiping blood and perspiration from her brow.

'You may have to,' he answered. 'There's bound to be some up there in their camp. Let's hope we get to it before these gods-botherers do.'

He spurred his mount forward, his head rocking back with the impetus. Coilla looked after him and joined in his wild charge.

Then they caught a glimpse of Krenad. He was hanging upside down, one foot caught in his stirrup as his horse rocketed away in fright, dancing between the broken ranks of fighters.

Stryke took Krenad's attacker with a swipe from the side while Coilla dashed after the enlistee. She managed to cut in front of his steed and haul it to a standstill. Helping him free his foot, she was glad to see that he could still smile shakily in thanks.

Then a shout from Rellston drew them like a magnet. A pocket of several hundred Unis had taken refuge in a hollow. It was defended by a thicket, and they were making sorties out of it then rushing back to take shelter in the thorny trees.

Krenad pulled himself back onto his horse and passed round a flask of some spirit Stryke didn't recognise. It tasted foul but it put new heart in him. He looked about him and saw Alfray coming towards them out of the murk.

Suddenly the old warrior stopped as though he'd seen someone in his path. Not an enemy but someone he had no beef with. Stryke could see the puzzlement on his corporal's face. Following Alfray's gaze, for an instant Stryke thought he saw a glimpse of white. A white stallion, with a wiry, auburn-headed man on its back.

Serapheim?

The vision was obscured by the mêlée.

'Right,' Stryke said, not quite managing to mask his super-stitious shiver. 'I want a real drink. Let's see what those sodding Unis have down there.'

The sun was low now, and Hobrow's surviving troops had been forced to retreat.

Some fool had fired the thicket hours ago, driving out the pocket of Unis but threatening to scorch anybody who wanted to get past. Smouldering leaves drifted in the breeze, setting odd little fires in unexpected places. At times the smoke was so thick it would have choked a dragon. All day the battle had raged, a losing one as far as the Unis were concerned, but fierce nonetheless.

Now the Wolverines and Krenad's enlistees were side by side, many of them on foot, all of them smeared with blood. For the lucky ones it was somebody else's.

As evening drew on, a wind sprang up, whistling down the valley on its way to the sea. It tore apart the pall of smoke just long enough for the orcs to see who it was who had so fortuitously come to their aid.

Jennesta.

'My gods!' exclaimed Haskeer at the same time as Stryke cried her name.

The irony of it was not lost on them. Nor, apparently, on Jennesta. From the platform of her distant chariot she glared at them.

Far away as she was, they knew she would be raging with naked hatred. A tiny figure way up on the hillside, she raised her hand as though to cast an invisible spear.

Stryke and his Wolverines scattered. They had seen enough of her magic to know she had balls of dazzling energy at her command.

They needn't have worried. With another unpredictable shift the breeze dropped the curtain of smoke between them.

'Don't worry,' Coilla said contemptuously. 'She won't risk her precious self down in the real battle. Now let's find that murdering Uni chief and then get the hell out of here.'

19

Kimball Hobrow had been behind his men all day, striding from place to place, urging them onward with increasingly desperate prayers. He'd shadowed them every step of the way, every hard-fought pace of the retreat. Now he was hiding out of sight behind an overturned wagon, still hoarsely shouting encouragement.

All at once he found himself with no one left to exhort. The last of his custodians sank to the ground with a tired sigh. Like a child falling asleep, the man gave up the ghost and died as the sun tucked itself behind the ridge.

The camp was off to one side of the valley. It should have been safe enough, hidden in a little dip lined with trees, a peaceful place for a man to make camp with his daughter. But he hadn't seen his daughter for hours. God alone knew where she was.

For the first time Hobrow wondered if God cared.

The Uni leader crouched lower, hardly aware of the splinters from the wagon board sticking into the flesh of his hand. His sword had long since vanished, dropped when a mob of howling savages came towards his gallant band. Now he had nothing with which to defend himself.

He spotted a couple of subhumans sneaking through the wreckage of his camp. They were wearing the uniform of the

Great Whore. Jackknifing up and down again, he snagged a torn blanket from the heap caught on the wheel and pulled it over his head. Perhaps if he squatted and kept really still, they might miss him.

Trying to hold his breath, Hobrow heard his heart as loud as hoofbeats in his ears. Surely they must hear it too? For it was obvious now that he had grievously offended the Lord, and the Lord had deserted him. Hadn't he been doing God's will? Hadn't he been zealous enough?

Apparently not.

Suddenly the two creatures pounced. Tearing the blanket off, they grabbed him as he blinked in the last of the daylight.

'Oh Lord, smite these unbelievers who dare to profane your instru—' One of the orcs clouted him casually over the head.

Hobrow lay stunned for a breath or two. When reality crowded back in on him, he heard the fat one say, 'Wonder if he's got anything worth looting?'

The tall one ferreted around in the pile of stuff that had fallen from the wagon. He tossed a holy book across the clearing, wiping his fingers afterwards on his jerkin. 'Nah. Just a pile of old crap.'

Hobrow forced himself up to one elbow. 'You can't say that!' he exclaimed, aghast.

The fat one backhanded him, splitting Hobrow's lip. 'Just did, lame-brain. You talk too much.'

'Let's cut out his tongue! I could do with a laugh.'

Hobrow scuttled backwards, his legs pedalling furiously. Before they could work out what he was doing he had crawled right under the smashed woodwork of the wagon bed.

The tall one vaulted over the broken traces and reached for him. Hobrow huddled in on himself beneath the broken planks, shrinking out of the orc's reach.

It made no difference. Casually, the fat one whacked the flat of his axe against Hobrow's knee. 'Quit playing hide and seek, scumpouch.'

Hobrow howled. 'Let me go! I'm the Lord's servant. You can't hurt me.' His tone tightened to a whine of self pity. 'Please don't hurt me!'

The fat one fastened his fingers in Hobrow's once-tidy hair and hauled him out. He dragged the cringing Uni upright, shaking him like a rag doll. 'Look,' he said to his companion as a stain spread steamily across Hobrow's pants. 'He's pissed himself.'

Hobrow closed his eyes, feeling the final indignity start to cool and stick clammily on his thighs. His captor shoved him aside. Hobrow fell hard against the wagon wheel.

'Reckon it's worth taking him back to Her Majesty, Hrackash?' his captor said.

The tall one stared at the Lord's servant with contempt. 'Nah. He can't be anyone important. He's got less spine than a jellyfish.'

Sunk in shame, Kimball Hobrow didn't even feel the knife that plunged into his heart.

As darkness came, Jennesta's troops fell back to their encampment. But unnatural howls floated across the shadowy battlefield. Furtive movements betrayed the fact that some of the Unis were making their escape over the ridge. Stryke wasn't aware that Mercy Hobrow was among them. But then, he had other things on his mind.

'We'd better get the last star and clear out,' he decided. 'That's Jennesta up there. I don't want to be anywhere near her come morning.'

'Why's she helping us?' Jup wondered.

'She's not helping us. She's just getting the Unis out of the way. It's us she's after. Coilla? Are you in on this?'

'Of course I am!' She hesitated as Alfray bound up a cut on her shoulder. 'It's just that . . . Well, you know, it doesn't seem right taking things from allies. It's not as though we've got that many friends, is it?'

'They owe us,' Haskeer stated baldly. 'Think of it as a reward.'

'Oh, charming,' Coilla said. 'So now I get to rob our allies' temple.'

A mass of tired riders shambled past them, heading for the town gates.

'Look,' Stryke said. 'These people don't stand a chance. When Jennesta comes through here in the morning, do you want her getting her hands on what might be a source of power?'

That clinched it.

The band made their way down to Ruffetts View, some of them limping, all of them weary.

Alfray grabbed Stryke's sleeve. 'Did you . . . did you see that human, Serapheim, in the battle?'

Stryke hesitated. 'I'm not sure. I thought I did, but—'

'But you're talking a load of bollocks,' Haskeer finished. 'Why would some wordsmith be farting around in a battle? Now let's get down there and find out how grateful these people *really* are.'

Inside the gates, the cheering rose up at them like a wall. Someone pressed tankards into their hands. Others passed them chunks of bread and meat. People were capering about, singing, carousing or praying as the mood took them.

Standing in a circle of torchlight by the pool, Krista Galby shone as clean and bright as a candle flame. Beside her, one arm thrust through his green sash as a sling, Commander Rellston leaned exhausted against the low wall. As the orcs put on a bit of swagger, the two Mani leaders called out to them.

'Once again, Stryke, you have my gratitude,' Krista said. 'We couldn't have defeated them without you.'

Rellston inclined his head stifffly. 'Let me add my thanks. I don't suppose you saw that swine Hobrow, did you?'

'No.'

Stryke made to carry on, but Rellston, determined to make up for his earlier mistrust, was summoning more flagons of ale.

It was the first time the Wolverines had felt like turning down a drink.

As soon as they could decently get away, they headed towards the fiery column of light on the hill. Krenad's band watched them go, cracking remarks about orcs who couldn't take the pace. Haskeer wasn't the only one who wanted to wipe the smirks off their faces.

With all the celebrations going on in the town, the area around the temple was practically deserted. The Wolverines made no pretence at finesse. As they strolled towards the temple door, they suddenly swung into an attack. It was the last thing the guards expected. They fell without a fight.

'Tie 'em up,' Stryke snapped, feeling a little guilty. But not enough to stop him storming inside.

On the threshold they halted. A votary lamp shone on the star on the column. It sat there, glinting steadily at them.

Coilla sighed and prepared to repeat her athletics of the day before.

'Fuck that,' Haskeer growled. Hurling himself at the massive plinth, he toppled it.

It crashed to the earthen floor with a thud that echoed around the temple. With everyone down at the celebrations there was nobody to hear it but the Wolverines.

Stryke watched the many-spiked star rolling across the floor, bouncing a little like the ones in his dream. If it had been a dream. Quickly he caught it up, thrusting it into his belt pouch with the others.

'Right,' he said. 'Let's get the hell out of here.'

They were in the stables before Coilla said, 'Aren't you going to tell Krenad and the enlistees?'

Stryke tossed a saddle onto his horse's back a little harder than necessary. The beast sidled in protest. 'They took their destiny into their own hands, just like us. They wanted freedom. They've got it. What they do with it is up to them.' He jerked the cinch tight.

'Not if Jennesta comes down here in the morning it's not,' Alfray reminded him. 'She'll skin them alive.'

'What do you want me to do? Try and hide with a whole army of orcs? Look, I don't like this any more than you do, but it's not as if we've got a lot of choice.'

Alfray said, 'We ought at least to warn them.'

Jup backed him.

Coilla was more forthright. 'Still scared you might start attracting a following?'

'What if I am?' Stryke whirled to glare at her. 'I never said I wanted to take on Jennesta! Or anybody else for that matter. All I want is to get out of this in one piece. Let some other bastard wave the flag.'

Alfray was disgusted. 'So you're just going to leave Krenad to Jennesta's tender mercies? You're not the orc I thought you were.'

Stryke stuck his face right in Alfray's. 'Wrong. That's exactly my point. I'm a leader of a warband and that's all that I am. You're the one who's trying to make me into something else. Coilla, go and find Krenad. No, wait. I'll do it myself. The gods know what sort of hash you lot would make of it.'

He found the enlistees' chief singing rude songs in a tavern.

'Come here.' Stryke said brusquely.

Krenad was too happy, and too drunk, to get off the barrel he was sitting astride. 'Wossamatter?' he mumbled.

Stryke hauled him outside and stuffed his head in a rainbutt until the deserter's eyes focused.

'Right. That's better. Now listen, Krenad. In case you didn't notice, the leader of the other army out there today was Jennesta.'

'Nah. Couldn't have been. Was a silly human in a skinny hat.'

Stryke held him under again until his sputtering grew frantic.

'Not him, you idiot! The other *Mani* army. The one on the hill. With the harpies. Remember?'

Suddenly Krenad was completely sober. 'Yes, sir. What time are we pulling out, sir?'

'*We're* pulling out now. You can pull out whenever you like.'

'You mean we're going to split up and rendezvous later?'

'No. Look, Corporal, don't think we haven't appreciated you being around for the battle. But let me make it clear to you one last time. I'm not recruiting. I never have been recruiting. And tomorrow, when we're far away from that murdering bitch, I still won't be recruiting. It's every orc for himself. Got that?'

Later that same night, far across the hills as the stars wheeled towards dawn, the look Krenad had given him still haunted Stryke.

As the sun tiptoed above the eastern wall of the stockade, Krista Galby stood aghast in the temple.

One of the guards, nursing a sore head, was saying, ' . . . and couldn't do a thing about it.'

For a long minute the Priestess kept silent, staring at the toppled pillar. At last she sighed and said, 'I don't imagine anybody saw them leave during the celebrations, but I suppose we at least have to ask.'

She paused, schooling her face to calm. Almost dreamily she said, more to herself than to the men with her, 'We have to find it and take it back. We built the temple to house it. It's been the centre of my life, and my mother's before me, and all the Priestesses right back to the time Ruffett first settled here. In fact, if it hadn't been for his finding the star in the pool in the first place, he never *would* have settled here.'

Unnerved by her preternatural tranquillity, the sore-headed guard mouthed into the silence, 'Shall I ask the Commander to get a troop together?'

Krista gazed at him. 'No. We don't want Stryke's band punished. Not after he saved Aidan's life.' Her voice trailed away, to come back stronger as she added, 'Round up all the temple guards who can still sit a horse. And saddle my mare for me.'

The man was horrified. 'You can't go, Priestess! Without the star we need you here more than ever.'

'Who else can explain why we need it? Don't you see? I *have* to go.'

In less than half an hour Krista was in the square before the northern gate. Sure enough, one of yesterday's widows had been mourning by her window. Long after the revelry had died away, she had seen a band of some thirty orcs riding out, with their horses' hooves muffled in rags. The gate-guard himself had no recollection of it. All he remembered was somebody coming over to offer him a drink and then clouting him on the back of the head.

Tenderly Krista hugged her son. Although he still couldn't walk far, his old nurse had asked one of the temple builders to carry him out to his mother. 'Be good, Aidan, and do what Merrilis tells you. We want you to get strong again, don't we?'

The boy clung to her arm. 'Don't go, Mother. Stay with me. There's bad things out there.'

'There are good things too. And I have these fine guards to keep me safe. Don't worry, my love. I'll be back before you know it.'

Krista looked at the old woman and the burly carpenter. 'Take care of him for me. And Aidan, pet, you can stay here and see the Queen ride in. Won't that be nice?'

The chief of the temple guard came up handed her the reins of a fine bay mare. Krista Galby blew her son a kiss.

Then she rode out with her followers as though a tidal wave was at her back.

Jennesta's chariot was decked with flowers.

She'd had the whirling knives removed. It wouldn't do to upset potential subjects by cutting their legs off. Now she nodded and smiled regally at the commoners lining the road to the gates of the squalid little town. What was it called again? Ah yes. Ruffetts View, or some such romantic notion. Though what was romantic about a collection of filthy hovels so far from her capital, she couldn't imagine. Behind her rode a fraction of her army, just to remind them who was who.

Men were cheering, girls were throwing late blooms, their bronze and crimson petals soon trampled into the muck. Jennesta glanced sidelong at Mersadion, sitting stiff in his saddle beside her, with his scars coming along nicely. At least he could see these unwashed peasants knew how to honour a queen.

Then a sunbeam lanced down, kissing the plume of magic with deeper fire. Her eyes were drawn upwards. The sight of such power brought a sly gleam to her eye. In her hands the reins fell slack and the horses slowed to a walk.

Their snorting brought her back to herself. Almost at the gates, a band of riders dared to cross her path. Without a word they pelted by at full gallop, hardly stopping to acknowledge her station.

But from within the gates came a roar as the townspeople saw her approach. Jennesta forced a smile to her lips and entered amid all the pomp she could muster.

In the very centre of the square was a muddy pool, rimmed with a low wall. Before it a man sat on a tall horse whose coat had been brushed until it shone. Despite the rapturous cheering, he seemed, of all things, to be glowering.

Rellston came back to himself with a start and bowed from the waist. His smile, Jennesta realised, was no more sincere than her own. But then, Rellston knew her reputation.

'Welcome,' he said unenthusiastically. 'And thank you for your timely aid.'

Mersadion tipped his head a fraction towards the Queen.

Rellston took the hint. 'Your Majesty,' he added.

'Think nothing of it,' Jennesta said, her voice like poisoned honey. 'Do you happen to have a band of orcs in here? I'd like to . . . *thank* them personally.'

'We did have. Your Majesty. But they've gone now.'

'How disappointing,' the Queen hissed. 'Did they happen to say where?'

'No, your Majesty. They left sometime in the night.'

Mersadion edged his horse away, waiting for Jennesta's volcanic explosion of wrath.

It didn't come. With monumental effort the Queen said between gritted teeth, 'And where is your High Priestess? Why is she not here to greet me?'

Rellston stiffened his back still further. 'She charged me with messages of gratitude, your Majesty. But I'm afraid she has . . . left on an errand. An *urgent* errand.'

The Queen stared about her vindictively. Suddenly, out of the crowd, came a beefy man carrying a boy pickaback. Not in the least afraid, unlike the other cretins who stood gawping at her, the boy was a handsome black-haired charmer. He looked too cocksure to be the child of someone unimportant.

'And who is the urchin on that big human's shoulders?' she enquired acidly.

Reluctantly Rellston said, 'It's the High Priestess's son, your Majesty.'

'Is it? Is it indeed?'

He didn't like the way Jennesta eyed the boy with sudden sultry interest. It made his stomach turn to see her smile at Aidan with all the lasciviousness of a hired courtesan.

In the shelter of the copse at the head of the valley, sat a tall, wiry human on a horse.

To either side of him bands of Unis were creeping away through the trees, but they didn't seem to see him. Nor did the few desultory scouts Mersadion had sent out on mopping-up operations.

The man's auburn hair gleamed in a dancing beam of sunshine. Thoughtfully, he observed the populace acclaiming Jennesta's triumphal entry into Ruffetts View.

Then he turned his stark white stallion and vanished into the woods.

20

Sickened, Rellston watched Jennesta all but drooling over the boy.

The Commander had felt obliged to offer her hospitality in the least damaged hostelry on the square. But the conversation wasn't exactly flowing, and she hadn't touched the goblet of mead the landlord had brought her. Aidan, however, was excited to be the centre of her Majesty's attention. But as the afternoon wore on, the young convalescent began to yawn.

Jennesta turned to him and said coldly, 'I bore you, do I?'

'*No*, your Majesty! I think you're beautiful.'

She preened.

Aidan yawned again.

Forestalling the Queen's wrath, Rellston intervened. 'Forgive him, your Majesty. He's not yet recovered from a wound he took two days ago. He was so badly hurt that for some time we didn't even expect him to live.'

She flicked her fingers in contemptuous dismissal, not even deigning to ask how he had made so astonishing a recovery. Indeed, the Commander realised, she lost all interest as soon as he himself had stopped glowering at her.

Chagrined at being made game of, he remarked, 'Your soldiers don't appear to have had much luck in searching for the objects you spoke of, ma'am. Perhaps you would care to join us in our meagre supper?'

Jennesta looked at him as though he'd crawled out from a latrine. 'I don't think so,' she announced imperiously, then stood up so abruptly her chair skidded across the floor of the inn. 'I shall return to my army. A good commander sees to her forces.'

Rellston bowed ironically but she missed it. She had already swept out.

As soon as her chariot was out of sight, he allowed his impatience and frustration free rein. He'd sneak out of Ruffetts if he had to. He'd do whatever he had to. But he couldn't leave the High Priestess out there with only a handful of men to protect her.

Late that afternoon, a ragged band of some thirty riders slowed to a walk. Before them lay a shallow incline but the horses were too exhausted to take it any faster.

Stryke looked at the slow, pewter waters of the Calyparr Inlet on his right. A brackish breeze rose to his nostrils. Not half a mile away lay the edge of the Norantellia Ocean but it was out of sight, behind a low, scrub-covered mound. That meant it was still several hours to Drogan Forest. He cursed and dismounted to give his horse a rest, leaning into the cold, sullen downpour as he plodded uphill.

'What's that?' Coilla whispered, pointing at a series of fast-moving shapes ahead of them.

'Unis, I think,' Haskeer replied. 'Fucking weather! Can't see a thing.'

'They don't seem to have horses,' Jup volunteered.

'Good!' Haskeer said. 'Serves the bastards right, having to walk in the rain they've brought down on us. I'd kill every one of 'em if I had my way.'

'We don't have time for that.' Stryke wearily informed him.

At last they breasted the ridge and climbed back into the saddle. At a trot they rounded a rocky outcrop.

Stryke pulled up sharply. Straggling across the road were some twenty of Hobrow's routed troops, but they had no heart to fight. Swords drawn, they backed out of sight into the dripping shrubs. The band galloped on.

With enemies everywhere, the Wolverines made the best time they could. The further they went, the more frequently they passed dispirited custodians. A time or two Jup, riding scout, urged them under cover as bands of orcs rode past, but whether they were enlistees or loyal to Jennesta there was no way of knowing.

Eventually, as the day died into a sad grey twilight, Stryke reined. They seemed to have outdistanced all pursuit. Dark along the northern horizon lay the line of Drogan Forest. A watery moon peeped coyly through the clouds.

Not risking a fire, let alone being able to find anything that might burn, the Wolverines lay down to rest until full dark. Soon snores were sawing across the darkness. Every now and then came a slap as a sleeper flailed at a whining insect, but there were no larger beings within the sentries' sight.

Unable to nod off, Stryke wandered down to the Inlet. For a while he sat on the bank, throwing pebbles into the water. With the rush of the flow he didn't hear Coilla coming up behind him. The first he knew she was there was when she plumped down beside him, arms around her knees. 'So what now, Stryke?' she asked. 'Do we push on to Drogan and seek Keppatawn's hospitality again?'

'Perhaps. I don't know.'

'Don't see where else we can go with Jennesta plaguing this end of the inlet.'

'Then again,' Stryke suggested, 'that might be the first place she'd come looking for us. Gods! I haven't a clue what we do now.'

Coilla threw a pebble of her own. It splashed into the Inlet. 'What's most important to you?'

'Just staying alive, I think.'

'What about the stars? Don't they matter any more?'

'Who knows? I wish we'd never started this.' He leaned back on a mossy boulder.

Twin pebbles splashed into the water. After a time Coilla turned to him. 'So what were you and Krista saying to each other back there while I was in the temple?'

'Nothing.'

'You stood there talking for half an hour without actually saying anything? I don't believe it.'

'The Priestess told me I might be a sport,' he admitted reluctantly.

'A *what*?'

'In my case it's an orc who can feel magic.' He took the stars out of his belt and flipped them between his hands as Coilla stared at him.

'That's not natural. Sorry, forget I said that. Did you tell her about the dreams?'

'I didn't have to. She seemed to think that was one of the . . . symptoms, whatever.'

'Have you ever considered that pellucid might be responsible for them?'

'The crystal? Course I have. For a while I kind of half believed it was. Now I'm sure it isn't.'

She changed tack. 'What are we going to do?' she repeated.

'Beats me.'

Stryke fussed with the stars, three in one fused piece and two still independent. Then he wearied of it and pushed them morosely across the grass.

For a time the two orcs peered through the moonlight at the puzzle. Neither of them could see how the instrumentalities were joined. The spikes melded them seamlessly together in a way that seemed to defy the laws of nature. There was something strange about the spidery mass, something that seemed to disappear into infinity.

Stryke took to fiddling with them again. Almost immediately the Ruffetts View star joined to the others with a dull click.

Coilla was impressed. 'How did you do that?'

'I've no idea.' He tried the last, the green, five-spiked one they'd lifted from Hobrow's settlement at Trinity.

'Here, give me that,' Coilla finally said and snatched it from him. She had no more luck than he did.

At last Stryke gave it up. He put the stars back into his pouch. 'I guess we'd better be getting back. The others will be worried about us.'

They hadn't taken a dozen steps when two figures stepped out from their hiding place and blocked their path.

Micah Lekmann and Greever Aulay.

'You're starting to make a habit of this,' Coilla told them.

'Very nice,' Lekmann said, his sword already naked in his hand. 'Couple of lovers on a secret tryst.'

'Shut up, Micah,' Aulay snapped. 'Why talk when we can kill?' He had his blade up too, its tip circling, as the orcs drew their swords.

On the banks of the Calyparr Inlet, two duels began.

Lekmann feinted at Stryke and slammed in a low hit. But the orc jumped his blade and spun to kick the bounty hunter in the knee. Lekmann swayed aside, almost overbalancing. Stryke's backhand stroke scored along his curving back, but Lekmann brought up his blade. It slithered along the edge of the orc's weapon, knocking it aside in a shower of sparks.

Meantime Coilla sprang back as Aulay drew something from under his coat. Then she watched, almost bemused, as he twisted his stump-cup free and plugged in a wicked knife. She leaped in at him but Aulay caught her blade on the long dagger he suddenly whipped out of his other sleeve.

'Gonna kill you, bitch.'

'Is that with or without your other eye?' she returned, the tip of her sword just missing his cheek.

With a snarl of fury he lunged. His foot landed badly on the uneven turf and as he fell, his blade caught against a buried rock. It snapped off near the hilt.

Coilla slashed down at his overextended arm. Blood gushed out. Not even the cloth of his coat could stem the flow.

Again he roared. Scrambling to his feet and backing off, he pulled the knife-blade out of his stump and snapped a vicious, two-sided hook in its place. It looked like something a butcher would use to hang a carcass.

'This is for Blaan!' he yelled, slicing the hook towards her.

She let it swing past then jumped in to seize his forearm. Taken by surprise, Aulay couldn't resist as she turned the hook in on his guts and disembowelled him. She gave the hook another twist. 'And this is for you, scumpouch.'

His face was a picture of stunned disbelief as his lifeblood trickled away.

All this time Stryke had been trying to drive Lekmann down towards the river. The rough ground was proving more of a hindrance than a help, and the orc was too tired for dancing. Once on a better surface, Stryke let rip. His blade a blur of icy moonlight, he cut the stocky man's defence to shreds.

Lekmann disengaged, gasping for breath. But Stryke had had enough. He sprang forward, his free hand slapping his thigh. The sound distracted his opponent for a brief second but it was enough. Stryke's sword plunged between Lekmann's ribs.

The orc put his foot on the bounty hunter's chest and pushed. Stryke's blade slid free of flesh and Lekmann hit the water with a splash. His greasy black hair fanned out around him as he lay face down in the wavelets.

The last Stryke saw of him, Lekmann was drifting along with the current, a deeper darkness spreading from his body.

Arms around each others' shoulders, the two orcs staggered back to their companions.

'I've had enough of quiet moments,' Coilla muttered.

They were about to approach the cold, dark camp when Stryke suddenly pulled Coilla into the bushes. With the rising wind she couldn't hear a thing. But she was beginning to trust Stryke's hunches.

Moments later, a band of riders thundered to a halt on every side of the half-asleep orcs. There wasn't a thing the sentries could do about it. Stryke thought his band was getting sloppy, but that was hardly the point now.

From their hiding place Stryke and Coilla watched as Krista Galby stared down at the Wolverines. 'Where is it?' she demanded bluntly.

'Where's what?' Haskeer blustered.

'Don't give us that!' the leader of Krista's temple guard said. He dismounted, never taking his sword's point from a line with Haskeer's throat.

'Jarno,' the High Priestess warned. 'These orcs were our allies. They fought alongside us. That old man there saved my son's life.' She held her hands out to her sides, then dropped them in a weary gesture. 'I don't want to hurt you. But you took something that belongs to us. It's important to us, a cornerstone of our faith.'

Nobody said anything. The wind blew its uncanny chill across the clearing. In the bushes Coilla and Stryke felt their own brand of guilt.

'We *need* it,' Krista added.

The uncomfortable silence stretched out.

Rellston's patience snapped. He had caught up with his Priestess's band several hours ago, and now a hundred men stirred restlessly around the Wolverines. The tension in the air was palpable. He dismounted and strode forward to stand over Jup and Haskeer.

Behind the screen of frost-browned leaves, Stryke whispered, 'I knew we shouldn't have stopped.'

Coilla nodded at the scene before them. 'So why isn't your girlfriend keeping Rellston on a tight rein?'

'Maybe that's as tight as it gets. Come on,' he said. 'If they'd wanted to kill anybody they would have started by now. Let's go and talk to her before Rellston gets out of control.'

They pushed their way out of the tangled leaves.

When Krista saw them, she said coldly, 'You've done me

two favours. Now I'll do you one. Give me the instrumentality and the Commander here won't exact a penalty for its theft.'

'What if I need them?' Stryke said, and instantly could have cut his own tongue out.

'*Them?*' Krista returned. 'You have more than one?'

'That's why we needed yours, don't you see?' He looked up at her, trying to read her face in the misty moonlight.

'No, I don't see.' It wasn't Krista who spoke but Rellston. He stepped in close, staring down into Stryke's eyes. 'If you've got another, you don't need ours. Give it back now.' The tip of his sword came up to rest against Stryke's windpipe. 'I knew I should never have trusted you. Orc trash.'

'Calm down!' Krista insisted. She reached over and gently pulled Rellston's sword point clear of Stryke's flesh. 'I'm sure we can solve this amicably.'

'I'm not,' Rellston growled, his anger barely in check.

All around them the Wolverines heard the restless sounds of men unsheathing weapons and climbing down from their horses. The orcs found themselves ringed by hostile townsmen. They began easing out their own weapons.

'Don't be more stupid than you have to be, Stryke,' the Commander said. 'You can't win. You're outnumbered. Just hand the thing over. That or I'll make you.'

'Yeah?' snapped Haskeer. 'You and whose army?'

'*This* one, lamebrain,' a man called out from behind him.

One of the grunts suddenly cried out as someone shoved into him. The grunt shoved back. All around the camp scuffles were beginning to break out.

'Stop it!' Krista shouted. '*Stop it!*'

'Calm down!' Stryke yelled, trying to cool the situation. A swift clash of blades almost drowned his words. Louder he said, 'You know us! We've fought alongside you. Do you really think a bunch like you can take us all?'

Rellston cursed, earning himself a hurt look from his Priestess. Then he said, 'At ease, lads. Let them go for now.'

'Wolverines, fall back,' Stryke ordered. His blade hung loosely in his grasp, ready to attack at any moment as he covered his band's withdrawal.

Almost all of them had faded back into the night when one of Rellston's men suddenly called, 'We can't let 'em get away! After 'em!'

Instantly, all was chaos.

'Don't kill anybody you don't have to!' Stryke shouted.

Their band's horses were out of reach, beyond the Mani force. Stryke yelled, 'Let's get out of here!'

He plunged into the bushes at his back once more, ducking overhanging branches and trying not to step on any rotten twigs. It helped that the ground was so waterlogged; the thick layer of mud deadened any sound. Straining his senses to the utmost, he tracked his warband by intuition.

It scared him. But it worked. Soon he'd passed through the thin screen of trees.

He found himself facing an open meadow and, in the faint light that came before the dawn, he saw the darker lines of footsteps painted on the rain-silvered grass. Sprinting along in their wake, he crested a slight rise and saw yet another thicket, with the last of the Wolverines just disappearing into its protection.

He raced up the shallow slope and into the trees. 'Should be safe here for a while,' he panted.

'Oh yeah?' Haskeer grumbled from the dappled shadows not an arm's length away. 'Take a look at that, then.'

That was the far side of the copse. And beyond it lay Calyparr Inlet, dull grey beneath the cloudy morning.

Stryke spun around. On every side but one the waters rushed past the little headland on which they stood. And the Manis were streaming up across the meadow at them, Rellston in the lead.

'What we supposed to do now?' Haskeer shouted in frustration. 'Swim?'

Jup snarled, 'Just open your big mouth and drink it.'

Oblivious of the Ruffetts View contingent bearing down on them, dwarf and orc glared at each other.

Coilla's temper snapped. 'This is you and your bloody stars!' she yelled at Stryke, slashing her knife through the pouch at his belt.

The pouch fell apart. Almost in slow motion Stryke watched the single, five-spiked instrumentality spinning through the air. One hand belatedly trying to hold the pouch shut, he threw himself forward. But it was too late. The four joined pieces also tumbled out. His fingertips just touched it, sending it cartwheeling across a narrow clearing beneath the trees.

As the Manis burst into the woodland, Stryke saw the single green piece seem to leap upwards as it bounced off the stony turf.

Neither he nor the other orcs were aware of a sodden figure crawling out of the water and into the fringes of the wood.

As Stryke's scrabbling hands reached out to scoop up the single star, he knocked it flying straight at the rolling meshed pieces. Pouncing on his hoard, he scooped them up against his chest.

He felt more than heard them click together. The puzzle was complete.

Then reality took a step to the left.

21

Blackness.

There was a feeling of intense cold and Stryke's stomach clenched as though he were falling. His ears were ringing too much for him to hear anything. He reached out to save himself but there was nothing to grasp.

Nothing beneath his feet.

Nothing at all.

Then abruptly he landed.

He tumbled forward, his hands plunging into something icy and dazzling. The shock brought him to himself.

Snow.

Snow, under a blanket of cloud so light it was almost as pale as the whiteness beneath him. Where it had been night just heartbeats before, now it was broad daylight. Low on the southern horizon hung a bleached disc that must have been the sun.

Panic threatened to overwhelm him.

He called out but he couldn't hear himself shout. For a moment he was terrified he'd gone deaf. Then sound came roaring back. An arctic wind was shrieking around him, tearing at his clothing. Squinting, he could just make out the huddled dark shapes that were the other Wolverines.

Tottering to his feet, he felt the gale pushing at him. He

scooped up the precious stars, which had again fallen from his grasp. Then he fought his way to Jup and Coilla, who were just making their first dizzy attempts at standing. Holding onto each other, they all began speaking at once. *'Where are we?'* and *'Where are the others?'* were the main questions.

Soon the other war band members staggered into view. They gathered in a slight depression nearby and it kept off the worst of the blast. Drifting snow blew in skeins over their heads and they had to bellow to make themselves heard.

'What the *fuck's* happening?' Haskeer yelled.

'I figure we're in the ice cap.' Stryke's teeth were rattling with the cold.

'What? How?'

Coilla, arms folded across her body in a futile attempt to keep warm, said, 'Never mind the philosophical debate. The real question is how do we keep from freezing to death.'

Several of the warband had managed to snatch up packs or bedrolls as they fled from the Manis. Some, however, like Stryke and Coilla. had been too busy fending off the humans' attack. Even sharing their blankets and spare clothes there wasn't enough to go round.

'Jup,' Stryke managed to say, through lips that were rapidly numbing with cold, 'are you up to trying to find a high point? To get some idea of where we are?'

'Right, Chief!' The dwarf stumbled off into the teeth of the wind.

Huddling together for warmth, the rest of the orcs tried to work out what had happened.

'It's those bloody stars,' Coilla muttered.

'If it was, they saved us from being cut to pieces,' Alfray pointed out.

'Yeah, so we can freeze to death out here.' Haskeer put in bitterly. 'Wherever *here* is.'

Stryke said, 'It's got to be the northern glacier field. The sun was almost due south of us, but I don't know whether it's morning or evening now.'

With stiff blue fingers he fumbled at his pouch, then remembered that Coilla had slashed it. Instead, he stuffed the stars inside his jerkin, just hoping he didn't fall on them if he tripped. At least he found his gloves tucked under his belt.

'We'll find out soon enough,' said Alfray. 'If we live that long.' A gloomy thought struck him. 'What if this is Jennesta getting her own back? It's just the sort of trick she'd play.'

'No.' Coilla's firm tone was marred by her shudders of cold. 'If she could do this, why didn't she just bring us all back to her camp so she could get her hands on us? And the stars?'

'This is pointless,' Stryke decided. 'We don't have enough to go on.' He pulled his fur jerkin tighter around him. It seemed utterly inadequate in this place. 'What provisions do we have?'

A short rummage amongst their salvaged possessions brought a few strips of dried meat to light, along with some crumbling trail bread and a couple of flasks of liquor. Not much to go around twenty-four hungry beings.

Trying to hide his disappointment, Stryke pointed to one of the grunts with a blanket. 'Go up and see if you can make out what's happened to Jup, Calthmon.'

Reluctantly the grunt waded up through the snowdrifts. He was almost knocked flying by the wind when he got above the rim of the depression. It wasn't that much longer before he returned with Jup following in his footsteps.

The dwarf hunkered down, rubbing his arms, then sticking his numb hands under his armpits.

'There's lots of crevasses,' he managed through chattering teeth. 'Some of them have got bridges of snow across them that won't bear an orc's weight. But I think I can see a way down over yonder.' He nodded towards what Stryke thought was the south-east. 'We're quite high up too.' As he spoke, his misty breath crystallised on his beard.

'Anything else out there?' Stryke asked.

'Not that I can see. No smoke. No signs of any houses. I did think I saw something moving. But whatever it was, it kept well away.'

'The sight of you would frighten anything with brains,' Haskeer told him.

Jup didn't bother responding to the jibe. That in itself told Stryke how badly the devastating cold was affecting them.

'Right,' he said. 'First order of business is to get the hell off this damned ice sheet and find shelter.'

In twos and threes they set off, with Jup trailblazing.

Within a short time the utter glaring whiteness had them seeing spots before their eyes. Limping, plunging through frozen crusts into snowdrifts as deep as an orc, they made their way east by south. It seemed like hours before they reached a bluff from which they could see quite a way around them.

Behind, to the north, towered the glacier, menacing in its vast solidity. It stretched from one side of the horizon to the other, a monument to the humans' stupidity in killing the magic of Maras-Dantia. Even at this distance it seemed to loom above them, threatening to crush them at any moment. As they watched, a segment of it fell away with a sound like thunder. Clouds of snow swirled into the air, and some of the heavier blocks must have bounced for half a mile.

Hastily they began to clamber down the southern face of the bluff. Not all of it was compacted snow. A huge granite boulder seemed to have been trapped in the ice. That made for solid footing, but the rock was slick with hoar-frost. Slithering and sliding, they cursed their way down to a plateau that couldn't have been more than a hundred and fifty feet above the frozen tundra.

They stopped to catch their breath. Here the rock kept the biting north wind off them. It also hid the intimidating bulk of the ice wall from view. That in itself was a blessing.

Below, in a curve between two thrusting glaciers, the land was flatter, pressed down, it seemed, by the weight of the advancing ice. It was grey with lichen and cut here and there by dark nets of streams that seemed threadlike at this range. Black against the horizon, there was a thin line that might or might not have been a forest. It was hard to tell with the sunlight glaring in their eyes.

'If we can make it down there,' Stryke said, slapping his gloved hands to bring back the circulation, 'we might find shelter. Fuel. Whatever.'

'*If*'s the right word,' grumbled Haskeer. 'I'm an orc, not a fucking mountain goat.'

But the trail down from the bluff wasn't as easy as it looked. Time and again they came up against a dead end, a drop so sheer they'd never make it.

'Is it me,' said Coilla as they stared at yet another barrier, 'or have you got that feeling there's somebody following us?'

'Yeah.' Jup rubbed the back of his neck.

Stryke, when consulted, said he felt it too.

'Maybe it's one of those abominable snowmen,' Coilla said, trying for levity.

'They're just myths,' Alfray stated flatly. 'What you've got to watch out for is snow leopards. Teeth the size of daggers.'

'Thanks. I really needed to know that.'

They trudged along in silence for a while.

'I see Jup's scouting is up to its usual standard,' Haskeer muttered as they backtracked yet again.

The way was narrow, crowded with orcs changing direction. Even so, Jup managed to press himself back against the cliff, letting the others pass until Haskeer reached him. Jup's hand shot out to grasp the orc by the neck. 'Think you can do any better, scumpouch?'

Haskeer shrugged Jup off. 'A blind man on a lame horse could do better,' he growled.

'Be my guest.'

Haskeer leading, they set off again. It still seemed to take forever to get down to the barren plain. A grunt slipped, only his mate's grip on his jerkin saving him from certain death. After that they stumbled along holding onto each other's clothing.

The sun rolled low along the skyline, rather than falling from its zenith. Whether they had been travelling all day or only half of it was moot. What was certain was that night was now falling, and with it came a bank of cloud. It blotted out the sun, dimming the long twilight as it raced overhead. A fine, stinging snow began to fall.

'That's all we need,' Jup muttered.

At last they were off the bluff. Haskeer jumped the final few feet and landed hard, grunting at the impact. Soon they were all milling on the level, staying in the lee of the glacier in the forlorn hope it might keep the rising wind off them.

'Did you see that?' Jup said. 'That light over there?' He pointed south towards the edge of the ice tongue.

'Nothing there now,' Haskeer said. 'Maybe you imagined it.'

The dwarf squared up to him. 'I didn't *imagine* it. It was there!'

Before a fight could develop Stryke stepped between them. 'Just a reflection, maybe? But it wouldn't hurt to find out. I'm not too keen on the idea of camping out if we don't have to. We'll give it half an hour. I want us to be settled before nightfall.'

Without warning, the glacier gave a mighty crack. A block of ice the size of a house began to fall away at their heels. The orcs fled out across the tundra, slipping and staggering. At last, safely out of range, they puffed to a halt. Alfray, almost exhausted, was some way behind the rest.

'We're safe,' Haskeer panted.

'No, we're not,' Alfray contradicted. 'Look!'

They followed his pointing finger. Racing towards them came a pack of creatures the size of lions. With their white coats they were almost invisible in the twilight.

'Form up!' Stryke yelled and pelted off towards Alfray.

Seeing Stryke dashing towards him, Alfray turned. The sight was enough to make anybody quail. With fangs like ivory sabres, five beasts were almost upon him.

Stryke cried out and whirled his sword. The lead snow

leopard, startled, missed his spring. He rolled head over heels, his claws giving him purchase as he sprang to his feet.

Not taking his eyes off the monster, Stryke shouted, 'This way!'

He had no time for more, because two of the leopards were now prowling around him, looking for an opening. The rest had swung round to herd the warband.

Stryke and Alfray backed away but one of the creatures bounded swiftly behind them. The smaller one feinted. At the same moment the dominant male leaped again. Distracted, Stryke almost fell to the raking claws but he got his sword up just in time. Blood sprayed from the beast's foreleg and with a savage scream the animal retreated.

For the moment the snow leopards circled just out of range of the orcs' blades.

In the meantime, Coilla was urging the rest of the orcs to shuffle closer in a body. Three of the leopard pack oozed sinuously around the defensive ring. The beasts faced a bristling wall of metal, but they blocked any attempt at rescuing Stryke and Alfray.

Again the pack leader came in at Alfray. Its claws spiked into his sleeve, knocking the old orc from his feet. But Stryke was there, his sword slashing out. The tip of his blade scored the beast's flank. A line of crimson darkened the creamy fur and the snow leopard bounded out of reach.

Stryke risked a glance. The rest of the warband were too far away to do him and Alfray any good. 'You all right, old-timer?' he panted.

'Yeah. But enough of the old-timer! Keep 'em off a moment, will you?'

Stryke didn't have time to argue. Again and again the snow leopards darted in, playing a deadly game. One after the other, they feigned attack. He knew he couldn't hold them off forever, but dared not look away to discover what Alfray was doing.

Cursing his cold, stiff fingers, Alfray fumbled with the buckles on his healer's bag. At last, desperate, he managed to find a large stone bottle. Splashing the contents onto the wet snow, he pulled back just in time. Turquoise flames *whoomped* up, singeing his eyebrows. The cats sprang back, dazzled and disorientated.

'What's that?' Stryke gasped.

Alfray didn't reply. Instead he hacked through a roll of bandages, spearing the cloth on his sword then dipping it into the pungent blaze. He flicked his wrist and the fireball whisked through the air, landing on the younger leopard's back. Gouts of fire sizzled through its pelt to the fatty layer beneath.

Then the whole creature went up in flames. It gave an unearthly scream and hurtled out of sight across the darkling plain. Meantime the strange blue fire dwindled until it went out in a pool of slush at Alfray's knees.

Warily the other cat circled then sprang at the squatting corporal. Stryke dropped, holding his blade upright. As the beast passed over him he stabbed upwards with all his might. The razor-sharp metal sliced right through the leopard's belly. Stinking guts spilled out on the orc below. Hastily wiping his eyes on his sleeve, Stryke saw the pack leader collapse just beyond him in a heap of tangled limbs.

He drew a deep breath and coughed as the stench hit his lungs.

Alfray got upwind of him and managed to gasp, 'Thanks, Stryke.'

'Can you do that again?'

Alfray shook the bottle. Liquid sloshed in it. 'Once or twice, maybe.'

'Then let's go.'

With no idea that salvation was trotting towards the warband, Coilla snapped, 'Give me that!' and grabbed a grunt's sword.

She stepped free of the sheltering mass of bodies and pitched it at the nearest leopard. The blade ripped through its spine, leaving the beast running on its front legs for a moment before it realised its hind legs were paralysed. Coilla came up on it from the rear and thrust her sword through the back of its neck. Blood pumped out onto the snow.

Two to go. With Stryke covering Alfray, the healer mixed his fire-brew again. They took out one of the leopards but the last drops of potion weren't enough to ignite.

The remaining beast panicked. It leaped away from the blazing body of its companion and found itself almost on top of Stryke. It had no time to lower its bony skull. Head up, it left its throat exposed.

It ran straight onto his blade, its momentum driving its body almost up to the hilt. The monstrous teeth were just a hair's breadth from Stryke's face. With a look of surprise in its green eyes it keeled over, bloody froth bubbling from its neck.

Its fall twisted Stryke's sword from his grasp. Swearing, he drew back, groping for his knife, but all the leopards were dead. He sat on the flank of the one who'd taken his blade and said tiredly, 'Butcher the damn things and take the fur. We might need it.'

The long northern twilight lingered. The snow shower blew itself out, leaving stars shining in the north above the ice sheet. As the moon rose, the band headed back for the lee of the glacier, finding enough light reflected from it to guide their steps.

Jup, in the lead, suddenly stopped. 'See?' he crowed. 'Told you I saw a light!'

Ahead of them stood a gigantic ice palace.

As they got closer they slowed in awe.

The palace was immense, its slender spires gleaming in the moonlight, its whiteness making the glacier behind it seem dirty. Flying buttresses cradled the central face in elegant curves. Statues stood in dark niches, impossible to make out beneath their coating of crusted snow.

It might have been a spectral vision of beauty if it had not been for the lights twinkling in the turret windows. Hardly distinguishable from the stars, the yellow glow of candles gleamed fitfully behind arched casements.

'If we'd come here in daylight we'd never have seen it at all,' breathed Coilla, gazing raptly upwards.

'Now that we have, let's get inside,' Jup suggested. 'This wind's freezing my bollocks off.'

The Wolverines walked towards it. Jup zigzagged towards it but it didn't seem as though anybody was guarding the place. The huge gates stood open. Dwarfed by them, the orcs crept into the courtyard.

In its centre was a frozen fountain. White mounds proved to be trees snapped off by the killing cold.

'This place must have been wonderful before the ice sheet struck,' Coilla said softly.

Haskeer wandered by. 'Yeah. Before the humans fucked everything up. Anybody found a way in?'

They hadn't. Jup and the others scouted around, sticking close to the walls, but they couldn't find an entrance.

Haskeer suddenly bellowed, 'Hello? Is anybody there?' His voice echoed back and a small avalanche slithered from a roof. But nothing answered.

Then a sharp wind slashed snow into their faces. Everything disappeared under a smothering blanket of white.

They were trapped outside in a blizzard.

Jennesta cursed and pushed back from the barrel of congealing blood. It didn't seem to be working. Her thoughts circled like a treadmill, ruining her concentration.

She suspected that the High Priestess of Ruffetts View had gone tearing off to track down the Wolverines, but she had no idea why. It was just that there was no other reason Krista Galby could have had for absenting herself from the royal audience.

What did it matter? Let the human wear herself out in sweaty pursuit. But first she needed information.

If only this vat of gore didn't keep scabbing over so quickly. All she kept seeing was white.

She snapped her fingers and a cowering flunkey handed her a goblet of spring water. Then, sighing, the Queen went back to her labours.

At first she thought it still wasn't functioning. Then she heard something. Someone. It was a woman's voice, pitched high, droning monotonously.

Sanara was talking to herself again.

Bending closer, Jennesta saw the vision expanding.

Sanara stood up, partially blocking a window. Now Jennesta realised what had happened. Her focus had been a little too high. All she had seen was the icy waste beyond. She realised she'd been seeing snow all along. Something – a distortion in the aether, perhaps – had been pulling her out of alignment. Now she shifted her viewpoint lower to see her sister's face.

On the point of speaking, Jennesta stopped. Ignoring Sanara completely, she stared past her and out into the night. Something was moving out there, something that exerted a strange pull on her.

Through the swirling flakes she saw the Wolverines huddled in the corner of a frozen courtyard. Some of them seemed to be covered in blood. Just the sight of it made her mouth water but she controlled her appetite. It wouldn't do to lose her concentration now.

Jennesta sent her essence floating among the spinning whiteness. 'How the hell did they get there?' she asked herself. 'It must be—'

She broke off. It didn't matter. The important thing was that she knew where they were.

Not a mile from the silken tent where Jennesta plied her necromancy with the blood of the Uni slain, Krista Galby and her weary troops rode in through the gates of Ruffetts View. Night was falling and the flickering torches were haloed by the rain.

The High Priestess cast a glance up at the pearly geyser of magic, feeling a pang of guilt, but there would be time enough to renew the invocations in the morning. Right now she just wanted to see Aidan, have a hot bath and go to bed.

She bade goodnight to Rellston and made her way home.

Jarno, the leader of the temple guard, accompanied her, but peeled off at her gate for his own house. She stepped inside her walled garden.

Then she paused, a sick feeling hollowing her stomach. At this time of evening there should have been lights inside, smoke from the chimney and cooking smells as Merrilis made dinner. She should have been able to hear Aidan's piping voice, perhaps raised in song or arguing with his motherly nurse.

She could hear nothing. And the house was dark.

'When I catch up with Merrilis I'll give her a piece of my mind,' she told herself. 'What does she mean by letting the fire go out?'

Forcing herself to face the worst, Krista Galby walked up to the door of her home. She didn't feel at all like the High Priestess now, more like a frightened mother.

The door swung open at her touch. The house seemed very empty now that its function as a hospital had ended, the patients moved elsewhere or dead.

She moved from room to room, searching the place, calling, 'Aidan? Merrilis?'

But only echoes answered her. The hearth was cold and her home was deserted.

What could have happened? Surely if Merrilis had stepped out for a minute, Aidan should still be there? But what if something had happened to him? If his illness had come back? If he was . . . dead? Instantly the picture formed in her mind of his lifeless body laid out in the old wooden temple that was still used. There'd be candles around his waxen corpse, their yellow light burnishing his ebony hair.

Past rational thought she ran out into the street, pounding on her neighbour's door. The house was empty.

Tears burning hot tracks down her cheeks, Krista drove herself onwards, asking every passer-by, 'Have you seen my son? Have you seen Aidan?'

But nobody had.

22

The orcs huddled together under a heap of blankets and bloody snow leopard skins.

In the corner of the courtyard, the wind found it harder to get at them. To either side deep drifts were beginning to form against the walls and snow whirled down around them. It was difficult to see more than a couple of feet.

There came a lull in the blizzard. Cautiously Stryke poked his nose up. A rift in the clouds showed a dark scatter of stars.

'Jup,' he said. 'Take a couple of grunts and find us a way in. If we have to stay here all night, we'll freeze to death.'

Haskeer grinned blearily. 'Yeah, earn your keep.'

'For that, Haskeer, you get to go with him. Now shut up and get a move on before it really starts snowing again.'

Picking two of the taller grunts, Jup and Haskeer set off through the thigh-deep whiteness. The rest of the Wolverines burrowed down again, their breath mingling under the furs. All things considered, it was a pretty chastened band who speculated idly on who, or what, had built this vast castle in the middle of nowhere. Coilla concluded that anybody who could design such breathtaking beauty must possess a gentle soul. The males were derisive of that.

Eventually they heard muttered curses above the hiss of

windblown snow. Taking another peek, Stryke said, 'Good. They're back.' He called, 'Did you find anything?'

Haskeer answered. 'Yeah! There's a doorway round the back. We'd never have found it if there hadn't been a light inside. I've left the grunts trying to get it open. If nothing else, it's more sheltered than this.'

In a welter of elbows and trampling feet, the warband hauled themselves upright, the lucky ones slinging the furs and blankets around their shoulders. The strange, muffled procession set off, retracing the footprints in the deep snow. All around them eerie silence held sway.

Keeping to the flat part above the steep bank of the palace's moat, they came to where the towering glacier gripped the structure. But Jup turned the angle of the wall and there was a deep crack in the ice. It was lit from within by a soft golden glow.

'You sure this is safe?' Alfray said, remembering his terror as he tried to outrun the avalanche.

'Safe as houses,' Haskeer replied gruffly. 'You think you can do any better, help yourself.'

Going deeper into the cleft, they heard hammering and swearing. Sure enough, as they clambered round a bend, there were Gant and Liffin, using their swords to hack at the ice sheathing an arched doorway. Soon a dozen orcs were at it. In the confined space the noise was appalling. Icicles and chunks of compacted snow began to patter down on them.

'Stop!' Stryke cried as a dagger of ice narrowly missed his head. 'This is stupid. We're going to kill ourselves before we get in.' He summoned Alfray through the crowd. 'Have you got enough of that potion to set fire to something?'

'Maybe.' He dug in his medicine bag. 'It's just liniment that Keppatawn's healer gave me. He warned me against it mixing with water.'

'Now we know why. Everybody! Get out anything you've got that's dry and might burn.'

The Wolverines began pillaging their knapsacks. Stryke set a couple of them to shredding ancient shirts and some of Alfray's precious bandages. Combined with the tinder from everyone's tinder boxes, it soon turned into a heap that stretched across the centre of the massive doors.

Alfray upended his flask of liniment and Stryke melted some snow in his hands. As it dripped down onto the makeshift kindling, peacock flames flew up. Soon a blaze was going, billowing thick smoke. Those at the front fell back to keep from choking. The grunts at the rear rushed forward to soak up some of the priceless heat. A chaos of pushing and shoving ensued.

All at once a massive slab of ice began to lean out over them. The Wolverines fled back past the corner of the crevasse.

With a great grinding roar the ice fell away, smashing onto the floor of the archway and filling the air with frozen missiles. At last the noise died. The orcs crept forward.

And stopped.

The great upswept leaves of the doors were exquisite. Made of some substance like frosted glass, they were inlaid with golden vines. The warm yellow light shone brightly through them. They were so cunningly wrought that the fruit and flowers seemed to stand out, though when Stryke dared to touch them they were smooth and flat.

As his fingers caressed the silken surface the doors opened on noiseless hinges. Almost reverently the orcs stepped over the sodden ashes and crossed the threshold.

In a hushed group they looked about them wonderingly. They were inside a vast hall whose vaulted ceiling rose so high it dwindled in the distance. Darkened doorways opened off it, and curving staircases of pure white marble. Every inch of the place was carved, but thick shadows stopped them making sense of the shapes. The air held a sad scent of autumn.

Jup moved forward cautiously. Even his soft footfalls were enough to set off echoes that came back to them, weirdly distorted.

'I don't like this place,' Coilla whispered.

Her words reverberated startlingly.

Stryke whipped around, feeling as though some unseen presence was creeping towards him. But there was nothing there. As he turned back to lead them deeper into the hall, he saw something halfway up the sweeping stairs.

It was a white-robed woman.

Poised tensely on a landing, her black hair flowing around her like a cloak, she seemed dwarfed by the chamber's immensity.

'Who—' He cleared his throat. 'Who are you?'

She didn't answer him directly. In a thin, pure voice she said, 'Leave this place. *Quickly.*'

'Into the storm? We wouldn't stand a chance out there.'

'Believe me,' she implored, 'the danger is worse in here. Go while you still can.' Suddenly she gasped, cowering against the banister. Sheer terror twisted her beautiful face as she cast a glance behind her. 'Go! Go *now!*'

'What's the matter?' Stryke said, moving to the foot of the staircase.

She didn't answer. He began climbing the steps, taking them two and three at a time.

When he reached her, he offered, 'We'll protect you.'

The woman gave a despairing laugh. 'Too late.'

Out of the doorway behind her came a pack of hideous creatures.

They looked like everybody's idea of demons, the tormenting spirits said to rule the halls of Xentagia with whips of fire.

Down in the hallway more of them poured out to surround the orcs.

No two of the creatures were entirely alike. Slithering, sidling, striding on spider-claws, their bodies subtly changed shape, moment by moment. Even their faces melted and reformed, now with one eye, now with tusks and snapping beaks. Some had wings like a bat, but without exception they all had fearsome claws. Their grey skin rippled continuously.

They were so hideous Stryke couldn't look at them without courting nausea.

They must have numbered fifty or more.

Every member of the band viewed them with superstitious dread.

'Throw down your weapons!' the woman urged.

'We don't do that!' Haskeer responded.

'But it's your only chance! How can you fight them? The Sluagh won't kill you if you don't attack.'

Stryke backed away from her and slowly retreated down the steps to his band. If he was to die, he didn't want it to be alone. Two of the beings undulated down the stairs behind him, snapping their fangs at his heels. As he reached the other Wolverines, the Sluagh reared above him, mouths agape.

'Do it!' Stryke snapped, throwing down his sword. It rang like a bell on the stone. His Sluagh guard drew back a little, coiling and uncoiling.

Outnumbered, the orcs reluctantly laid down their arms. The creatures stayed close until every last weapon rested on the floor at their feet.

'I thought the Sluagh were just fireside tales,' Coilla whispered.

'I thought they were creatures from hell,' Alfray said.

Looking at them, it was easy to believe that they were.

Fear surrounded them like a miasma. Out of their dark aura thoughts slicked into Stryke's mind. He whirled around but could not locate which creature had spoken.

'*Give us the instrumentalities,*' it said.

From their startled reactions, it was obvious that the whole band heard it, if heard was the word.

Stryke said aloud, 'I don't have them.'

This time the voices seemed to come from behind. '*You lie! We can feel their power.*'

'*They reach out to us.*'

'*They call to us.*'

'*Give us the instrumentalities and we may let you live.*'

Dizzy, the Wolverine leader fumbled beneath his tunic. His hand were clammy, slipping over the spiky mass. Nevertheless, he managed to break one of the stars from the meld. The rest were stuck as solidly as if they'd been soldered together. He touched the single one. It was the five-spiked green object he had first rescued from Hobrow in Trinity. It seemed an age ago. Gingerly, he held out the group of four.

A snaking tentacle plucked it from his grasp.

Something like a sigh whispered echoing to the ceiling.

'*And the other? Where is the other?*'

Stryke swallowed. 'We haven't got it.'

'*Then you will suffer for all eternity.*'

Agony gripped Stryke's head. He felt like a firebrand had been thrust inside his skull. Clutching his temples, he fell writhing to the floor. Around him, the other Wolverines were equally in pain.

'Wait!' Stryke managed to say. 'I meant we haven't got it *here*. But we can get it.'

The anguish lessened. '*When? When can you get it?*'

'It's with the rest of our band,' he lied. White heat jolted through his brain. 'They're coming, they're coming,' he gasped.

'*How soon?*' the hissing voices demanded.

'I don't know. We got separated in the blizzard. But they'll be here. Tomorrow, if the storms hold off.'

'*Then we can kill you now.*'

'You do that and you'll never get it!'

'*If they are coming here they will not be able to stop us taking it.*'

'If we don't give them the signal, they won't enter this place.' He directed a cold gaze at the nearest Sluagh. 'I'm the only one who knows what it is,' he bluffed. 'And I'll die before you get it out of me.'

On the fringes of his mind Stryke heard them conversing but he couldn't make out what they said.

At last a pug-faced demon said, '*Very well. We will let you live until tomorrow.*'

'*At dusk,*' another one said. '*If we do not have the instrumentality by then, you will never leave this place alive.*'

'*And you will loathe every heartbeat that you live.*'

The Sluagh herded them up the stairs. As they passed the white-robed human, she started as though coming awake. Silently she fell into step between Stryke and Coilla.

It was a long way up. The woman was visibly shaking with exhaustion by the time they reached the top. No doubt they were in the top of one of the turrets that had reared so high above the plain. If anything, the air was even chillier up here than it had been down in the hall.

As the first Sluagh reached the tiny landing a door swung open without a touch. Stryke saw that it had no handle, no latch. He stored the information for later, gazing into the circular chamber beyond. Again it was filled with golden light though he couldn't see where it came from, unless the air itself was glowing. Once more the walls were covered with carvings, hideous gargoyles this time that looked like Sluagh captured in stone. Long yellow curtains hung at random from the arched ceiling.

Now the demons crawled aside. Taking a deep breath Stryke led the band through the gilded door, the woman collapsing immediately with her back against one of the drapes.

Once they were all inside, the door slammed shut. Abruptly the pain left them. Jup ran back to where the door had been. Before he even touched it a wall of light threw him halfway across the crowded room.

Alfray came to kneel beside him. 'I think he's just stunned. At least I hope so. His heart's still beating.'

They fanned out, looking behind draperies for another exit. There was nothing but endless carvings. For all their probing they couldn't find a key, a knob, anything that would let them out.

Eventually they gave up and slumped down to rest. The woman hadn't moved.

Shivering in the unnatural cold, Stryke wrenched a curtain loose and wrapped it around him like a shawl. Some of the grunts did likewise.

'You knew there was no way out, didn't you?' Stryke said, coming to sit beside the woman.

'But I still hoped you'd find one.' Her voice was high, ethereal. 'And now you want to know who I am.'

Coilla came to squat at her side. 'You bet we do.' Her tone was harsh.

'Can't you see I'm just as much a prisoner as you are?'

'You still haven't told us your name,' Stryke said.

'Sanara.'

Realisation took a few seconds to soak in. 'Jennesta's *sister* Sanara?'

'Yes. But don't judge me by her, I beg you. I'm not like her.'

Coilla snorted. 'Says you!'

'How can I convince you?'

'You can't.' Coilla stood and walked away.

'You are not like her,' Sanara told Stryke. 'I sense the power of the land flowing around you, like the orcs of olden days. But that child has none of it.'

'I wouldn't call Coilla a child to her face,' he replied shortly.

She shrugged miserably. 'What does it matter? At sundown tomorrow she'll be dying just the same. You didn't really think the Sluagh would let you go, did you?'

'I'd hoped they might.'

'Dream on, orc. They thrive on the pain and suffering of others. They'll spin your life out in endless agony until you're begging to die, but still they'll feast on your terror.'

'My name's Stryke. If we're going to die together, we ought at least to be on first name terms.'

In answer she waved a languid hand.

'So, Queen Sanara,' he said at length, wishing he could pierce her shroud of indifference to find some answers that might get them out of here. 'Am I supposed to call you your Highness or something?'

As she shook her head a faint perfume of roses wafted from her hair. 'No. I haven't been called that in a long time. Not since the humans ate the magic of my land.'

'*Your* land?'

'My land. My realm.' She smiled sadly. 'Jennesta had the southlands, Adpar the nyadd domain. This is what my mother willed to me. But you see what it has become; a desert of snow and death. Whole cities lie imprisoned beneath the glaciers. Once this land was rich and good, a place of forests and meadows. Every single one of my subjects fled or perished when the ice swept down. It started when I first came to the throne, coming closer day by day. How could they not think it was my fault? Do you know what it's like, to be blamed for the death of the land? Can you imagine how sad it is seeing your friends, your lovers turn away from you and die one by one?' Her eyes misted. 'I tried to counter it but I have very little power now. All that remains of my capital, Illex, is this fortress.'

'Why didn't Jennesta help you?'

She made an all too human sound of derision. 'If you know my sister you know she doesn't help anybody but herself. That was why Mother sent her away. She hasn't been back to my realm for generations of your kind.'

'Your mother?'

'Vermegram.'

'The sorceress? *The* legendary Vermegram of old?'

Sanara sighed and nodded.

'Then you're not as human as you seem.'

'Indeed not, no more than my brood sisters. But Vermegram died many winters ago. And I was watching when you saw Adpar die by Jennesta's power.'

'How did you know I was there?'

She gazed at him mysteriously. 'I've had my eye on you for

a long time, Stryke.' But when he pressed her, she wouldn't say why.

Not liking where the conversation might be heading, Stryke fell silent for a time. At last he said against a background of orcish snores, 'How come you let the Sluagh in?'

'What a strange question! How could I keep them out?'

Stryke conceded the point with a grimace. 'Where did they come from? And why are they here?'

The former Queen sighed again and lay down, pillowing her head on her arm. She looked up at him with limpid green eyes that reminded him a little of Jennesta's. There was no scaling on her face though, just soft, milky skin. 'They're an ancient race from the dawn of time. What they are is evil incarnate. You think Jennesta's bad? Compared to them, she's just an amateur. And they're here because they knew that sooner or later Jennesta would find out about the instrumentalities. They've held me prisoner here for longer than you've been alive. And I'll still be here when the Sluagh are chewing on your bones. They thought that she would seek them out—'

Trying not to dwell on the image of his demise, Stryke said, 'She tried.'

'And then the Sluagh would bargain me for them.'

'Why do they want them?' he asked. 'What do you know of the stars? The instrumentalities?'

Sanara seemed to look through him to some place that only she could see. Lost in her reverie, she hardly noticed Jup and Coilla drifting back to Stryke's side.

'They want to use them, of course,' the pale Queen said dreamily.

'What for? What do they do?'

'All together they exist throughout the planes.'

Jup thought he grasped some of that. 'Is that what they do then? Move about from place to place? Is that how we got here?'

Sanara brushed her hair back from her face. 'They don't

move. I told you, once they're joined they exist throughout the planes.'

The Wolverines looked at her, baffled.

'Throughout space,' she said. 'Throughout time.'

'And they brought us here?' Coilla asked, casting a bitter glance at Stryke.

'I presume so, if you did not walk.'

'And is that time thing why it was night when we left and day a heartbeat later when we arrived here?'

The Queen nodded.

'Is that what they're for, then?' Jup wondered before Coilla could get another word in.

Sanara shook her head. 'No. That's just . . . a side effect. It's not their main function.'

'What *is* their main function?' the dwarf said.

'It is beyond the mind of mere mortals.' She didn't seem to have taken to the dwarf.

Before any of them could respond, the perspective on the far wall shifted. It seemed to retreat into blue distances before snapping back into place.

Then a figure stood where before there had been nothing. He was swathed in shadows that obscured his face but could do nothing to disguise his height.

'On your feet!' Stryke cried. 'Intruder!'

The orcs had no weapons. But there were almost thirty of them and only one opponent.

Besides, they were ready for a good fight.

23

The figure stepped out of its cloak of shadows, hands held up in a gesture of peace.

As it approached, the room's buttery light showed its face, revealing a human. The silver embroidery on his jerkin glinted and his belt held no scabbard.

It was Serapheim.

One or two of the warband shuffled back, casting sideways glances at each other and reaching for their swords, only to remember their sheaths were empty.

But their surprise was nothing compared to Sanara's. She turned even paler, if that were possible, and one hand went to her throat. Green eyes wide with shock, she sagged into Stryke's arms.

Serapheim moved forward to take her weight, folding his arms tightly around her. Her hands encircled his waist and she rested her head briefly against his shoulder. Almost at once she recovered her poise, drawing herself up as if to maintain some long-forgotten protocol. 'I thought you were dead,' she told him.

'You know this human?' Stryke said.

Serapheim and Sanara exchanged a look, laden with a meaning the Wolverines couldn't read. Then she acknowledged the question with a nod.

'How did you get in here?' Coilla asked, blazing suspicion.

'That's not important now,' Serapheim replied. 'We have more significant issues to deal with. But what I can tell you, I will. You must trust me.'

'Yeah,' Haskeer sneered cynically.

'I might be your only hope,' the human said, 'and you have nothing to lose by hearing me out.'

'We do if you're going to spout nonsense again,' Jup replied. 'We've no time for your fairy tales.'

'It's true I have a story. But it's no yarn spun by wordsmiths.'

'So cut to the payoff and save us some grief.'

Serapheim took in their expectant faces. 'All right. How about, you've stolen a world?'

While the rest puzzled over that, Coilla exclaimed, 'What? *Us?* That's rich coming from your kind.'

'Nevertheless, it's true.'

'This does sound like another of your tales,' Stryke judged. 'You'd better explain yourself, Serapheim, or our patience gets revoked.'

'There is much *to* explain, and you'd do well to attend. That or face death at the hands of the Sluagh.'

'All right,' Stryke relented. 'Long as you keep it quick and clear. What's this about stealing worlds?'

'What would you say if I told you Maras-Dantia wasn't your land?'

One or two of the grunts laughed derisively.

'I'd say you humans haven't got it all yet.'

'That isn't what I meant.'

Stryke was beginning to show his frustration. 'What *do* you mean? And no more riddles, Serapheim.'

'Let me put it this way. Do the Sluagh seem to you as being of this world?'

'They're *here*, aren't they?' Jup countered.

'Yes, but have you ever seen anything like them before? Up to now, did you believe that they existed? Or were they the stuff of legend to you?'

'Take a look around Maras-Dantia,' the dwarf advised. 'You'll see one hell of a lot of very different races. Apart from being plug ugly, what's special about the Sluagh?'

'In a way, that's my point. How do you think this land came to be shared by so many different races? Why do you think Maras-Dantia's so rich in the kinds of life it holds? Or should I say Centrasia?'

'Only if you want your throat cut!' a grunt called out. 'This is *our* land!'

Stryke shut him up. Turning back to the human, he said, 'What kind of a question is that?'

'Probably the most important one ever put to you.' He held up a hand to still their response. 'Bear with me, please. You'd understand me best if you concede for a moment that all the elder races came here from elsewhere.'

'The way the humans came here, you mean, from outside?' Alfray asked.

'In a sense. Although we mean different things when we say . . . outside.'

'Go on,' Stryke said, intrigued despite himself.

'The elder races came here from other places. Believe that. And the artifacts you call stars are part of how they came here.'

'This is making my head hurt,' Haskeer complained. 'If they, us, don't come from here, then where?'

'I'll try to put it in a way that can be grasped. Imagine that there are places where only gremlins dwell. Or pixies, nyadds and goblins. Or orcs.'

Stryke frowned. 'You mean lands where only these races live? No mixing? No humans?'

'Exactly. And were it not for the instrumentalities, none of you would be here at all.'

'Including humans?'

'No. We have always been here.'

An uproar ensued. Stryke had to use his best parade-ground roar to stifle it. 'A story like that's all the better for proof, Serapheim. Where's yours?'

'If my plan succeeds, you'll have it. But we can't afford much more delay. Will you let me finish?'

Stryke nodded.

'I understand your disbelief,' Serapheim told them all. 'This place is all you've ever known, and your parents before you. But I assure you, much though you believe we humans are the invaders, we are not. The truth of what I'm saying lies here, in Illex, and if we help each other it can be confirmed. Perhaps used to your advantage.'

'Put some flesh on the bones,' Coilla said, 'and maybe we'll see it differently.'

'I'll try.' He took counsel with himself, then continued, 'That truth has to do with the abundance of magical energy here in what you call Maras-Dantia.' Many present resented his choice of words, but they held their tongues. 'Or at least the richness of energy there once was. Generations ago, as you know, humans began crossing the Scilantiun Desert in search of new land, and settled here, leaving their homes on the other side of the world. They came on foot and on horseback, trekking across the burning sands, leaving their dead behind them with their graves to mark the way. Only the strongest came, the most determined. 'With this lush continent providing everything they could possibly want, they had no need to breed cautiously. If this patch of earth was exhausted, why not move on to another? After all, who else was using it? Nobody who *settled*. Nobody who put down roots in one spot, or mined its riches. So they built, and they dug, and they burnt the forests for their crops. Most of them having no sensitivity for the earth energies, for the magic, they had no idea of the havoc they were causing. To them magic was just some sleight of hand, a little conjuring, a firework or two. Only a very few, who took the trouble to acquaint themselves with the elder races, knew this not to be so. That was the origin of the Manis.'

'And you are one such,' Alfray divined.

'I'm not a Mani, or a Uni either come to that. But yes, a practitioner of the art. One of the few my race has produced.'

'Why are you telling us this? Why involve yourself with our troubles when you could just stay clear?'

'I'm trying to rectify wrongs. But this isn't the time to say much more. Soon the Sluagh will wake from their slumbers in the ice. We have to act.'

'Can you get us out of here?'

'I think so. But simply trying to escape isn't my plan. And where would you go in this icy waste?'

'What *is* your plan?' Stryke wanted to know.

'To retrieve the stars and have them effect your leaving this place.'

Sanara spoke up then, reminding them all of her presence. 'The portal?'

'Yes,' Serapheim responded.

Stryke frowned. 'And what's *that?*'

'Part of the mystery I seek to open to you. But first you must lend your sword arms.' He looked around at them. 'Let me guide you,' he appealed. 'If you see no benefit in what we're doing, what have you lost? You can abandon me and go your own way, brave Illex's fury and try to reach warmer climes.'

'When you put it that way,' Stryke reasoned, 'I'm inclined to go along with you.' He allowed his tone to become menacing. 'But only so far. Any hint of treachery, or if we don't like the way things are heading, we will go it alone. And you'll be paying with your life.'

'I expect no less. Thank you. Our first task is to get to the palace cellars.'

'Why?'

'Because there lies the portal, and your salvation.'

'Believe him,' Sanara added. 'This is the only way.'

'We'll go along with it for now,' Stryke agreed. 'But talk of cellars is all very well when we can't even get out of this room.'

'I can take myself out, the same way I came in, but nobody else,' Serapheim said. 'The dying of the magic has depleted my powers as much as everyone else's. And no, I can't open the door from the outside. Only the Sluagh can do that. I'm sure I

can find how in their minds, but I don't want to get that close
to them. My idea is to find and lure one in here. But once I
have, it'll be your task to overcome it.'

'They can be killed then?'

'Oh yes. They are not invulnerable or immortal, although
they are incredibly tough and long-living.'

'What about their pain weapon?'

'That's where Sanara and I come in. We'll assault it mentally
while you attack it with whatever comes to hand. Though of
course you have no weapons.'

'We're good at improvising,' Jup assured him.

'Good. Because you must not underestimate the Sluagh's
powers. You must attack without let and in numbers.'

'Count on it,' the dwarf said.

'Then ready yourselves. It begins.'

Serapheim moved back into the shadows.

He kept to them once he was outside the room.

His boots made no sound in the thick dust of the corridors.
He opened door after door, ready to flee at an instant's notice,
but as he suspected the Sluagh had not yet risen from their icy
cradles.

At last, as the sky began to lighten the south-east, he felt the
rumble in his mind that meant Sluagh were talking nearby.
Flattening himself against a wall's marble slabs, he peered around
a corner.

There were four of them, their grey shapes shifting from one
ugly conformation to another.

Cautiously, Serapheim withdrew.

He had hoped for fewer, but there wasn't time to search
anymore. Steadying his resolve, he stepped boldly out in front
of them, touching fingers to brow in a mocking salute.

Instantly pain whipped out at him. But he'd been expecting
it and took to his heels.

They came after him. Two had fearsome insect limbs that
propelled them swiftly along the passage. A third threw out

scaly wings that creaked as they slapped the air, but the passage was too narrow for it to extend them fully. Instead it barely rose, floating ponderously above the last one, a slug-like being that left a shining, rancid trail.

Serapheim outpaced them. Pelting along past open doors, he headed through a long, dusky gallery. At the end of it he leaned panting against the wall.

Now he had reached the spiral staircase. It was like a nightmare, running throughout eternity up a neverending flight of steps, and with each stride he was slower. His pursuers were catching up to him. Serapheim was beginning to think he'd never make it.

He gasped and forced himself to greater speed, lungs burning, legs as heavy as logs. It was all he could do to put one foot in front of another. He grasped the banister and used that to haul himself higher. A glimpse over his shoulder showed him clawed tentacles reaching towards him. Terrified, he put on another spurt. Around and around the spiral stairway he staggered, thinking he'd never make it close enough to the room to transport himself inside. The Sluagh were almost at his back.

Pain lashed through his mind. His shields were weakening.

Inside the room at the top of the tower, Stryke looked around. They'd tossed their furs and their packs against the walls, clearing a space to fight in. There was nothing resembling furniture and all their weapons had been taken from them.

'We can always throw Jup at 'em,' Haskeer suggested. Coilla swatted his head.

Stryke had an idea. 'You and you!' he snapped at a couple of grunts. 'Climb up those gargoyles and bring down the curtain poles. And the curtains as well, come to think of it. Then stand ready.'

Time seemed to pass too slowly. The Wolverines were beginning to eye Sanara suspiciously, wondering if she was in on some plot with the human.

At last Serapheim wavered back into view, like a mirage

turning to solid flesh. He took a couple of tottering steps and dropped to his knees on a pool of yellow cloth between Coilla and Haskeer.

'They're coming,' he panted. 'Four of them.'

A heartbeat later the door burst open and slammed back against the wall. The entrance wasn't wide enough to accommodate more than one of the beings at a time. Stryke saw the others out on the landing, one hovering in mid-air on its rippling grey wings.

'Now!' he yelled.

The two orcs hurled their poles like javelins. They were flung hard enough to penetrate even the Sluagh's unnatural skin. Sticky black ichor began to flow from the nearest one's chest. It swayed in the doorway, blocking its companions as it changed from a six-limbed wolf to a snake that dropped in coils to the floor.

A gang of grunts rushed in and commenced stomping it enthusiastically. Their boots began to steam, but that didn't stop other orcs from joining in. One and all, they took out their frustrations on the slithering serpent. Little by little its strivings ceased, though its beady eyes continued staring at them implacably.

Flickers of pain rippled through the warband's minds. Then the winged Sluagh arrowed down at them with its pinions folded behind it like a stooping hawk. Coilla and Haskeer sprang into action, holding the curtain up between them. The monster flew straight into it. Quickly they wrapped it then Haskeer dropped onto the bundle with all his weight. Another orc thwacked the netted Sluagh with his rod of iron. Foul stains began to seep through the yellow cloth.

All that time Serapheim hadn't moved from his place beside the door. Now he stepped forward, Sanara at his shoulder. Fingers intertwined, they raised their hands in a gesture that was far from peaceful. There were no flashes, no puffs of coloured smoke. In fact, nothing seemed to happen at all.

And that, Stryke realised, was the point. Though the two dead Sluagh were still in the room, the others hadn't entered.

'Cover us,' commanded Serapheim.

Stryke and the others moved forward despite the fierce aches that rolled and retreated through their skulls.

Jup took a peek and bobbed back inside. 'They're having a powwow about half a dozen steps down. No others about.'

'Any advice?' Stryke asked the humans.

Serapheim shook his head. 'No. Now that we've pushed them that far back, it's up to you.'

Wielding his metal rod like a club, Stryke led the band out in a wild charge.

Orcs catapulted off the banisters and into a headlong dash down the stairs, or whipped round on the inside of the stairs with one hand around the newel. The Sluagh fled, the slug undulating obscenely and his insect-like fellow stilting away at high speed.

Down and down the band went, spiralling endlessly inside the shaft of white stone. Stryke raced down the middle of the stairs, flailing his curtain rod in hissing arcs that would have broken the neck of a dragon. But the Sluagh moved surprisingly fast. They kept well out of range in what seemed like heedless flight.

Nevertheless, when the demons reached a landing, they whipped round. Agony flared through the orcs' heads. Most of them fell to their knees, or rolled down the stairs in a whirl of limbs. Now, half the warband were helpless on the level space, unable to back up without trampling their companions.

Coilla's head smacked into the piers of the banister, her helmet tumbling down into the void. Sick, racked with pain, she lost hold of her weapon and it too clanged downwards from step to step until it wedged itself in an angle far below.

Now the Sluagh began to advance. 'Use your magic, can't you?' Stryke grated.

'We are!' Serapheim yelled back. 'That's why they're coming so slowly.'

'Call that *slow*?' Squinting through the whorls of light that tormented his sight, he swung his weapon once more and hurled it with all his might.

It tangled in the insect-Slaugh's segmented legs. The monster tripped and stumbled, not even its six limbs enough to steady it until it bowled off the landing and down a half spiral. It landed on its back, rocking and waving its legs in the air, unable to turn itself in the tight space. An enraged fire roared in Stryke's ears.

Then the last monster reared to an awesome height. It seemed to draw itself up and out until it almost filled the width of the stairs. Before their horrified gaze it changed from a slug-like thing. Its lower part forked, forming claws on its massive hind feet, while a tooth-filled mouth gaped in a soundless roar. Tentacles sprouted from its torso once more, wreathing around it. The taloned paws clicked on the stone, then it built up speed and charged.

Haskeer threw himself flat on the floor, face upwards, the curtain rail pointing straight at the charging beast just as Stryke had done with the snow leopard. The Sluagh extended its legs and strode over him untouched. It used its tentacles to hurl other warriors aside, not even bothering to watch where they fell. Intent on reaching the humans, it trampled on the uncon-scious orcs in its headlong rush.

That was its undoing. The beast's talons caught in a Wolver-ine's jerkin. Just for a second, but that was long enough to unbalance the monster. Crashing to lie dazed on the stairs, it couldn't even shapeshift. A groaning trooper rolled over, yellow cloth draped over his arms. Another came to help him and just as the demonic creature jackknifed upright, the curtain billowed over his head.

At once it too began to transform into a snake but, by now, enough of the orcs had recovered to give it a pounding. The stink of its black blood rose thickly into the air. Steaming faintly through the fabric, it died.

With that, the dazzling pain was lifted from the band's minds.

Most of them were able to stand, or at least to hang on to a less injured comrade. This time it was Jup who led the way, advancing one step at a time on the overturned insect that obstructed the stairs beneath them. He brought down his weapon on its neck but the metal clanged off its jointed scales. Acid filled the Wolverines' minds again, its keenness quickly dampening as Serapheim and Sanara came down as close as they dared.

'*You dare to challenge me?*' the Sluagh shrieked into their minds, so fiery it darkened their vision. It renewed its frantic scrabbling but still couldn't right itself.

'Damn right, I dare,' Jup snapped, hammering at it blindly.

His blow tipped it over a fraction. Before the dwarf could blink it was spidering straight up the wall above his head. A scorpion tail slashed down at him.

That was its undoing. The extra weight made it bottom heavy. It skidded downwards and landed on Haskeer's rail. Its own weight drove the makeshift spear through its body. The top burst through the dome where its skull should have been. A pulpy mess fountained out, raining down in sticky black globs.

Stryke sank down onto a step, leaning his back against the balustrade. 'Good work, everybody.'

The orcs were rejoicing, slapping each others' backs or just grinning as they tottered to their feet.

Serapheim spoiled it. 'Don't celebrate too soon. It's almost dawn and we still have to make it down to the cellars.'

24

Trying not to get any of the disgusting ichor on them, orcs and humans clambered down over the Sluagh's body. It wasn't easy on the spiral stairs, but they managed it, eventually reaching the floor of the great hall where they were captured the day before.

Crouching behind the railing, Stryke watched a dozen Sluagh going about their business. In ones and twos they were heading sluggishly in different directions. All would be lost if just one decide to come their way, but miraculously none did. Then the last group had crossed into one of the shadowy arches and none of the hideous creatures was in sight.

Serapheim hissed, 'Quick! This way!' and they set off at a lope across the vast hall. They made for another staircase on the far side and began running up it.

'Hold on,' Stryke said. 'I thought we were heading for the cellars. Why are we climbing stairs?'

'A small diversion for weapons.' He motioned for the orcs to be still as they reached a wide gallery overlooking the hall. 'See that corridor about halfway along? It leads to the armoury. Stay alert. There are other Sluagh about.'

Indeed there were. Once more, grey-skinned horrors were going about their daily activities below. Crouching, the Wolverines kept in the shadows as they tiptoed along the gallery.

Typically, the way to the armoury was a maze of stairs and passages. But at least this part of the palace seemed to be deserted. The yellow light was patchy here, the dust deep underfoot, muffling their footsteps.

Serapheim and Sanara drew to a halt by yet another bend. The man made a gesture to Stryke, who peered round at what lay ahead.

'Two of them, either side of a door,' he reported in a whisper. Using the band's hand signals, he split his forces. Jup, Coilla and Haskeer were to take the further creature. He and Alfray would lead half the grunts against the gryphon-headed monster nearest them.

This time the fight was brief. It was much easier to attack when all the warband could come at the Sluagh at once. The creatures themselves were pinned against the wall with no place to retreat. Despite the lancing headaches it didn't take long before the monsters were no more than an oozing mush.

Stryke gestured to Serapheim to go first. The humans opened the door onto an armoury like no other. More than half the weapons weren't even things the orcs recognised. They headed straight for the ranks of spears and pikes clipped to the wall. As they went further, daylight from an iced-up window reflected off a heap of metal on the floor.

'My axe!' Jup exclaimed joyfully, sweeping up the butterfly-headed weapon. Soon, each of them had back the arms the Sluagh had taken the day before. In the more exotic part of the armoury Sanara and Serapheim helped themselves to bulbous tubes of what looked like glass.

Pillaging done, Serapheim guided them down a different way. Stryke got the feeling that this had once been the servants' area, for the stairs were of rough granite and the walls were plain.

The air, already cold, began to grow damp. There was a smell of decay, and mould began to appear in corners. It was beaded with frost. The square windows no longer showed daylight but the strange blue of the glacier outside. Then there were no more windows and they realised they were underground. Eventually they found themselves in the palace's cavernous cellars. Creeping through a labyrinthine series of tunnels, they had to watch their footing, for ice slicked the stone. Ahead there was more of the yellow glow. The band stopped while Jup scouted cautiously. 'There's eight Sluagh in front of the weirdest doors you've ever seen,' he reported.

Again Stryke detailed the band to separate targets. With swords, pikes and axes the Wolverines felt much happier about attacking a large force. Even so it was a bloody struggle. The Sluagh came at them with claws and webs of agony. Serapheim and Sanara edged round the walls, trying to get behind the monsters. When they did, their glass tubes began to glow eerily. Bolts of light shot from them. There was a deafening explosion and suddenly it was raining Sluagh blood. Then it was all over.

'Useful weapon,' Coilla remarked admiringly.

Jup had been right. The doors formed a circle set deep into the rock. Once again, there was no obvious handle but ten little dimples were set into the frosty metal. It was Sanara who matched her fingertips to the depressions and pushed.

The doors swung back. Ducking, Serapheim led them inside. They found themselves in a doorway that must have burrowed ten feet through the rock.

Inside was the portal.

It stood, a platform canopied in granite, within a ring of standing stones. Here and there jewels winked in spiral patterns on the floor of the dais. Others glimmered from all the stones but one, which looked somehow dead. Some of the gems were the size of a pigeon's egg.

Haskeer bent down to caress a huge sapphire but recoiled, a look of confusion on his features as coloured lights swirled up into the musty air.

There was no hint of what the portal might do, but Stryke shivered all the same.

Coilla stopped. 'What the hell is *that*?'

Serapheim said absently, 'Something that's stood here for a long time.'

The last of the warband crowded into the room. 'Secure these doors,' Stryke ordered.

It took five grunts to do it. When the doors slammed shut a hollow boom shook the ground. Now the only light was the rainbow flicker from the jewels.

When it was done, Stryke turned to the man, who stood with his arm around the Queen's shoulders. 'All right, Serapheim. It's time you explained things.'

Serapheim nodded. He and Sanara sat on the edge of the jewel-encrusted platform. 'Think of this world as being just one of many others.' he began. 'An infinite number. Many of them would be more or less like this one. Many more would be unimaginably different. Now picture all these worlds existing side by side, stretching out forever. As though they had been laid out on an endless plain.' He checked the faces of his audience to see if they were following. 'Long ago, something fractured this plain. It left a gap, if you like, a corridor that beings could use, like mice between the walls of a house. This portal is one entrance to that corridor.'

'So it was made by mice then?' Haskeer piped up.

The brighter ones took a moment to explain it to him in a more basic way. Finally he seemed to understand.

'Who found the portal, I don't know,' Serapheim continued. 'Nor who might have adorned it in this way. That was long ago, too. But the sorceress Vermegram, mother of Sanara here, and Jennesta and Adpar, rediscovered it in more recent times. She also discovered that with the aid of her magic she could actually see some of the other plains, as Stryke unwittingly has.'

'What do you mean?' Stryke said.

'Your dreams.'

'How did you know I've been having dreams?'

'Let's just say that I am attuned to the energies of the earth, and knew you had made that connection.'

Stryke was speechless.

'The point is that they were not dreams. They were glimpses of another place. A place of orcs.'

'I had another dream recently,' Stryke confessed. 'It wasn't about the . . . orc world. I was in a tunnel at the start, then I broke out of that into a strange landscape. Mobbs was there.' By way of explanation he added, 'A gremlin scholar we met.'

All this was news to the Wolverines, and Stryke could see he'd have some explaining to do later.

'That dream would have been inspired by the instrumentalities' power too,' Serapheim ventured. 'The tunnel represents death and rebirth.'

Stryke didn't know about that. He only hoped Mobbs would find peace.

'But the point is that this portal has been here since before the ice came,' Serapheim went on. 'The Sluagh's numbers have been dwindling since the climate changed. They have tried in vain to activate the portal in order to return to their world.'

'And you want to *stop* them getting away?' Coilla said.

'I want to stop them having control of the portal. It would enable them to send conquering hordes into untold other worlds. That's unthinkable.'

'This is a load of horse-shit,' Haskeer sneered. 'You said you'd *show* us something.'

'That's why I brought you to the portal,' Serapheim replied. 'Without the stars, I can't activate it. But the vortex within can be made to give a view of the parallel worlds.' He moved to it and did something at one of the stones. They couldn't see what.

Stryke's jaw dropped. There were gasps and exclamations.

A picture that moved, like a window on to a landscape, had appeared in the air. The scene it showed was unmistakably the world of Stryke's dreams. The verdant hills and valleys, mighty full-leafed forests and sparkling blue seas. There were hundreds of orcs battling in the sort of raid that blooded young warriors. Then views of orcs in rough-gamed carousing before roaring fires.

Stryke's strongest thought was that he wasn't insane. What he had been seeing was a vision of . . . home.

The picture dissolved in a glitter of golden motes and was gone.

'Now do you see?' Serapheim said. '*All* the elder races have their own worlds.' He stared straight into Jup's eyes. 'And that includes dwarfs.'

Now the scene showed orc hatchlings laughing as they practised with their first wooden swords, their birth-mothers looking on proudly from the doors of longhouses.

'In the beginning the portal was just a kind of window that let Vermegram see as you are seeing. But as she observed the orc world, she conceived the idea of using your naturally militaristic race for her own ends. At last she . . . found a way to bring a number of your race through the portal, activating it with magic. She wanted to establish an army of super warriors she could control by sorcery.' He paused. 'The next part you might not favour. Something went wrong and the orcs she transported were altered in the process. They remained just as warlike but their intelligence was diminished, a defect that continued through subsequent generations.'

Haskeer thrust his jaw out belligerently. 'You saying we're stupid?'

'No, no. You're . . . as you should be. The one who is a throwback is you, Stryke. A sport. You're the closest to the orcs on your race's home world.'

'If orcs were . . . changed going through that thing in the first place,' Alfray pointed out, 'what's to stop it happening again? Is it safe?'

'Quite safe. The accident, shall we call it, happened because of Vermegram's inexperience with the portal. The instrumentalities prevent it occurring again.'

Suddenly they heard a heavy pounding on the door.

'It will take time for even them to get through that,' he judged. 'Let me finish quickly. Vermegram meant only to bring orcs into this world. But activating the portal meant that beings in other worlds who had access to their own portals could also come here. I suspect that for most it was an accident. In its natural state, an invisible cleft in space and time, a portal is often impossible to detect. It would be easy to be swept into one unawares.'

'Just a minute,' Coilla interrupted. 'Vermegram was a nyadd, wasn't she? So how could she be here before the—'

'No, she wasn't a nyadd. She was human.'

'But everybody says . . .' She cast an eye at Sanara. 'Her offspring. They're symbiotes, aren't they? Where did they get their nyadd blood?'

'When they were in her womb. A nyadd colony had been established here by then.'

'I don't understand.'

'She found a way to insert nyadd seed into the forming child she was carrying.'

'Why would she do such a thing?'

'What interested her was the fact that nyadds always give birth to triplets. She wanted that too, and thought she had isolated the tiny particle of nyadd matter that caused it. Shortly after, the sole child she carried mutated into a triple birth. This was done as much in a spirit of curiosity as a desire for three offspring.' He gave Sanara a sympathetic smile.

'She sounds a charmer,' Jup said.

'What did she want orc warriors for?' Stryke asked.

'To help her defeat a warlock called Tentarr Arngrim. He had watched power corrupt her, make her cruel and meddlesome. When he tried to stop her, she turned on him. The irony was that Vermegram and Tentarr Arngrim had once been lovers. They even had a child together before she became evil.' He pulled Sanara into an embrace. '*This* child. My daughter.'

259

There was general uproar.

'This is too fucking much,' Haskeer complained.

'You're asking us to swallow a lot, Serapheim,' Alfray told him.

Serapheim held up his hands for silence, and got it. 'I am Tentarr Arngrim, once a mighty sorcerer, now much reduced.' The sheer force of his words held them. 'It was I who made the instrumentalities, who fashioned them from alchemy and tempered them with magic when the power was full in me.'

'Why?'

'To make it possible for the elder races to return to their home worlds, should they so choose. For that I needed control, and in essence the instrumentalities were a key. I brought them here. But Vermegram had her warriors steal them and hide them away. That led to war between us. She died with only a fraction of her powers, but I was depleted too. By the time my body had recovered from its wounds, the instrumentalities were scattered, the magic all but lost. The stars became stuff of myth, and I was never able to make any more. I have waited aeons for them all to be found. But I knew they would be. I knew when the right beings came they would hear the music of the stars.'

There was a renewed clamour at the door. They hardly noticed.

'I told you they were singing to me!' Haskeer exclaimed.

'If they were,' Serapheim told him, 'then you must have a brain . . . *something* like your captain's. There's a bit of sport in you too, Sergeant.'

Haskeer grinned, full of himself.

'That could be the most amazing thing you've told us,' Coilla remarked dryly.

'I don't say your comrade has as highly sharpened a mind as Stryke—'

'No,' Jup said, 'he's a dolt.'

Haskeer gave him a lemon-suck look.

'Unpolished diamond might be a better description,' the wizard concluded diplomatically.

Again the Sluagh assaulted the door. Thick as it was, a tiny crack appeared between its two halves. 'Now we must move for the other stars and activate the portal.' He could see that doubts still lingered. 'What is there for you here? You must accept that this world belongs to my kind, whatever their faults or virtues.'

'And leave humans to wallow in their own shit after all the destruction they've wrought?' Coilla remarked.

'Perhaps it won't be that way forever. Things just might improve.'

'You'll understand we find that hard to believe.'

Thin, worm-like tentacles began to creep through the gap in the doors. Sanara aimed her weapon at them. The bulb of the tube filled with light, then shot out in a beam of golden power. A shriek echoed through the warband's minds. The worms had turned to smoking shreds.

'Some of you will need to stay and guard the portal,' Serapheim suggested, 'while the rest go after the instrumentalities.'

Haskeer liked the sound of that. 'Now you're talking. All this jaw-wagging's doing my head in.'

Stryke picked the grunts to stay with the portal, along with Sanara and Serapheim, and added, 'You'll be here too, Alfray.'

'Leaving the oldest out of the action again, is that it?'

Stryke drew him aside. 'That's why I want you here. We daren't lose the portal. It's too important. I need somebody experienced to steady this crew. You can see how jumpy some of them are.'

Alfray seemed to accept that.

Sanara joined them. 'Hear me on this, Stryke. I know you won't like the idea, but you should leave the one star you have with me.' She headed off his protest. 'It will help me draw power from the portal to keep your men safe. Besides, now you're attuned to the song of the stars the Sluagh will not be able to hide them from you. But they could if your mind was filled with this one's presence.'

She was right, he didn't like it, but it made sense. He took the star from his jerkin and handed it to her.

As the raiding party formed up, Coilla and Serapheim found themselves standing apart from the others. Something was troubling her. 'You talked about redeeming yourself. But from what you've said, this whole mess was Vermegram's fault.'

'Not all of it. You see . . . Well . . . you were loyal to Jennesta at the time and . . .'

'Spit it out.'

'I commissioned the kobolds to snatch the first instrumentality from you,' he confessed.

'You devious *bastard*,' she hissed.

'As I said, you were loyal to my daughter then. Or at least I thought you were. I'd just made the decision to try re-gathering the stars and—'

'And using the kobolds seemed a good idea. But they double-crossed you, right?'

He nodded.

'So you got us into this in the first place. Well, you and our own lack of discipline after the raid on Homefield.' She glanced at the band. 'I can imagine their reaction to *that* piece of news. But I won't tell them until we're through this. If we *do* get through. We've got enough on our plates.'

He quietly thanked her.

At that moment, the door gave. Serapheim hurried towards it. Sanara joined him. They levelled their glass weapons at the mass of Sluagh trying to get in. Blasts of searing yellow light sliced into the creatures. There were hideous shrieks. A stink of burning flesh filled the air.

'That's the last of these,' Serapheim announced, throwing his glass tube aside, 'they're drained. You're on your own now, Wolverines.'

'If we get separated, meet back here,' Stryke instructed them. 'Now *move!*'

The band set out, wading through the mass of pulpy bodies.

Stryke wasn't aware of the strange mental tug that called him back to the star he'd left below until it faded. By that time they were on their way out of the cellar's labyrinth.

But as they ran up yet another flight of steps, he was aware of the first notes of a celestial song somewhere above. Seconds later, they reached another dimly-lit corridor, with a large open chamber in front of them.

It was filled with demons.

Something like a triumphal chord crashed into his mind as Stryke led the charge.

The Sluagh never knew what hit them. They seemed deaf and blind to all but the joined stars, sitting on a table in their midst. Spears sliced the air, lancing through demons hanging down from the ceiling. Jup's axe bit deep into a shaggy grey back while Coilla decapitated another Sluagh with a frenzy of hacking.

Now the monsters began to fight back. Perhaps a dozen of them turned, their limbs flowing into new and deadly shapes. One, a serpent, instantly formed a dragonlike maw and whipped round, its hideous jaws salivating. Once again the Sluagh began to pour their foul acid pain into the orcs' minds. Some of the grunts toppled, hands battened to their ears, but the rest fought grimly on.

At last the remaining Sluagh gave way before the Wolverines' onslaught. Most of the demons were bleeding darkly on the floor. Scattered limbs were still twitching. The last two monsters had been pushed back towards the far wall. In one last desperate welter of claws and fangs they tried to get back to the stars, but half the Wolverines were between them and their goal. Defeated, dripping ichor from a score of wounds, they turned and fled, undulating rapidly down through an open stairwell.

As they disappeared, so did their gift of pain. The Wolverines pulled themselves together, astonished to find themselves alive. Haskeer turned to scoop the stars from the table.

They weren't there. Neither was Stryke.

In the mêlée, he had seen a Sluagh snatch the stars and scurry to an open balcony with them. Dextrously, the creature began climbing the outside of the palace. Now Stryke was bounding up a staircase, a spear in his hand, hoping to catch up with it.

Above him the stairs split, leading off in two different directions. And there was the Sluagh, spidering downwards on the farther side, not twenty paces from him. With all his strength he hurled the spear. The creature dropped like a stone.

It was wounded, not dead. Pushing out a claw to the stars it had dropped, it tried to pull them closer. Stryke dashed forward and sliced its limb clean through. But the Sluagh wasn't finished. It shot out a blade-like appendage and gashed his shoulder. Stryke quickly retreated, clutching the wound, and watched the thing die. Then he grabbed the stars and ran.

As he reached the point where the stairs branched he heard sounds of combat. He threw himself into the shadows. A pack of Sluagh slithered into sight, and they were retreating from a greater force. He blinked through the gloom, trying to make out who. Then he saw them.

Humans and orcs.

Manis.

Stryke was almost shockproof after recent revelations, but this new twist took some beating. The only comfort he could take was that, although he had no idea what they were doing here, the Manis would put more pressure on the Sluagh. Allies, but not necessarily friends. In a moment they would reach the joining of the stairways and block his downward flight. Tucking the stars into his jerkin, he took the only course open to him and went up.

Closing his mind to the pain of his wound, which was

troublesome but far from the worst he'd taken, he paused to listen at the next landing. The echoing clash of weapons was fading away. Presumably the Sluagh and Manis had gone down, the way he'd intended travelling. Moving quietly, sword at the ready, he continued climbing upwards, looking for a way to outflank the strangers and get back down to the portal.

He thought he must be somewhere near the palace's broad front. By a window, he stopped to knot a tourniquet round his upper arm. Then movement outside caught his eye. He peered through a broken pane, past the fringe of icicles on the casement.

A seething army sprawled across the wintry plain. Columns of soldiers were heading towards the palace. Others clustered around the entrance below.

The sound of halting footsteps drew him from the sight. He turned, his blade up and ready.

Somebody limped out of the gloom.

Stryke couldn't believe it. Nor did he exactly need it at a time like this.

'What does it take to kill you?' he said. Though in truth, the one he addressed looked half dead anyway.

'It ain't that easy,' Micah Lekmann replied. Insanity blazed in his eyes. 'I don't know how I got here, or you neither, but I can't believe I've been given another chance to kill you. Maybe there are gods after all.'

The man was clearly deranged. Stryke thought of him tracking them through snow and ice in his skimpy clothes. His eyes were red-rimmed, the fingers of his left hand blackened with frostbite.

'This is crazy, Lekmann,' he said. 'Give it up.'

'No way!' His sword lashed out, low and dangerous. Stryke jumped out of its path. The bounty hunter, a crazed grin plastered on his face, kept coming, thrusting again and again with the fury of a madman.

Stryke parried and fought back. His counter-blows seemed feeble for all the effect they had. Lekmann drank them up and kept coming. They battered it out, up and down the corridor, Stryke desperate to find an opening and end another distraction he didn't need. It wasn't proving easy. The human seemed to have dispensed with fear and caution. He fought like a ravening beast.

Suddenly Stryke was blinded by an intense flare of light. Bewildered, he pulled back out of range, straining to recover his vision. When it returned there were motes in his eyes, as though he'd been staring at the sun. But that didn't obscure what he was looking at.

Lekmann stood in front of him, quite still, his sword at his feet.

He had a gaping hole in his chest. Broken ribs showed white in the spilling gore. The edge of the wound was charred and smoking. Through it, Stryke caught a glimpse of the wall beyond.

Almost casually, Lekmann lowered his head and stared at the damage. He didn't look as if he was in agony, though he must have been. The expression he wore was one of dazed affront-edness. Then he disgorged a mouthful of blood, swayed like a drunk and went down, face first. Smouldering.

As Stryke gaped, trying to make sense of what had happened, another figure moved from more distant shadows.

Jennesta's mouth twisted in an ugly grimace as she saw him. The scream she let out, equal parts rage and triumph, cut through him like a blade. Her hands came up, presumably to deal him a similar fate.

He was already moving. Even so, he barely managed to avoid the dazzling gout of lightning she flung at him. It struck a carved pillar a hairsbreadth away, pulverising the marble and sending shards flying.

Stumbling, in pain, he vaulted down the next staircase. Another bolt hit, over his head, bringing down a plaster shower. He half-jumped, half-fell down the broad flight of steps. In a corridor off the landing below, Mani troopers were battling more Sluagh. He dodged past them and pounded down the next flight, letting the song of the stars guide him back to the portal.

The odds were against him making it.

25

'Do you sense something?' Serapheim asked, without looking round.

His back to the gemmed portal, he stared about the chamber. Nothing moved, though faint vapours were rising from the downed Sluagh at the entrance.

'Yes,' Sanara answered. 'They're close.'

'Who are?' Alfray said.

As if in reply, one of the grunts near the door signalled urgently. Seconds later, the hunting party ran in.

Alfray scanned their ranks. 'Where's Stryke?'

'We were hoping he was here,' Coilla told him. She explained what had happened.

'For what it's worth, I have felt no disturbance in the life web indicating he might be dead,' Serapheim declared.

Haskeer said, 'What?'

'A question of sensitivity. There's no time to explain now. The stars?'

'I don't know,' Coilla admitted. 'Maybe Stryke has them. They went missing the same time he did. But listen! There's a whole army of Manis storming the place. They're engaging the Sluagh.'

'You confirm what my daughter and I already suspected,' Serapheim revealed. 'Jennesta's here.'

'Gods!'

'We have to find Stryke,' he continued. 'And do what we can to sow discord in the ranks of her forces. Jennesta mustn't get the upper hand.'

'I'll take a group to search for him,' Jup offered.

'Sanara will go with you. From this end I should be able to channel power through to her.' He turned to his daughter. 'Are you willing, Sanara?'

'Of course.'

'How's she going to help us find Stryke?'

'She's not. But if your troops can get her to a safe place as near the interlopers as possible, we might be able to do something about Jennesta. Trust me.'

'But what about *Stryke*?' Coilla demanded.

'Perhaps you'll find him while you're escorting Sanara.'

'That's not good enough! We can't abandon one of our own.'

'Then I suggest you split into two groups. But you must hurry!'

'Reafdaw!' she shouted. The grunt came over to her, blood trickling from a cut above his ear. 'You stay here with Alfray. Haskeer, we'll go after Stryke, all right? The rest of you, follow Jup.'

The Wolvermes readied themselves. Some shared their last dregs of water, others patched their wounds.

Then Haskeer, as officer in charge, barked the order and the two groups set off again.

Trying to reach the cellars drew on all of Stryke's reserves of skill and stamina.

With Manis and Sluagh battling at every turn, there was chaos in the palace. He tried to stay clear of conflict, sidestepping fights and skirting any challenging him.

His luck ran out when he rounded a corner and found himself confronted by a pair of orcs. For a second he dared hope they might think he was part of Jennesta's horde. But they obviously knew his face.

'That's Stryke!' one of them yelled.

They advanced, weapons raised.

He tried diplomacy. 'Whoa! Just hold it.' He lifted his hands to mollify them. 'There's no need for this.'

'There is,' the first grunt told him. 'You're top of our mistress's wanted list.'

'She was my mistress too. You must know she's no friend of orcs.'

'She fills our bellies, gives us shelter. Some of us have stayed loyal.'

'And how loyal do you think she'd be to you, when it comes to it?'

Stryke thought the one who hadn't named him seemed to waver.

'She'll reward us for your head,' the first trooper said. 'That's more than you'd do, if we let you keep it.'

'We shouldn't be fighting each other. Not us, not orcs.'

'The brotherhood of orcs, eh? Sorry, not this time.' He began moving forward, adding, 'It's nothing personal, Captain. Just doing my job.'

The second trooper called out, 'Careful, Freendo, that's Stryke you're up against! You know his reputation!'

'He's just an orc, ain't he? Like us.'

He charged in, slashing with his sword. Stryke tensed, ready to meet him. But even now he wanted to incapacitate, not kill. If that was possible. From the corner of his eye he saw that the other grunt was holding back.

Their blades clashed, the sound ringing through the dusty corridor. Stryke battered at the other's sword, trying to dislodge it. His opponent's intentions were obviously more lethal. He was doing his best to reach flesh.

They sparred for a moment, Stryke on the defensive, but he was growing restive. He had no time to waste on a couple of boneheads. If he had to put them down, so be it, they'd had their chance. Powering in, he went for a kill. His foe, the lesser swordsman for all that he was an orc, started backing, a look of alarm filling his face.

Then Stryke saw his chance. The grunt had tried a low sweep. It left his upper body unprotected. Stryke sent in a sideswipe with the flat of his blade striking the orc across the mouth. He heard the crunch of broken teeth. The orc bounded backwards, almost falling, spitting blood. His sword was lost. Stryke advanced, kicking the fallen sword to one side. The grunt, his face whitening, waited for the killing blow.

'Now fuck off.' Stryke told him. He sent a menacing sneer the way of the waverer too.

They stared at him for a second, then turned and fled.

Stryke sighed and resumed his journey, reflecting on the irony of fighting fellow orcs, and humans he was until so recently allied with.

Jup's group, surrounding Sanara to protect her, fought their way to the top of a tower.

They found an empty stone chamber there with an open balcony. While some guarded the stairs, she stepped out on to it, Jup beside her.

Jennesta's army was spread out across the icy wilderness below. There was a scrum at the palace's gates as details rushed to get in. Then someone cried out and they looked up to see dragons in the sky.

'Shit, that's all we need,' the dwarf proclaimed gloomily.

But then the dragons dived and began spitting gouts of flame at Jennesta's troops. A ragged cheer broke out in the tower.

'That's got to be Glozellan,' Jup guessed. 'Good for her!'

He turned, beaming, to Sanara. Her eyes were closed, and as he watched she slowly began to raise her arms.

The band stared at her, mystified.

In the cellars, Alfray and Reafdaw looked on as Serapheim seemed to go into some kind of trance. His eyes were glazed and his arms were raised, and for all the notice he took of the orcs they might have not been there.

Then a hum, strange and low, issued from the area of the portal. Gingerly, Alfray approached it. He held out a cautious hand and felt a warm, tingling sensation caressing his palm.

He stepped back and exchanged baffled expressions with the grunt.

Stryke was passing a stove-in window when something extraordinary caught his eye.

He looked out and saw Jennesta's army, their vast number covering the ice to the middle distance. But it wasn't that which held him.

There was something in the sky.

The best he could liken it to was a canvas. But its picture moved, and changed to other views as he watched. He realised it was like the vision Serapheim had conjured at the portal, only writ enormously across the leaden heavens. It showed similar scenes of orc tranquillity and verdant splendour.

There were roars below. But they were not the battle cries of stoked-up warriors. They were shouts of wonder, followed by discontent.

He saw the magician's plan. What better way to sow discord in the ranks than by showing them the lie of their existence? That, plus filling them with dread at this supernatural manifestation. It would likely baffle them as much as turn their loyalties, but that could be enough to buy the time they needed.

The sound of running feet came to him. He readied for another clash. But it was Coilla and Haskeer's group that dashed along an adjacent corridor.

'Thank the gods!' she cried. 'We thought we'd lost you!'

'Jennesta's here!'

'We noticed,' she replied dryly.

'Then let's get to the cellars!'

They crashed down to them, broaching all opposition, cutting down any in their way. They sliced through the turmoil like knives through chickens' necks.

Eventually, breathing hard and sweating despite the cold, they arrived at the portal chamber and rushed in.

Serapheim held his trance-like pose, with Alfray and Reafdaw looking on. A small version of the picture glowing in the sky outside hovered in the portal's circle.

Almost at once the magician snapped out of his reverie. The picture flickered and died. 'We can do no more,' he panted, looking like a man who had engaged in hard physical toil.

'It was a smart trick,' Stryke complimented him. 'Now what?'

Before Serapheim could answer, Jup's group returned, still marvelling aloud at the display. They were bloodied, breathless, but whole. Sanara ran to her father's arms.

'Give me the instrumentalities,' Serapheim said.

Stryke handed over the four that were fused and got the single loose artifact back from Sanara. With nimble fingers Serapheim swiftly united them.

'There is one thing I haven't mentioned,' he confessed.

'What's that?' Coilla asked warily.

'Activating the portal will liberate a vast amount of energy. It will likely destroy the palace.'

'*Now* you tell us.' She glared at him.

'Had I said so earlier, it might have influenced your decision.'

'Will it stop us using the thing?' Stryke said.

'No, if you go through swiftly.'

Most of the band had doubt in their faces. Serapheim indicated the increasing sound of discord above. 'Your choice has narrowed. Use the portal or face anarchy up there.'

Stryke nodded assent.

Serapheim went forward and picked out one of the larger bejewelled stones. He laid the five-part star on its surface.

'Is that it?' Haskeer said.

'Wait,' the human replied.

The space above the portal's dais suddenly transformed into something wondrous. It was like an inverted waterfall of millions of tiny golden stars, whirling, flowing, never still. And there was a throb of energy they could feel through the soles of their boots.

All present were transfixed by the fantastic sight. The myriad stars threw off a glow that reflected on their faces, their clothes, the walls around them.

'I need to attune it to your destination,' Serapheim explained, approaching the circle.

'It's beautiful,' Coilla whispered.

'Awesome,' Jup reckoned.

'*And mine!*'

Everyone turned.

Jennesta stood at the door. General Mersadion, his face ravaged, was beside her.

Serapheim was the first to recover. 'You're too late,' he told her.

'It's nice to see you too, Father dear,' she replied sarcastically. 'I have a contingent of my Royal Guard at my heels. Surrender or die, it's all the same to me.'

'I think not,' Sanara said. 'I can't see you passing on the opportunity to slay those you think have wronged you.'

'You know me so well, sister. And how pleasant to see you in the flesh again. I look forward to despoiling it.'

'If you think we're giving up without a fight,' Stryke declared, 'you're wrong. We've nothing to lose.'

'Ah, Captain Stryke.' She cast a disdainful eye over the warband. 'And the Wolverines. I've relished the thought of meeting you again in particular.' Her voice became granite. 'Now throw down your weapons.'

There was a sudden flurry of movement. Alfray rushed towards her, a sword in his hand.

Mersadion leapt in to counter it. His blade flashed. Then it was buried in the corporal's chest. The general tugged it free. Alfray still stood, looking down at the blood on his hands.

He swayed and fell.

There was a moment of shock that rooted them all to the spot.

The spell shattered. Haskeer, Jup, Coilla and Stryke all rushed at Mersadion and unleashed their frenzy. Every grunt in the room would have done the same but for the crush.

Mersadion didn't even have time to cry out. He was cut to pieces in seconds.

The band turned from his mangled corpse and moved Jennesta's way, ready to further sate their fury. She was weaving a contorted pattern in the air with her hands.

'*No!*' Serapheim shouted.

An orange fireball like a miniature sun ignited between her hands. She flung it. The band scattered. With blurring speed the firebrand sailed over their heads and exploded against a wall with a shattering report. Jennesta began forming another.

But Serapheim and Sanara had found each other, and together they faced her. Their hands lifted and a sheet of ethereal flame appeared like a shield in front of them, masking the room and its occupants. Jennesta hurled the new fireball at it, but saw its intense energy absorbed by the blazing barrier.

The portal's display of splendour continued unabated. But its destructive bent was becoming apparent. A deep rumbling had started to shake the castle's foundations. Unheeding, the band gathered around Alfray.

Coilla and Stryke went down on their knees beside him. They saw how severe his wound was. Coilla took his wrist, then looked into her Captain's eyes. 'He's bad, Stryke.'

'Alfray,' Stryke said. '*Alfray*, can you hear me?'

The old orc managed to open his eyes. He seemed comforted by the sight of his comrades. '*So . . . this is how . . . it ends.*'

'No,' Coilla said. 'We can tend your wound. We—'

'*You have . . . no need to . . . lie . . . to me. Not now. Let me . . . at least have the . . . dignity of . . . truth.*'

'Hell, Alfray,' Stryke whispered, his voice choking. 'I got you into this. I'm so sorry.'

Alfray smiled weakly. '*We got into . . . this . . . together. It was a . . . good mission, eh, Stryke?*'

'Yes. A good mission. And you were the best comrade an orc could have, old friend.'

'*I take . . . that as a . . . compliment to . . . be proud . . . of.*' Now his lips were working but no sound came. Stryke leaned close and put his ear close to Alfray's mouth. Faintly he heard, '*Sword . . .*'

Stryke took his blade and pressed its grip into Alfray's trembling palm. He closed the fingers around it. Alfray gripped feebly and looked content. '*Remember the . . . old ways,*' he rasped. '*Honour . . . the . . . traditions.*'

'We will,' Stryke promised. 'And your memory. Always.'

The ground gave another bass rumble. Showers of plaster fell from the ceiling. Off to one side of the vast chamber Jennesta and her kin battled on in a blaze of supernatural radiance and flashing lights.

Alfray's breath was thin and laboured. '*I will . . . drink . . . a toast to you . . . all . . . in the . . . halls of . . . Vartania.*'

Then his eyes closed for the last time.

'No,' Coilla said. 'No, Alfray.' She started shaking him. 'We need you. Don't go, the band needs you. Alfray?'

Stryke took her by the shoulders and forced her to look at him. 'He's . . . gone, Coilla. He's gone.'

She stared at him, not seeming to comprehend.

Orcs weren't supposed to be able to cry. It was something humans did. The mist filling her eyes belied that.

Jup had his face in his hands. Haskeer's head was bowed. The grunts were struck dumb with the shock of grief.

Stryke gently took back his sword. Then he looked up at the magical duel and rage began to return. They all felt it. But they felt impotence too. There was no way they dared intervene in the exchange of sorcery, nor could they pass it.

No more than a minute later their quandary was resolved.

Jennesta cried out. Her fiery magical shield flickered and

died. She staggered, her head down, looking exhausted. Damp locks of ebony hair were plastered to her face.

The enchanted, flaming buffer protecting Serapheim and Sanara vanished too, snuffed out like a candle. He darted the few steps separating them from Jennesta and seized her wrist. Drained by the efforts of their duel, she put up little resistance as he began dragging her toward the portal.

Leaping to their feet, the band made to charge and vent their wrath on her.

'*No!*' Serapheim bellowed. 'She's my daughter! I have a responsibility for all she's done! I'll deal with this myself!'

Such was the force of his outburst that it stopped them in their tracks.

They watched as Serapheim pulled her the last few feet to the portal's edge. As they arrived, she came to herself a little and realised where they were. Her eyes moved from the dancing grandeur of the portal's vortex to her father's face. She seemed to devine his intention, but she showed no fear.

'You wouldn't dare,' she sneered.

'Once, perhaps,' he returned, 'before the full horror of your wickedness was brought home to me. Not now.' Still holding her wrist in an iron grip, he thrust her hand near to the portal's cascading brilliance, the tips of her fingers almost in the flow. 'I brought you into this world. Now I'm taking you out of it. You should appreciate the symmetry of the act.'

'You're a fool,' she hissed, 'you always were. And a coward. I have an army here. If anything happens to me, you'll die a death beyond your wildest imagination.' She flicked her gaze to Sanara. 'You both will.'

'I don't care,' he told her.

'Nor I,' Sanara backed him.

'Some prices are worth paying to rid the world of evil,' Serapheim said, pushing her hand nearer the sparkling flux.

She gazed into his eyes and knew he meant it. Her cocksure expression weakened somewhat then, and she began to struggle.

'At least face your end with dignity,' he told her. 'Or is that too much to ask?'

'*Never.*'

He forced her hand into the vortex, then let go and retreated a pace.

She squirmed and fought to pull her hand free but the gushing fountain of energy held it as sure as a vice. Then a change came upon the trapped flesh. Very slowly, it began to dissolve away, releasing itself as thousand of particles that flew into the swarm of stars and spiralled with them. The process increased a pace, the vortex gobbling up her wrist. Rapidly she was drawn in to the depth of her arm, which likewise disintegrated and scattered.

The band was rooted, their expressions a mixture of horror and macabre fascination.

Her leg had been sucked in now, and it was melting before their eyes. Strands of her hair followed, as though inhaled by an invisible giant. Jennesta's disintegration speeded up, her matter eaten into by the surging vortex at a faster and faster rate.

When it began to consume her face she finally screamed. The sound was almost instantly cut off as the energy took the rest of her in several gulps. The last of her matter gyrated for a moment in the spinning energy field before it became nothingness.

Serapheim looked as though he was going to faint. Sanara went to him and they embraced.

Coilla punctured the awed silence. 'What happened to her?'

Serapheim gathered himself. 'She made contact with the portal before it was set for a destination. She's either been torn apart by the titanic forces it contains or flung into another dimension. Either way, she's gone. Finished.'

Stryke wasn't the only one who felt a pang of pity for him, despite their hatred of Jennesta. 'Is that how *we'll* go?' he asked.

There was another rumble beneath their feet, deeper, longer than any before.

'No, my friend. I will set the location. Your transition will be profound, but not like that. It will feel just like walking through a door.' He disengaged himself from Sanara. 'Come, there's no time to waste.'

He made his way to one of the stones surrounding the portal and fiddled with the instrumentalities.

'What about you?' Coilla said.

'I will remain here in Maras-Dantia. Where else would I go? Here I can witness either the end of things or try to do some good if the land recovers from its blight.'

All present knew that his real choice was death.

'I will remain here also,' Sanara said. 'This is my world. For better or worse.' Tears stained her cheeks.

The earth grumbled more persistently.

'Come, Jup,' Serapheim urged. 'We'll send you to the domain of dwarfs first.'

'No,' he said.

'What?' Haskeer exclaimed.

'This is the only world I know too. I've had no visions of a dwarf world. It sounds tempting, but who would I know there? I'd really be a stranger in a strange land.'

'You won't change your mind?' Stryke asked.

'No, Chief. I've given it a lot of thought. I'll stay here and take my chances.'

Haskeer stepped forward. 'You sure, Jup?'

'What's the matter, miss somebody to argue with?'

'I'll always find somebody to do that with.' He regarded the dwarf for a moment. 'But it won't be the same.'

They exchanged the warrior's clasp.

'Then please take Sanara with you,' Serapheim said. 'Protect her for me.'

Jup nodded. Then with a last look at the band he escorted Sanara from the chamber.

'Now we must move with all speed,' Serapheim announced. 'Into the portal.'

Everybody looked sheepish.

'I promise you that no harm will befall any of you.'

'On the double!' Stryke barked.

Gleadeg stepped forward.

'In you go,' Stryke told him. He added more softly, 'Have no fear, trooper.'

The grunt took a breath and moved into the portal. Instantly he vanished.

'Come on! Come on!' Stryke shouted.

One by one, the remainder of the grunts passed through.

Then it was Haskeer's turn. He leapt in, a battle cry on his lips.

Coilla, taking a last look at Serapheim, and then turning her eyes to Stryke, went next.

Stryke and Serapheim stood alone in the trembling chamber. 'Thank you,' the orc said.

'It was the least I could do. Here.' He pushed the stars into his hand. 'Take these.'

'But—'

'I have no further need of them. You do with them as you will. But don't argue now!'

Stryke accepted them.

'Fare thee well, Stryke of the Wolverines.'

'And you, Sorcerer.'

He stepped to the lip of the vortex. The palace began to fall. Serapheim made no move to escape. Stryke hadn't thought he would. He lifted an arm and gave the human a clipped salute.

There was a moment of chaos and transition. Somehow, perhaps via the dreadful power of the stars and their portal, he had a brief flashing vision of many wondrous things.

He saw Aidan Galby, walking hand in hand with Jup and Sanara across a pastoral scene. He glimpsed Mercy Hobrow astride a unicorn. He knew again the allure of his orc homeland.

His last thought was that the humans could have their world, and welcome to it.

Then he turned and stepped into the light.